BORROWED

A NOVEL

LUCIA DiSTEFANO

ELEPHANT
ROCK
BOOKS

For information about permission to reproduce sections from this book, contact Permissions at elephantrockbooks@gmail.com. Elephant Rock Books are distributed by Small Press United, a division of Independent Publishers Group.

ISBN: 978-1-7324141-0-5

Library of Congress Control Number: 2018948499

Printed in the United States of America

Cover and interior design by Fisheye Graphic Services, Chicago

First Edition
10 9 8 7 6 5 4 3 2 1

Elephant Rock Books
Ashford, Connecticut

For Greg,
whose music will forever
live in my heart

Last night I reached into the oven to slide out a lemon cake I'd put in an hour earlier, but the cake had disappeared. Instead, the aluminum pan held a human heart. Still beating.

I pressed a palm against my sternum, shifted it left and up. No echoey thwump, no reassuringly steady rhythm. Just silent bone. And somewhere outside of me, a robo-voice reciting in an endless loop:

"The human heart beats approximately seventy-two times per minute . . . The human heart beats approximately seventy-two times per minute . . . The human heart beats approximately seventy-two times per minute."

I palpated my chest again. No heartbeat. Then no rise and fall. As if my lungs had been scooped out, too. The only thing alive was the cake-panned heart sitting in blood and closed like a fist.

The human heart beats approx—

I had to get it back inside my chest while it was still alive. Without it, I was nothing but the husk of a girl with memories of a sick past and with no hope of a future. I watched it shudder. I watched its beats slow.

The human heart beats—

"No!" I sputtered, the word as hollow as me. "It's *mine*."

I grabbed the cake pan with both hands, blood sloshing over the rim. The scorching-hot metal singed my palms. I screamed and dropped it.

The human heart—

I jolted up in bed, drenched in sweat, my fingers digging into the mattress, the ghost scents of butter and citrus and my own burning flesh crowding my head.

A dream is just a dream, right?

Not when the heart you carry isn't really yours.

I

The heart devours what it cannot understand.
—John Mellencamp

LIN1EA

"Go on," I say, nudging the plated cupcake toward Alma. "Take a bite."

Alma pulls a suspicious face. "Why do you sound all wicked stepmother pushy?"

"Since when do I have to convince you to eat something I baked?"

"Since bikini season started. This year I'm turning that lifeguard's head at Barton Springs if it kills me."

"And him," Julie says from the family room sofa, where she's lost in a novel. Not so lost that she can't eavesdrop, apparently.

"Nobody asked you," Alma says.

Because she's lying flat on the couch, we can't see Julie from the kitchen, but her snort travels over loud and clear.

"Okay, fine," Alma says, peeling off the cupcake's paper wrapper. "What're friends for?" She takes a big bite. Instead of the involuntary moan I usually hear when she first tastes something I made, she chews, knits her brow, and sets the remainder atop its crumby liner. She knuckles frosting off the tip of her nose and reaches for her *Keep Austin Weird* mug.

"What's wrong?" I ask.

"Wrong? Nothing's wrong." Her statement is awash in a mouthful of peppermint tea.

"Alma, it's obvious you hate it."

"I didn't say anything."

"Your face said it all."

She assesses the cupcake. Even spins the plate around. We're sitting at the breakfast bar, the pendant lights painting our shoulders a buttery yellow. As if to mirror the plate spin, Alma swivels the stool one complete revolution.

You'd think I'd try my own cupcake, but this morning I woke up in no mood for sweets. I craved bacon. And I'm not the kind of vegetarian who craves bacon. Maybe I have a cold coming on or something.

"Linn," she says, "it looks beautiful as ever . . ."

"But . . ." I prompt.

"It tastes . . . um . . . off." She squinches her face. "Sorry."

"Opinions don't require an apology." But my voice feels stitched too tight.

"The frosting's great. Maybe you forgot to put something in the batter?"

I laugh curtly. "Not a chance. I've made this recipe a thousand times." A Texas bourbon cake with praline buttercream frosting.

I drag the plate to me. It looks like it always does: the cake golden brown and poofy, the frosting a swirled crown of shimmer. Smells like it always does: nutty and sweet with a darker undertone (courtesy of the booze). And even though I've been known to make fun of people who eat cupcakes with a fork (just as, I imagine, a New Yorker would mock people who morsel out pizza like steak), that's how I take my bite. As if I don't want to touch it.

Although I wouldn't call myself a person bursting with confidence (missing more than half your school career due to illness and being assigned a tutor who oozes pity will trample on anyone's self-esteem), I do claim to know my stuff when it comes to dessert. I'm the pastry chef at Basement Tapes in Austin, which may not be L.A., but which does have a buzzing food scene. And my boss, Nicola, is infamously picky. She went through six pastry chefs in as many months before she hired me four months ago. She doesn't miss a chance to remind me that I'm only seventeen and if I don't get waylaid by "drugs and dudes," I just might have a sweet career ahead of me. (Pun intended.)

I'm just glad to have an "ahead of me" ahead of me. A year ago I didn't think I did.

So I take that bite and expect to prove Alma wrong. Or at least be able to ask her if she snuck one of her "occasional" cigarettes before she tasted. Nicotine and tar can scramble any palate.

Instead I have to lean across the counter and spit the gummy mess into the bowl that's holding eggshells and butter wrappers. "Ugh, that's awful."

"You said it, girl, not me."

"This isn't good at all," I mumble. I'm talking about more than the cupcake. My audition for the Illinois Institute of Art's Baking and Pastry School is just a month away. I can't blow this. Nicola is sponsoring my interview, even though she says if she were smarter she'd keep me all to herself.

But even more urgently, I woke up determined to bake and get the dream residue off me, to reassure myself that what you slide into the oven is what you slide out.

"Jules," Alma calls.

"Yeah?" Julie keeps reading. She never goes anywhere without a book. It used to insult me, but I've figured out that a book to her is like an inhaler to an asthmatic.

"Give your eyes a break," Alma says. "We need your taste buds."

"No thanks," she says as she turns a page. "Y'all don't sound like you're having fun."

"These are my baseline cupcakes," I mutter. "If I can't do this—"

Alma touches my shoulder gently. "It's kind of comforting to know that you can fuck up like the rest of us."

I retrace my steps. Sifted flour with baking powder and salt. Folded sugar into butter. Beat three eggs into butter mixture, one at a time. Stirred in vanilla.

Or did I?

"Maybe I missed the powder. Or the salt. I couldn't have missed the sugar. Could I?" The sugar canister is on the counter, its lid beside it, the scoop inside. Otherwise mute.

"You've got a lot on your mind," Alma says. "My abuelo says too much on the mind means a muddled dish."

"Kind of a life metaphor," Julie says. So she was listening.

Alma's at the sink, rinsing out her mug. "He also says the dish will tell you what it needs, but you have to be humble enough to listen."

"Thanks, Al, but your grandfather's a savory cook. You can revise right up to the end with savory."

"Savory, sweet, it all gets shoveled into your face hole anyway."

"Gross," says Jules. She rests her book on her lap, facedown, and cracks her knuckles. "So make 'em over, Linn."

"I plan to." I'm scraping the sad remains of this batch into the trash.

Alma groans. "You two know it's spring break, right?"

"Duh." That's Julie behind the book.

"Weather's gorgeous. Let's not be cooped up baking and reading."

"Linnea has to practice," Julie says, stealing the words from my mouth.

Mom bustles into the kitchen, carry-on bag over her shoulder, suitcase wheels clacking against the tiles. I wish I could present her with a fresh cupcake. An edible truce.

We had a big fight this morning, about the usual. She claims I'm pushing too hard, trying to prove I'm healthy, trying to make up for the lost years when I was in bed and Alma and Julie were at Six Flags or Schlitterbahn.

"White-water rafting?" she had sputtered when she found out about the latest (only because she talked to Alma's mom). I had lied and told her that Alma and I were in San Marcos so Alma could check out Texas State.

"Yeah, so?" I had said.

"But Linnea, you can't swim."

"That's what life jackets are for."

She threw up her hands. "I don't know which I'm more upset about, the fact that you lied or that you risked your life."

While I was slamming down the rapids in this little raft, Alma's hair whipping behind her and into my face, I had the weirdest feeling that I did know how to swim. I mean, I knew I'd never swum before. Not ever. (One of the side effects of being a sick kid.) But in those moments I'd felt like

I'd swum hundreds of times, could even feel my body slicing the water, as if my muscles and bones and skin held a memory my mind had forgotten.

"If you'd rather me not go," Mom says now, for the fiftieth time this week, "I'll cancel the whole thing."

"You don't have a choice, right?" I won't embarrass her with a discussion of our finances in front of the girls, even though they know it all. How the money from Pop-Pop's estate has dwindled after all the time Mom's had to take off. How we need a new roof, and soon the water heater will go, and we have an outstanding balance on our property taxes.

Mom squeezes my forearm, peers into my face in that way that makes me feel like she's trying to capture a piece of me. "Does that mean you'd rather I stay?"

"No, it doesn't. I'm fine. I'm almost eighteen."

"Eighteen in three months is not 'almost.'" She glances at my Basement Tapes T-shirt, but I know she's seeing beneath it to the scar that bisects me.

"Two and a half months. And I'm feeling good. Great, actually." In my socked feet, I ballerina-twirl on the tile floor. "Besides, what kind of college recruiter doesn't leave the state?"

Her boss finally gave her an ultimatum: get back on the road or find a new job. He'd been accommodating for so long. Through the desperate waiting for a donor match. The surgery. A happy day for us, but a funeral for someone else. And then through the dicey recovery, loads of anti-rejection meds and the slow march of time when I could only hope my body got the *accept or time's up* memo.

"I'm fine," I repeat. I don't mention I might be getting a cold. Colds for transplant patients can be lethal, though I'm less worried about that one year out. "I'm perfect. It's only a week."

Please go. Please let me breathe on my own.

"Okay," she finally says, the word dragging its shoelaces. "But we'll talk every day, right?"

"Uh . . . I thought we agreed to talk sometimes but text every day."

She tilts her head as if she's weighing something. "And by the time I get back you'll be finished with all the practice tests. Right?" She taps a newly manicured fingernail on my GED study manual where it sits on the counter, regrettably flour-dusted and batter-spattered. Alma and Jules have another year of school once the current one ends in June, but it was pointless to keep trying to do school the traditional way with as much as I missed.

"Yes, Mom," Alma and I say in unison. Alma giggles.

"Mrs. S.," Alma says, stepping up and linking her arm in mine. "I promise we'll take good care of Linnea. You know how levelheaded we are."

"Levelheaded," Julie repeats from behind the pages of *Catch-22.* "Ha."

Later, the three of us are in my room. I'm folding laundry. Julie is on the bed—reading, naturally—and Alma is at my desktop, opening a hundred windows and bouncing between them. And that's Alma without caffeine.

There's a giant Austin City Limits Fest poster on the wall above my desk, a bird's-eye view of the festival with its throngs of people, jumbotron-flanked music stages, food vendors, litter, porta potties, life. Julie and Alma have gone the last two years and wanted me to go so badly to the last one, but I was only six months post-op, and the thought of walking around Zilker Park in the heat, in the middle of thousands of people who might jostle the new heart inside my chest, sent me into a spiral of panic. I was relieved when Mom said absolutely not.

"Would it be tacky to ask you to bake for your own party?" Alma asks.

"What party?" I drag my eyes away from the poster and back to my task. I cuff a pair of paisley socks together.

Alma twirls the desk chair around to face me. "You know, the one-year thing."

"That's sweet 'n' all, but remember? I said I didn't want a party."

"You don't think that's selfish?" she says.

"How's that?" I peel a dryer sheet away from a neon-pink tank top; the crackle of static zips up my fingers and settles in my palms.

"Me and Jules were out of our minds with worry." During the surgery, she means. Or maybe she means before too. "Weren't we, Jules?" She bounces onto the bed.

"I knew she'd be fine," Julie says, closing the book on her finger.

"Admit it, you were worried," Alma says.

"Maybe I was." Julie sits up, using a finger to trace one of the armadillos stitched onto my duvet. And then another. "A little."

"See?" Alma says. "We need a party for *us*, Linn, even if you don't. Don't they say getting to the one-year mark is key?"

"If by 'they,' you mean doctors, then yes, that's what they say." I don't need the calendar to tell me this heart is mine, though. I can feel it.

It's not my body that worries me . . . it's my mind. Last night's dream wasn't an anomaly. For the last month, my dreams have been starting ordinary and ending with a heart where it doesn't belong (in a bucket of sand at the beach, behind bars at a zoo, in a display case at a jeweler's). And my real heart, the one that's safely tucked into my chest, is always pinballing wildly when I wake, as if it's looking for an exit chute.

So maybe I'm kidding myself about feeling that ownership.

"I guess we could order the dessert," Alma says, "even though it wouldn't be half as good as yours. But if you're sick of baking—"

"Ahem," I interrupt. "Transplantee here. Saying she doesn't want a party." Getting through the first year without my body realizing the heart is an aftermarket part is a measure of tricking the universe as it is. I don't need to stick out my tongue at fate via party hats and streamers, too.

"Yeah, okay, the transplantee has spoken," Jules says, rolling over onto her stomach and flipping through the unread pages of her book to peek at the end.

Alma huffs. "What a blast you two are." She goes over to the window, pops out the screen, and leans it up against the wall. She's been crawling out onto the roof for years, at first just because she couldn't at home in her single-story house, and then later, to smoke. I can't even stick my whole head out of my unscreened window without feeling vertigo and imagining myself splattered on the sidewalk below.

Alma settles herself on the roof, her knees pulled to her chest. A bee jitters through the open window and into my room. I try to shoo it back out, but that only seems to agitate it.

"Some help, Jules?"

She swats at it with her book. "Looks like a wasp."

"They're all bees to me," I say.

"Good one." She's already reading again. Julie is a great friend to have if you're worried about your social skills. You can't help but look good in comparison.

I go over to the window to put the screen back in. I brace myself for the quick grip of panic at being near a large hole to the outside two stories up. No panic. Instead, a tug. A pull. Outward. Toward the roof. I toss the screen aside. I stick my head out and lean. No terror. Just excitement. I breathe in, deeply. I climb out. All the way out.

"¡Qué tienes!" Alma slides a few inches down the roof's gentle pitch and steadies herself by gripping the window frame. A cigarette hangs off her lip as she gapes at me. "What are you *doing*?"

"Living a little." I sit and press my palms against the roof, liking the pebbly warmth against my skin.

"¡Tan loca!" she says, more to herself. She holds her hands out like she's ready to catch me. "You okay?"

"Yeah. I am." There's no frantic clutching in my belly. No biscuit-sized lump in my throat. I can't explain it, but there it is. I love seeing the neighborhood from this perspective, the leafy crowns of the cedars, the bricks in the chimneys stacked like layer cake, the distant field thick with bluebonnets that looks like a body of water from this height.

Alma whoops with delight. "Way to trounce your fear, girl!"

An easy smile lifts the corners of my lips. "That's a good way to put it."

"Hey," she says, pointing into the distance toward a guy walking a bunch of dogs. "Isn't that Dave or Demeter or Dexter? The neighborhood new guy?"

I block the sun with my hand. Daniel's right on time. Inwardly, I smile.

"Spill," Alma says. "You've talked to him, haven't you?"

"Maybe." I have, just once—not that he remembers. Daniel's from Michigan. He's not in high school either. Graduated. And more than cute, if you like the hopelessly disheveled look, which I guess I do. I'm disappointed that he takes a left instead of a right and moves away from the house. I want him to see me up here and think I'm kind of badass.

Alma squints. "He's easy on the eyes."

"You must have Supergirl vision."

"I do when I want to." She pats my hand. "Just looking, by the way. I would never try to steal a guy you're sniffing around."

"Sniffing? I don't sniff."

"*Yet*," she says. "Where there's a yet, there's hope."

Daniel snaps the tangle of leashes as the dogs weave in four different directions. The fact that he can't control his charges makes him that much more interesting.

Julie's at the window now. "Holy shit, Linnea. WTF?"

I laugh. "The only way past a fear is through it, right?" A bee zips over, zags around my face. I backhand it away.

With a twisty wrist, Alma snuffs her cigarette out on a roof shingle. She turns away from me and exhales one last mouthful of smoke.

"Bum a smoke?" I ask.

"What?" The breeze plays her hair across her face, and she looks at me through it.

"A cigarette. For me."

"Linnea—"

"I thought my mom already left. And yet, here you are."

Julie sticks her head farther out the window. "But isn't smoking like the worst thing . . . you know . . . for your . . ."

I lean over, surprised that the shift in weight doesn't trigger an internal alarm. The cigarettes are under Alma's knee. I grab a corner of the crinkly pack and slide it toward me. Alma is too stunned to do anything. I tap one out and bring it to my lips.

"A light?" I ask.

She sets her jaw and shakes her head.

"C'mon," I say. "Don't make me go back inside just for matches."

"That's fucked up," Julie says.

Alma touches my knee, her voice soft. "You're supposed to take better care of it."

"It? You mean my heart? So *you* can smoke, and it's okay—"

"It's not okay," Julie says. "It's disgusting. She stinks."

Alma glares at her.

"But it's worse if *I* smoke," I say, "because it's not my heart. Is that what you guys mean? I'm supposed to take better care of it because it's on loan?"

"Well, that's a strange way to put it," Alma says. She stands her lighter between us and picks at a loose roof shingle with her thumbnail.

Somewhere down the street a lawn mower starts. Chattering squirrels race up a tree. Kids shout playfully in a nearby backyard.

Julie takes a deep breath. "Yeah, that is a weird way to say it." She extends her hand, and, after three heartbeats, I drop the cigarette into it. "Because when you borrow something," Jules says, "you have to give it back."

Maybe that's what I'm afraid of.

And maybe that's what my dreams are trying to tell me.

MAXINE

Every day is the same.

I get up in the dark—sometimes after barely sleeping—and brew the coffee double strength. Once I've downed two cups, I wake the boys and get them ready for school. Then two more cups. After school for them and sometimes for me (depending on whether or not I bother going), the goal is to fill up the hours before bed in a way that makes my brothers think they're in a normal family.

They always ask about Harper.

"Why won't she come back?" one of them will ask through a square meal or toothpaste foam or a damp facecloth.

"Remember?" I'll say, trying not to let my gritted teeth grind my words to dust. "She can't come back, sweetie."

"But *why*, Max? Doesn't she love us anymore?"

"Of course she loves us. *Loved* us. But when it's somebody's time to go to heaven, they can't come back anymore." I don't believe in a fated time to go, like a trapdoor on a calendar. And I sure as hell don't believe in heaven. But I'm learning that part of parenting is leaning on the kindness of lies.

The boys are old enough to understand death. I've even talked to their teachers about it. It's just that they don't want to accept it, thanks to one of Race's schoolmates, who told my brother about a movie where people crawled out of their graves. Hungry. And just in case Race might've dismissed this as make-believe, the lousy little snot said his grandmother knows it's true because it's in the Bible. "You just hafta believe enough, Max," Race parroted. "You're not supposed to forget."

So my brothers have started dragging an extra plate out of the cupboard at dinnertime. They clang utensils against it. Float a napkin over it. And drop glances at it during the meal.

It kills me to see that empty seat. That empty dish. That motionless fork and knife. But the boys are too invested in it for me to sweep it all off the table with one quick arm and yell that Harper is nothing but bones by now.

Mom's chair is empty, too. But that's different. And they're used to that, a year later.

And me? What am I used to a whole year later?

The days are all the same. One by one. Shuffling footsteps without a destination.

Sunday, 3:30. I'm drinking coffee and reading the boys' spring break day camp schedule. They're watching something on TV that Mom would've never allowed a year ago, something peppered with explosions.

ABOUT	DAY CAMP	CONTACT	REGISTER

SCHEDULE:

Monday a.m.	Tick, tock, campers! Go back in time to see what life was like for the first settlers in the Hill Country! (Including a horse-and-buggy wildflower tour!)

I should be grateful I don't need to wash clothes by beating them with rocks in the crick, but I just can't muster the enthusiasm. Vaguely, I wonder whether the time travel will include accurate history. As in native-peoples-brutally-wiped-out accurate. Since you can't be taller than a fourth-grader to attend this camp, I'm thinking not.

There's a knock on the back door. Shelby breezes in a second after the knock.

"How about waiting for 'come in'?" I say, but I don't mean it. Shelby walking in like she lives here is a whiff of normal.

She greets me with a side hug. "If I thought you might be doing something you needed privacy for, I would've. Something involving the f-word. Remember that? Fun?"

"Vaguely." The last time I hung out with Chris was fun. Mostly, though, it's the other f-word—forgetting—that is the only way I can get to fun.

There's a muffled thud above our heads. Shelby points to the ceiling, quirks a brow, and mouths *Mom?* I nod.

I showed up at the hospital for Mom on Friday, as planned, but she refused to change into her street clothes. So I did what any loving daughter would do: I gave up and led her to the car in her bathrobe.

I wonder if it's comforting for the boys to know she's home, even if she's mildly catatonic behind the closed door of Harper's bedroom, wearing Harper's clothes and muttering to herself in Harper's mirror. I guess the hospital fixing her is too much to hope for. I know it must be worse for her—I *know*—but sometimes I hate her for leaving me with everything.

"Have I got the color for you," Shelby says, all car-salesman smooth, rooting in her enormous pleather purse that smells like waiting room furniture.

"Does this have something to do with fun?"

"I was just at the Estée Lauder counter."

"I was thinking you look especially glam," I say. She does, her wide blue eyes expertly lined and shadowed, her short platinum hair sleekly blunt against her shimmery jaw. "Don't tell me—while the Estée elves were plying you with samples, you helped yourself to something with a price tag."

She scowls. "Miss Morality all of a sudden." She pulls out a shiny gold tube of lipstick and pulls off the cap with a pop.

"Just observing . . . not judging."

"Pucker," she says and cradles my chin in her hand.

I pull out of her grasp and glug the coffee down the drain. I don't even like coffee. Harper did. Running a damp sponge over the counter, I slow down near a coffee ring stain on the old chipped white Formica, not sure if I caused it or if my sister did. Wishing I could say for sure it was hers.

"You're pretty," Shelby announces, like it's a diagnosis. "It's time for you to start acting the part."

"Shel, you know I hate lipstick. It's like eating crayons. Gradually."

"But it's Seduction after Dark."

"Looks like orange."

"You used to be daring, Maxine."

"I'm feeling judgment," I warn.

"Just observing." She plunks the uncapped lipstick down on the counter. It looks like a tiny, poised missile. "Okay, well at least let me do something about those bags." She goes back to digging through her purse.

I look around. "What bags?"

It's telling that I think grocery bags.

"The ones under your eyes."

"How do you know I'm not perfecting those for a makeover photo shoot? The before part, naturally."

"Ha. You're exhausted, Max. I get it. But until you can get beauty sleep, you've got to rely on Products." (Yes, she says it capitalized. Products possess divinity for Shelby.)

I sit at the kitchen table, anchor my elbows on a sticky placemat, and prop my chin in my hands. Shelby squeezes my shoulders, causing the chair to wobble against the linoleum. I feel the exhaustion draining from my limbs as I sit still, but it doesn't leave me entirely. It pools somewhere around my heart.

"Don't," I say, "unless you want me to fall asleep right here."

"You have kolache-sized knots in here." She digs into the back of my neck with an expert knuckle.

"By design. Tension keeps me awake." I grab her hand. Shelby's planning on going to massage school. While I may need a massage, I don't have time for one. "When you have to get your practicum hours or whatever, I'll be a guinea pig for you. But I'm good for now."

"Lawd, let me help you, girl." She frees her hand.

"You help me plenty," I say. "You bring the normal."

"Hey, I know!" She releases my hair from its ponytail and lifts sections of it away from my scalp. "I'll do something about this listless hair." She keeps sectioning, which feels like a mini-massage.

"It's clean. Volume is a luxury I don't have."

"Think maximizer and chunky auburn highlights," she says.

Race pads into the kitchen. "Shelby!" He grabs her waist and squeezes, even though his arms don't reach all the way around. He's five, which is a developmental world away from Will's eight. So Will is much harder to distract.

She ruffles his hair fast, like she's determined to create static. "You being good for your big sister?"

"Watch out," I say to Race. "Before you know it, you'll have chunky auburn highlights."

He squirms out of the hug and looks up at Shelby. "Did you bring me something?"

"Race," I say, "don't be rude."

"Of course I did," Shelby says. "Don't I always?" She snatches the lipstick off the counter. "A special crayon. Goes on extra thick."

"Cool! Do I have to share it with Will?"

"I think I have something in here for big brother." She digs in her purse again and comes up with an elegant box of eye shadow in bruised sunset colors. "A tiny box of paints. They work best if you mix them with water."

I cringe at the thought of wet eye shadow streaking the walls. But seeing Race's delight at the "gifts" changes my cringe to a laugh. "Remember, that stuff stays on paper only. And tell your brother dinner will be ready soon."

He sniffs the air. "I don't smell anything."

I stand up. "That's because it's still all up here, wise guy." I tap my temple and wink. Glad he's small enough that I can still do this, I scoop him up and plant a kiss on his cheek. The kind that makes him wipe it off. And to think a year ago I thought little half brothers were pesky cohabitants I had to steer around. To think a year ago I was annoyed their totally out-of-the-picture father never gave us a break from them.

Clutching his spoils, Race runs out of the room.

"How's Will?" Shelby asks.

"You know . . . the same." I bite my thumbnail. "Has nightmares sometimes."

I don't look at Shelby, because I don't want to see how bad it all is, reflected back to me. Dinner. That's something to do.

I open the fridge and hope for inspiration or ingredients. Nada. Just cold and empty. I knee it shut and am faced with one of the pictures magneted to the front. Harper and Ezra, last year's prom. She wears a stunning satiny one-sleeve royal-blue dress and a dazzling smile. Her dark brown hair is loose and wild and ridiculously lush, whatever the polar opposite of "listless" is. She has her arm around Ezra in this effort-less, relaxed way, and although she's looking at the camera, he's looking at her. She's so unselfconsciously alive in the photo that I always lapse into present tense when I look. I correct myself: *Wore. Was. Had. Loved.*

"Should I order pizza?" Shelby asks.

"Absolutely."

She opens the junk drawer and paws through it for the right menu.

Race patters in again. "Will wants to know what we're having—he said he's flamished."

"Pizza pie!" Shelby says proudly, like she invented it.

"Cool!" He turns to leave and deliver the news, but stops and calls over his shoulder, "Don't forget to get half with mushrooms. For Harper."

And he runs back out.

Shelby blankets me in a look I wish I could shrug out of. One part helplessness, one part pity, it says, *Shit, it really* is *as bad as all that.*

Yes, and tomorrow will be more of the same.

Trying to fill emptiness with nothing but two hands and one heart.

LINNEA

I'm alone. Finally.

I'm sitting on the roof, relishing the lightness of the air on my skin. The tarry shingles retain the day's heat, even though the sun is sinking. I have a Bic lighter in one pocket of my capris and a pack of Mom's super-secret-stash cigarettes in the other. I'm trying to talk myself out of lighting up.

Mom thinks she's hiding her occasional habit from me, and I wouldn't tell her otherwise. I get it: this year has been über-stressful. There were times in the early months after my surgery where she'd run out for groceries and come back with few items but with more energy and a whiff of ashtray. It didn't take me long to discover her hiding place—a box in the garage marked *2013 tax receipts*. (The giveaway? The top of that box was less dusty than *2016 tax receipts*.)

Smoking is the worst thing for any heart, and I don't have just any heart. Mine had to be coaxed to work with a circulatory system it just met. Before today, I had never even thought about smoking. Before today, I had never craved a cigarette, the sharp, burned bitterness crouched on the back of my tongue like a dare.

Julie was expected at home for Sunday night dinner with her parents, and though that's a standing family-only thing, she called them and asked if I could come too. I think she was worried about leaving me alone. I hated disappointing her, but alone was exactly where I wanted to be. I thought about studying for the GED and got as far as de-flouring the damn book. I couldn't make myself care about the causes of World War I with a war raging in my head.

Alma had to visit her great-grandmother in San Antonio and invited me to come along. That was harder to turn down; I feel more comfortable around Alma's family. Julie's mom and dad treat me like I've got a stress fracture running through me instead of a surgical scar, and any second the fissure will erupt, leaving me to crumble before their eyes.

Alma and I drove down to San Antone last November to celebrate the last two days of Día de los Muertos with her great-grandmother, and though I thought it would be creepy and morbid, it was exactly the opposite. It was this cool space where art and memory and faith intersected and let you feel sadness right alongside joy. When we got there, Señora Gutierrez took one of my hands in both of hers, held my gaze for a long while, and then beamed at me like she had seen my alma (my soul) . . . and had approved.

There were three small altars set up in her home: for her husband, one of her sons, and one granddaughter. After I'd added the biscochitos I'd made to all that she'd already arranged (stuff like photos, handwritten poems, candy, bread . . . you know, the ingredients of a life that seem ordinary when you look at them from one direction, spectacular from another), she asked me to help her light candles for the loved ones she'd lost. I was surprised by all the beauty waiting in the small places: the soft scratch of the wooden match against the box, the wick catching like a sudden bloom, the tremulous quiver of the new flame. Then we lit a candle for the heart donor (her idea), and she said a prayer for the donor's alma in Spanish that was more beautiful to me for not being translated, and then she turned to me, laughed gently, and told me I needed to eat more. And since Alma's grandparents own two restaurants in San Antonio, that's not hard to do when I'm there.

But as fond as I am of Alma's whole family, I get the sense I'm supposed to be on my own today.

My hair is tied up in a paisley bandanna smeared with buttercream. I redid my cupcakes, and they came out perfect. As good as ever, if not better than ever. The bad batch meant nothing.

I lean over the roofline, expecting to feel the familiar plummet in my belly. The clamminess in my palms. The flutter in my throat.

They're not there, though. There's just me, relaxed, admiring the red poppies swarming the mailbox post. I'll pick some for the mason jar on the kitchen table.

A wasp crashes my inner peace party. And then another. Maybe they're after the sugar residue on my head. I yank the bandanna off and whip it into my room.

But the damn bug still hovers around me. And another. And another. *Really?*

Scanning the eaves, I locate a papery nest—no bigger than my fist—suspended above my window. If it weren't packed with little insect bodies, I might see it as lovely and delicate, a dark bedtime story or a strange dream catcher. More yellow and black bodies wriggle out and creep in. "You've got to go." For a second, my voice sounds unfamiliar to me. I shake it off and get to work.

Searching the cobwebby garage shelves, I find a rusted can of hornet killer. Should work on wasps, too, right?

The spray claims to shoot a forty-foot stream of poison. The instructions say not to get too close to the nest when you douse it. Poison blowback and the risk of angry hornets exiting before mass extermination. So rather than go back onto the roof, I plan a land-based assault.

I walk to the side yard beneath my window, aim the nozzle, and press. Nothing.

I shake the can and try again. A weary spit of foam dribbles onto my hand. I run the dispenser under water from the outdoor spigot and try again, but it won't stream like the picture promises. Finally, just about ready to give up, I try again, and a gush of chemical sneezes out. No way it's forty feet, though. I'll have to get closer.

I go back to the garage and drag the ladder over to the house. I'm sweating like it's my job. As I struggle to hoist the ladder upright against the siding, something furry brushes against my bare leg. I jump. The ladder crashes to the ground.

"Sorry!" I hear from down the street. "He's friendly."

Oh.

Oh.

It's Daniel. With his dog posse, chasing after the escapee. A midsize black-and-white dog, twining itself around my legs. Not a toddler-size wasp.

My legs! When was the last time I shaved? Why didn't I choose jeans instead of capris? Stupid summer-in-April Texas! But it's dusky out. Will the hair be noticeable? Oh. My. God. My hair. It must look terrifying. It was smashed under a bandanna all day. Flat and greasy.

I want to crawl up the ladder and hide in the wasps' nest, but I still haven't managed to get the ladder pointing upward. So I sit on the grass, crisscross my legs, and pull the dog onto my lap. That'll hide my neglected legs. With one discreet hand, I try to fluff the top of my flattened hair.

Daniel stands over me. He's slightly out of breath, though he seems to be trying to hide it. He unwinds the coil of leashes, leaving a red band of skin over his knuckles. The scattered stubble along his jaw makes him seem older today. He was clean-shaven that day a couple of weeks ago when I first met him. I had been leaving for work and saw the U-Haul truck in the driveway three houses down. I spotted a cute guy, my age-ish, lugging boxes out of the truck and into the garage. So I stopped and introduced myself, even though that is *so* not like me.

"So you live here?" Daniel asks.

"No, I'm just trying to break in. I hear the owners are away."

He laughs, and I want to grab the sound from the air and wrap it around me.

"You really love dogs, huh?" I say. An old black lab with a gray chin squats and pees on my lawn. She's one of four on leashes. The dog in my lap makes five.

Daniel points at the escapee and scowls. "Socks, I thought we had an agreement."

Socks looks up at me and stops panting long enough to whimper. I imagine he's saying, "Save me, save me!"

"Socks, huh?" I say, sizing up his white legs and paws. "Not the most original name."

"I know, right? But don't look at me. He's not mine." He clips a leash on Socks, who flips belly-up and rubs his back on the grass christened by the lab.

I scratch Socks's underside, much to his squirmy delight. "Are any of them yours?"

"Yup." He stoops to pat a pensive-looking Jack Russell.

"And . . ." I say, "his name?"

"Nietzsche."

"Touché." I laugh. "So, you're a dog-walker?"

"Yeah, but not a very good one at the moment." He looks around him at the stalled bunch, expressing their displeasure in barks and whines. "I'm Daniel."

Oh great. So he doesn't even remember talking to me. I'm *that* memorable.

He reaches out his hand, and my heart beats in happy terror. Is he trying to shake my hand or help me up? I decide to assume it's both and manage to gracefully rise, still holding onto his hand. "Sorry I was preoccupied when you stopped by the other day," he says.

"No problem. Moving does that to people."

"Yeah, well. It was nice of you to say hi. I couldn't remember if I ever got around to actually introducing myself."

"You did, and I'm Lin—"

"Linnea," he finishes. "I remember. You don't hear that name too often. It's nice."

I turn into a heap of frosting sliding off a warm cupcake. I let go of his hand since the shaking / helping up must be officially over by now.

"You're from Michigan, right?" I say.

"Hey, you remembered." He seems genuinely pleased.

Come up with something better than *I hear it's cold up there*. "How are you liking Texas so far?" Marginally better.

"Where I'm from, it's still cold as hell in April, so I like this."

"Good deal."

"Plus y'all are really friendly," he adds.

A loud motorcycle roars down the street. I let it pass before I speak. "Is that a good thing or a bad thing?"

"Oh, I think it's a good thing."

"And you got the 'y'all' down," I say. "That'll serve you well here."

"I'm getting that impression. I studied my Texisms before we moved. The one I don't think I'll ever find a use for, though, is—"

A *yipe* cuts him off. We assess the pack. Socks has grown bored and is nipping at the legs of a poodle-looking mutt that yelps again in protest.

"I should get the gang home," he says. "Do you need any help?"

"Huh?" That's me, of course. The queen of natural, compelling convo.

He gestures toward the still-horizontal ladder. "You're painting, right?"

"Oh, that. No, there's a wasp nest up there."

"You have spray?"

I nod.

"It's best to wait 'til it's darker," he says, "'til they're all back in the nest for the night."

"Oh. Okay."

"I can help," he says.

I don't want to insult him by turning down his offer, but I don't want to appear damsel-in-distress either. I leave it open to interpretation. "Thanks."

"I know I seem incompetent." He looks up at me, grins, and reveals a lone dimple, which now officially makes me unbearably self-conscious about my appearance. "But I'm usually pretty good with them." Standing straight, he drags his hand through his hair and tugs the leash of a basset hound sacked out on the grass and chewing on blades. He easily hefts the ladder off the ground and leans it against the house. "I'll run them all home, and then I'll be back."

Daniel twirls around, pulling the pack down the street, the exhausted basset slowing the pace. He backward-glances and catches me looking. He lifts a leash-clutching hand in a wave.

Will it look too obvious if I change before he gets back? Wash my hair? Bake him a cake?

Just be yourself, I tell myself, wondering who exactly "myself" is. The one Mom accuses of overcompensating, or the timid one who would never send back a bad meal because she doesn't want to stress out the server?

Better to go ahead and kill the damn wasps, prove you don't need a man to get the job done.

I concentrate on climbing up the ladder, and the sound of my feet on the rungs focuses my thoughts, most of which start with *Daniel*.

Halfway up is close enough. I start my assault. The spray nozzle fires and the stream hits the nest. There's a wasp hovering around my face as if trying to ID me as the assassin. I use my free hand to wave it away. It stings my cheek.

"Ow! Hey!"

My soles start to slip off the rung. Instinctively, I grip the sides of the ladder with both hands, losing the can of poison.

There's another wasp on my wrist. I shake my arm, trying to bounce it off.

"Really?" I need to get off this ladder.

As I descend, I feel one under my shirt. Legs and wings. Ew. I grab the hem of my tee and parachute the fabric so the bee will fly out, but it stings me on the stomach anyway.

And then time goes noodley. Vengeful needles with teeth, more bees sting me: legs, arms, neck. I'm feeling woozy now, not sure whether the house is receding or I am. I'm lower down on the ladder but not on solid ground yet. My footing gives out, and I fall back on the grass, the air knocked out of my lungs in a percussive heave.

I press a palm against my chest to steady the smacking inside. I try to get up, but my body's too heavy to move. Except for the erratic squeak of bats, I'm alone.

My throat closes in on itself. The light filtering into my vision narrows down to the thinnest straw. I'm vibrating with a relentless buzz-ingbuzzingbuzzing . . . is it my heart?

Where is my heart?

MAXINE 4

The four of us are at the kitchen table, two pizzas our centerpiece. Race is picking mushrooms off his slice and heaping them onto Shelby's. "Look at my spoils!" she crows each time. Darkness has gathered outside, and I glance at the window, the old tasseled kitschy spoon-patterned curtains (badly in need of a wash) pulled aside so the glass is a mirror. I see us all flanking the oval table and want to imagine we fill in the missing parts.

The fridge kicks on. The rattle that I thought had gone away is back and louder than ever. It gives me a headache. Not the noise itself, but what it predicts. A big withdrawal out of the savings account with no big deposits in sight. If it weren't for Mom having a decent enough job before and always putting some aside, I don't know how we could've gotten through the year. Even if I did pull the plug on school, I wouldn't be able to earn enough to cover childcare for the boys. And I certainly can't leave them with Mom. This week's day camp is a gift from Shelby's parents. Race and Will attended last year and loved it; they've been asking about it since Christmas. I hate taking charity, but I'm glad they don't have to be disappointed.

"It sounds like it's lifting off," Race says, pointing to the fridge, "to outer space!"

"Yeah, well, I wish it would send a better one back to take its place," I say.

"It's already cold in outer space," Will says. "Nobody needs fridges there."

Shelby's on her feet. "Anyone want anything while I'm up?"

"Gummy worms?" Race tries.

"Fat chance," I say.

Shelby opens a cupboard, a drawer. She navigates the kitchen comfortably, but something about the way the light hits her (and there's a bulb out; I'll have to get to that), or the way her flawless makeup contrasts the cabinets painted a rough teal blue (we left the boys' messy brushstrokes on the lower half), makes her seem like an actor on a set. Like she'll go home to her real world eventually. Which, of course, she will. I feel a lump of envy rise in my throat and send dough and cheese in to push it down.

She comes back to the table with more napkins and a fork and knife. "Is it just me, or is the pepperoni particularly greasy tonight?"

"It's delicious," Will says, and pats it with careful fingers.

"Harper said eating pizza with a fork is like drinking water with a spoon," Race says. "She says it's cheating."

Shelby's eyes flit to mine. Without moving a muscle, she's holding my hand.

I smile at Race, hoping he doesn't notice the tension glazing the smile. "I think Shelby gets a pass since you've cheated by unloading half your toppings onto her plate."

Will watches Shelby cut up her pizza. He drops another crust into the box and announces: "Somebody brought a knife to school."

"Cool!" Race says.

"No, not cool," I say. "Will, when did that happen?"

"On Friday."

"And why didn't you tell me about it?"

He looks confused. "I just did."

"I mean when the bus dropped you off. Remember, I asked how your day was, like I always do? And you said 'Good,' like you always do?"

Will shrugs and scrunches up his marinara face. "I didn't think of it then."

Tossing my balled-up napkin onto my dish, I stand up and start clearing the table. I drop saucy napkins in the empty box, close the lid on them.

"This is Texas, after all," Shelby says. "Only a state that allows you to walk around with automatic *guns* in public places is one where a third-grader would think it's okay to bring a knife to show and tell."

"Don't mess with Texas!" Race shouts, leveling a crust at his brother. Will grabs a self-defense crust from the other box.

"You don't have permits for those weapons, so they have to go back to being pizza crusts."

Race giggles. I pinch his cheek.

"The girl who brought the knife was a fifth-grader," Will says. "And it wasn't for show and tell. They don't have that in fifth grade."

"He was a she," Shelby says. "Even more depressing."

I move to the sink, stop the drain, and fill it with soapy water. The dishwasher's been on the fritz for a while. Even guided by YouTube videos, Ezra couldn't fix it. "Boys, pick up your rooms and get your PJs out. Baths in ten."

"Our room's too heavy for us to pick up," Will says. Race falls off his chair laughing.

"Ha ha, my little smarty pants." I hand Will a napkin. "Wipe those fingers, please."

"Can't we have a half hour of TV first?" Race pleads.

I peer out of the window above the sink. The neighbors' speedboat is like a reverse shadow, a boat-shaped hole in the dark. I can't help but see my own reflection superimposed on it. As if finding freedom is just a matter of owning something that can motor you away.

"Aunt Shelby says you can have fifteen minutes of mush-the-brain time," Shelby tells the boys. "And only a show with zero chance of knives or guns."

"Aunt?" Race repeats.

Shelby takes his hand. "That's right, kiddo. I've decided I want to be an aunt. I'm getting older, you know."

As she leads them to the living room, there's a thud from above. I tug the curtain on its rod 'til it covers the window, plop a slice of pizza on a plate, and head upstairs. I pass the open door of my dark room, the pale sheets of my unmade bed like a raft on a silent sea. I step over a puddle of loose Legos in front of the closed door of my mother's room, which hasn't been slept in for a year (unless you count Mom's college roommate who came from Vermont for the funeral). Across from that is the boys' room, their bunk beds against the one emerald-green wall.

And at the end of the hallway, Harper's room.

I turn the handle and push, but something stops the door from swinging open. Not again.

I press my mouth to the crack in the door. "Mom, can I come in?"

Silence.

"Mom, are you okay? We heard something."

More silence. Then, an inhale and, tersely: "I dropped a book."

"Can I come in?"

Pause. "Why?"

Because I can't take your word that it was only a book. Because I can't be sure you haven't found a way to hurt yourself. "Because I need to talk to you. Boy trouble," I lie. It's so hard pretending I'm still the child in this relationship.

"Why didn't you say so?" Her voice is deceptively strong. "Come in."

"You pushed the dresser up against the door again?"

"It does seem to be there. But I didn't put it there."

"I really need to talk to you, Mom. No one else understands." The kindness of lies.

"Hold on a minute." I hear her slippers ski the wood floor. And then the scrape of the furniture, a trek that will leave gouges.

I open the door, and there she is, my mother and not my mother.

She's wearing a weird mishmash of Harper's clothes: earth-tone paisley cardigan over neon-orange tank over pilled black yoga pants. Only the slippers are hers.

But at least she's clean today. And she's looking right at me instead of past me. I'll take what I can get.

"Mom, how about some pizza?"

She shakes her head. I set it on Harper's desk, next to the soup I delivered hours ago. All Mom eats anymore are protein bars (peanut butter), probably because one was in Harper's bag the night she died. Mom's doctor says there are worse things she could be surviving on. And for weeks after Harper's death, Mom wasn't eating at all, so this is an improvement.

My sister's collection of neon-haired troll dolls glower at the untouched food, the neat row of them against the wall belying the wildness of their hair ("Pink, orange, and green, oh my!" Harper used to say when she'd tickle the boys with them). Above them are words calligraphed by Harper onto the plaster wall: *I took my power in my hand and went against the world.* Emily Dickinson was one of Harper's heroes, which is ironic when you consider Emily was a shut-in, and Harper considered a night at home a major case of missing out.

"Is Christopher treating you well?" Mom asks.

Huh? Oh yeah: I feigned boy trouble to get in. "Yes, sure he is."

"Then what's wrong?"

I scramble to make something up, but something benign so she won't worry. "Well, I think he wants to get serious already."

She presses her lips into a straight line. "You're too young for serious."

"That's what I figured."

I wait for more. The parental wisdom I desperately need. I get silence.

As always when I'm in this room, my gaze is pulled to where Harper's most alive, her Austin City Limits music festival wall. Pastel thumbtacks hold up an official poster from every year of the four she attended, along with each of the wristbands, carefully cut off her wrist at the end of the weekend. And something I thought particularly weird at the time, the paper triangle from her first and last blue raspberry shaved ice of each festival. All pinned above her Yamaha electric piano.

I went with Harper to the last two ACLs and didn't see why it was her idea of heaven on earth. She'd always been musical, which is why she stuck with piano lessons and I didn't. True, some acts were great (like

Louis the Child, the xx, Milky Chance), but still, I was never convinced trudging around with like a hundred thousand profusely sweating people in ninety-degree mugginess made the acts worth it. She promised I'd like it better my second year, when I wasn't a music fest virgin. She was wrong.

So six months before she died, long before the artists were announced, she reserved only one early-early bird wristband for the following October's fest. When it came in the mail last September, it blindsided me. Holding the smooth fabric in the bowl of my hands, I couldn't stop sobbing.

Thinking I could erase some of the pain, I threw the wristband away. And regretted it the minute the garbage truck drove off. Whenever I look at that wall, I can't help but see the hole where that last memento should be.

"Ezra and Harper are made for each other," Mom says finally. "Don't you think?"

"Yeah, Mom, I think." Present tense. Her doctor said to go with it.

"She lights up for him."

"That she did," I mumble. "Does."

"And he clearly adores her."

"No doubt." Mom is in a period of "traumatic bereavement," not uncommon in the cases of untimely deaths of children. Her psychiatrist can't tell me when the period will end, or even *if* it'll end. But he said for there to be any chance of her coming back to us, I need to be patient with her.

"It would do your sister some good to be a little more serious. Ezra's a good influence on her."

The room feels stuffy. I wish I could open a window, but Ezra had to nail them shut when we discovered Mom had been crawling onto the roof to smoke.

"But you're already serious enough." Mom's tone is of someone who hates math trying to work out a math problem. "So you should just have fun for a long while."

I swipe a shiny protein bar wrapper from Harper's duvet into the trash and take a seat on the bed.

Mom yelps. "I wish you wouldn't sit on your sister's bed."

I hop up. That's new. "Sorry."

"It's just that she has nothing left, and you have everything, so the least we can do is keep her bed nice."

I don't point out to Mom that she sleeps in it every night, since that might make her sleep on the floor. "You're right."

I look around for what caused the thud. It seems like it was a book after all. *Journey through Chemistry*. Harper hated chemistry, cracked up at how the publisher added "journey" to make it seem like an adventure. "If you hate it so much, why didn't you turn the book in at the end of the year?" I'd asked. She rolled her eyes, as if explaining the obvious to her slightly (thirteen months) younger sib was such a chore. "Duh. I hated it so much that I *had* to keep it. To remind me of how nothing else will be that torturous. It'll cut down on life complaining overall."

"Is it okay if I pick that up?" I point to the book.

"Naturally." She blinks fast. "Why wouldn't it be?"

I scoop it up and hug it to my chest. I bring it up to my face, inhale through my nose. But it only smells like book. "Mom, we all miss her."

She tenses up. "You have your whole life in front of you, Maxine."

"And you still have Will. And Race." I don't add "and me," because I don't feel like any kind of prize.

Her voice is tight. "Are you trying to make me feel guilty? About not spending more time with the boys?"

"God, no. I'm not, Mom. I wouldn't. I just . . . I just wanted to let you know that we love you. We all do."

"You'll all leave, eventually."

"I'm not going anywhere." I slide the book onto the shelf, spine out. Her eyes fill.

I drape an arm around her; we're the same height so we fit together like wild-haired rubber troll dolls. Since Harper died, I can't full-on hug my mother. I learned that the hard way once; she nearly hit the ceiling when I embraced her and accused me of trying to drown her. Now she leans against me. I kiss her on the temple. Her skin is warm and soft.

"You take as long as you need," I whisper.

We stay that way for a little while. She straightens up, her voice flattened under tears. "I'm tired now, okay, Harper?"

That shouldn't hurt as much as it does.

"Of course, Mom. Let me help you get into bed."

And I do.

Before I head downstairs, I sit at the computer desk tucked in the little nook behind the hall closet. Harper had set up this old beater desktop for the boys to play games on a few weeks before she died. It's the perfect cranny for a work cubby, but I would've never noticed that on my own. Harper had a gift for showing people things they'd otherwise miss.

Three days after she died, I threw my laptop across the room when Shelby told me the pain would hurt less in time. "Like you would know!" I yelled. "Like you've ever felt this!"

Weeks later, I apologized to her for my computer violence, but she hugged me and said there was nothing to apologize for. "You could demolish a hundred laptops and I'd still be here." I wonder what kind of friend I would've been if the tables were turned.

I didn't have the money to replace my laptop, so I've used this clunky desktop for bill paying, which is getting more depressing each month. I keep hoping for a loaves-and-fishes miracle.

I bounce over to my e-mail to dilute the bill-paying experience. There's the typical smattering of spam, something from Chris (subject: thinking of you), which I'll read later. It's sweet he takes the time to send e-mails when really we get along fine with texts. Kind of retro and romantic.

"Where's Maxine?" I hear Race ask from downstairs.

"She's with your mom, sweetie," Shelby says.

"TV time is wrapping up!" I call out. "It's bath time for urchins."

Will groans.

Race says, "I'm not an urchin anyway. Am I, Aunt Shelby?"

Shelby murmurs something I don't hear, but her tone is warm and full.

I'm about to close out of my e-mail when a message catches my eye. And my breath.

Subject: your sister's death.

LINNEA

I'm underwater.

My lungs scream. My limbs flail. The water seals my eyes shut. Suddenly I remember I can't swim. A memory that floods me with terror. But then I hear a voice. Garbled into nonsense by the water in my ears, but then clearer. Someone's name.

"Linnea? Oh my God. Linnea?"

My name.

I try to open my eyes, but only one will obey. The other's stuck.

"Can you hear me?"

Daniel? Where am I? I hurt, yet I'm floating too. Am I floating on air? On water?

"Can you hear me?" His voice tugs at me when I need to float. "You're stung."

I try to say something, anything, but there's no room in my throat for words. Or for breath. I'm choking. Am I choking on water? No, that can't be. Only air touches my skin. Shit, I can't *breathe*. I'm on the ground, outside my house. And I can't breathe. I gasp.

"Yes, breathe," he says.

My lungs are thick, heavy, useless. Wasps. Everywhere. I close the one working eye because it hurts to keep it open. My cheeks have turned into cannibal potatoes that have swallowed my mouth.

My heart lurches with the memory of tumbling off the ladder. A thousand pinpricks. *My heart?*

"Linnea!"

Daniel's hands are on my hips. Patting, patting. Is that good touch? Bad touch? Why is he patting me like I'm one of the dogs?

"Linnea, where's your phone?"

My fingers stretch and clutch, blades of cool grass between them.

"Linnea, what about your pen? Where do you keep the pens?"

My fingers go slack. I start to float again, since that's when the pain floats too. Floats off and away from me.

"Shit," he says. "*Shit*. I'll be right back."

And then there's the sound of feet running and breath trying to squeeze into my chest.

I run my fingers over my scar. My heart beating. That's all that matters. The heart. *My* heart.

"Linnea." Daniel's out of breath. "Goddamnit, I have to do this."

Do *what?*

I hear a rustling. The air hits my skin differently, pockets of breeze in the damp stillness. And then there's a sound like a tiny cork being popped out of a tiny bottle, and a sound like Daniel sucking in his breath.

"I'm sorry," Daniel says. "I'm really, really sorry."

Sorry for wha—

The pain starts small but fierce—a mean, confident puncture— and gathers momentum, little fists inside my skin punching up my thigh and into my hip. A flower of space opens petals in my chest, rinsing my lungs with air.

"Linnea?"

My throat loosens. And I can open both eyes now.

"That's better," he says.

Daniel is kneeling beside me in the dark, the porch light behind him. His face is twisted with panic. Did I do that to him?

"I must've dropped my phone out here," he says. "I can't find it. Where's yours? I'll call 911."

"No!" I manage to say.

"But you were almost—"

"Please," I plead. "No ambulance."

"Okay, your mom then."

"Oh, God, that would be worse." She'd never leave me alone

again. Never let me go downtown, never mind to Chicago for school. She can't know.

"Dad?" he tries.

Anonymous sperm bank donors aren't dads. But I don't share that fact of my existence with people I just met. "My mom's away for work. She can't afford to get turned around."

"I don't know . . ."

I struggle to hike myself up on my elbows. "I'll be fine." The porch light looks good on Daniel, making his face one of summits and hollows. "See? I'm better already."

"Well, at least let me help you inside," he says, brow furrowed. "Make sure you're really okay."

"Deal."

"Hornets are the worst," he says once I'm on the couch, throw pillows that he adorably fluffed up for me propping me into a stiff right angle. He insists I recline and elevate my feet. "You didn't stand a chance."

"So does that mean I can't say, 'You should see the other guy'?"

There's his smile again. "How you feeling?"

"Good. See? No paramedics needed." I try to display an optimistic smile, but my cheeks are still puffy enough that it feels unnatural. Not only am I gritty with dirt (the couch will have to be steam cleaned), but there are red welts up and down my arms, my calves, I bet on my thighs under my capris too.

"Do you have any baking soda?" he asks.

I snicker.

"What's funny?" he says. "Did my northern accent show?"

It does, but that's cute, not funny. "Baking soda is one of the things I'd never run out of."

"You like to bake?"

"Something like that." I look down. My neck kills when I do. I point to my restaurant tee. "I work here. Desserts."

He smiles. "Cool. You're looking better, by the way."

"Better than what? Wait, don't answer that." I try to discreetly read-just on the couch so I'm not so stiff-looking. But then I feel like I'm getting ready to model lingerie. "What are you making with baking soda?"

"You'll see," Daniel says. "Point me to it."

"In the pantry." I point to the door with the ceramic four-leaf clover on the wall above it the size of a head. Mom's idea of luck.

"Is this part of the deal?" I say. "You bake something now?"

"If you tried my cooking, you'd rather take your chance with the wasps again."

He opens the pantry door, ducks inside. It seems surreal, this guy I've admired mostly from afar, in my house. Oh my God. He's the first guy-guy I've ever had in my house. Like a guy-I'm-interested-in guy and not a repair guy or please-sign-for-this-delivery guy. Dating is pretty low on the priority list when you're told your heart won't make it to prom.

I'm afraid to look around the room and see, like, a bra draped over a chair. Or a paperback with a windblown couple on the cover, man baring oiled pecs, woman barely containing trembling cleavage. Not that I'm a drape-bra-on-common-area-chair sort of girl, even when Mom's away, but romance novels . . .

What does make me cringe is one braless chair in particular: a ratty recliner, stuffing spilling from a seam like sneaky laughter no matter how many times I've sewn it. The same ratty recliner I wouldn't let Mom give away because I spent the first two months post-op in it, streaming cheesy rom-coms and napping during *The People's Court*, and so I swear it's good luck. Well, if it's not the furniture that carries the luck, it's the heart-shaped stone I slipped into a tear in the arm.

I found it (the stone, not the chair) at a farmer's market in Austin a month before the heart dropped into my life, when I was so sick I needed a wheelchair to go short distances. The last place I wanted to be was one mobbed with sunshiny people taking life for granted, but my friends were right: it was good for me. I got to snark on the vegan cupcake baker's sloppy deco job. I got to watch Alma hit on a (strangely receptive) guy whose girlfriend came charging over from the goat-milk soap tent. And I got to discover this stone at the Rock Lady's booth.

Thanks to the forevers of sand and water, the rock is naturally heart-shaped—subtly rounded and sloping—not fake pointy like Valentine's candy and emojis. The Rock Lady wouldn't take any money for it. "The luck will be strongest when it's a gift," she said, pressing it into my palm and closing her fingers around it. She recognized I was in need of luck. If the wheelchair didn't give it away, the oxygen tank sitting on my lap like an obedient spaniel and the cannula softly whistling into my nostrils sure did. Even though she was old and old people are supposed to have poor circulation and therefore colder extremities, her hands were warm against my cold one. But if she noticed, she didn't flinch.

After the surgery, I must've pulled that stone out from its hiding place a hundred times a day to warm it between my palms, to memorize its bumps and grooves and smooth spots. As if getting to know that heart could help me get to know the stranger's heart in my chest.

"I need a bowl and spoon," he calls.

"Bowl in cupboard to left of fridge, spoon in drawer to right of stove."

I prop myself up on my elbows for a better view. I watch the ropy muscles move under his shirt as he reaches into the cupboard and slides open the drawer. Does that make me a perv? Redirecting my attention, I glance down at my legs. Despite the fact that I can't pinpoint when I last brought a razor into the shower, they don't look overgrown. Maybe I have the mercy of mud to thank for that. I run my fingers through my hair in an attempt at tidying and come away with some mesquite leaves. I stuff them behind a cushion.

I hear the water run, hear the spoon against the bowl. I hear him hum softly. A tune I can't identify.

Daniel comes back over to the couch, a dish towel slung over his shoulder. He proudly lowers the bowl, showing me the white gluey paste inside.

"Oh, yum," I say. "Is this the starter, or are we going right into the entree?"

"It's a poultice. It soothes the inflammation and draws the stingers out."

"What? They leave their stingers behind?" I'd like to crawl out of my skin now, please.

"Imagine how pissed at someone you'd have to be to die inflicting pain on them."

"I hope I never am."

He sits in the ratty recliner (cringe!) at the end of the couch and points at my socked feet and says, "May I?"

It's such an old-fashioned thing to say that I can't help but say yes. Though I'm not 100 percent sure what he's asking permission for.

He sets the bowl down on the ottoman near his knee, gently takes my left foot in his hand, rests the heel on his palm. He spoons out some muck from the bowl and dabs it on a welt above my anklebone. The white paste is cool, soothing. Using his fingers, he rubs little circles of it into my skin, transferring the warmth of his hands along the way.

My leg muscles relax. He finds another wasp wound higher up on my shin and then one lower, on the side of my leg, and takes care of those too. If only my brain could relax in the moment half as much as my leg.

To break the ice, I say (after rehearsing it three times silently first), "So, which saying do you not imagine having a use for?"

He looks up at my face almost as if he'd forgotten anything above my leg existed. "What's that?"

"Before you had to take the dogs home, you were saying you found one Texism that . . ." I lose energy. Or nerve. Good icebreakers don't require backstory.

"Oh, yeah!" He plunks the spoon in the bowl. "Promise you won't, you know, think less of me for it."

"Cross my heart." As I cross it, I feel bee stings under my shirt. Those I will have to poultice on my own.

"Okay, you were warned. Here it is: 'He's so ugly his mama takes him everywhere she goes just so she doesn't have to kiss him goodbye.'"

My own guffaw surprises me. "Did you make that up?"

"I swear I didn't." It's his turn to cross his heart. "Found it in a book."

"*Peculiar Putdowns? Distinctive Disses?*"

He smirks. "*Lonestar Lingo.*" When I make a *really?* face, he says, "Really. I'll bring it over sometime. It's the size of a trussed-up hog, so it'll take some doin'."

"Impressive real-life application!" I say, mock teacher style.

"My neighbor gave it to me before I moved. She said language is the window to the culture."

I picture his neighbor misting the pages with her signature perfume, maybe planting a few lipstick silhouettes in random margins for him to discover later, showing up at his door bearing the book in a bikini and the skimpiest of wraps. Okay, so if he left Michigan in March, maybe that outfit wouldn't be doable. I revise my image to parka and cute knitted cap, but she's still gorgeous and vibrant in winter wear, and of course they'll do the long-distance thing until she follows him here to attend UT. I sigh.

"For the last few years," Daniel says, "ever since her husband died, I'd been doing her yardwork and getting groceries for her and stuff. She can't drive. Cataracts. I even demolished a few hornets' nests, too."

"Ah." I'm sheepishly relieved, until I'm back to second guessing. Is that what this attention is? He can't help being a good neighbor?

There's an extra beat of silence before Daniel picks up the bowl again. "Where were we?" His voice is gentle, soft. As soft as his eyes—if I had to pick a color for them, I'd choose gray suede.

His gaze climbs higher up my thigh searching for welts.

"I can take it from here." I reach for the bowl.

His face falls. "Oh. Okay."

"I just want to . . . you know, carry my own weight."

He relaxes, hands me the bowl. "Then you shouldn't fight bees without your trusty EpiPen on you."

"Ah. That's what that was," I say, more to myself.

He nods. "My little brother has a serious nut allergy, so we have 'em all over the house."

"I'm not allergic." I glop some paste on my arm and press it down so it doesn't slip off and onto the sofa cushion under me.

"I hate to break it to you, but you are."

I decorate myself with another dollop of white goo, this time onto an angry montage of stings at the crook of my elbow. I'm sure I'll never look at baking soda in the same way again. "But I've been stung before. Wouldn't I know if I had an allergy?"

He paste-dabs a welt on my calf. "You've never had a reaction?"

"Beyond 'ow, that hurts,' nope." I reach into the bowl, and our fingers touch. There's that smile again. It makes me feel as gluey as the poultice.

He says, "How are you feeling now?"

"Embarrassed."

"Good, that doesn't require medical intervention. And physically?"

"Mortified," I say.

"You hungry?"

"Nah," I lie. I'm ravenous, actually. But him taking care of me like this is making me feel antsy. You'd think I'd be used to people watching out for me by now, but it's different when it's your mom. Or people paid to keep you alive.

He stands up. "Well, do you mind if I get something, then?"

"Of course not! I can name every sweet thing under this roof, but if you're looking for savory you'll have to rummage."

"You like pizza?"

"Yep. Dessert and otherwise. No topping off limits. Well, maybe except for the poor, maligned anchovy." And yet, even as I say that, it feels like a lie. I'm flooded with the sharp memory of the soft salty fish on my tongue, of liking it, of tasting it against a backdrop of sauce and cheese.

"I'll get an East Side pie. And I'll stop at Ace on the way to get more spray and finish off that nest."

"Hey, is this your way of keeping an eye on me?"

"Don't give me too much credit. Just hungry, is all."

But as he looks away I catch something in his eyes, or maybe it's technically around his eyes, that says he's happy I noticed.

Once the door latches shut behind him, I swing my feet to the floor and start to stand up, but a rush of dizziness and light-headedness makes me fall back against the cushions.

The skin on my arms feels less inflamed under the baking soda paste. But the skin around my heart is stretched with ache. I rock back to my feet and stand before the mirror in the hallway. The one mom calls her "how's my hair before the UPS driver sees me" mirror.

Tentatively, I lift my shirt, afraid of what I'll see. There's a constellation of welts splashed across my torso, a particularly thick cluster of inflammation in the heart area, as if the bees were going right for the newest, healthiest part. The skin pulses with heat and pain.

I drag two fingers through the poultice, scoop up a comfort's worth, and gently pack it over my heart. Groaning with relief, I close my eyes as the mixture draws the burn out and leaves coolness in its place.

I hear something. My eyes snap open.

Oh, God. Daniel is standing there. "I'm sorry," he says. "I should have knocked."

I grab the dish towel and fling it across my chest like I'm putting out a fire. Thank the queen of bees I'm at least wearing a bra, though I wish it were the nice black Maidenform with scalloped edges instead of the cotton-candy pink Barely There that's little more than a bra-shaped T-shirt. Only after I stupidly complete the dish towel conceal do I realize I can simply lower my shirt.

Daniel, gentleman that he seems to be, has turned around by this point, so his back is to me. "I forgot to get your drink order," he says.

Sheepishly, unless I'm imagining that part.

"Uh, Sprite?" I ask. Literally asking. Should I request something stronger? Where are your wise(r) friends when you need them?

I force an unconvincing laugh to show him (or maybe me) that it's all good. "You can turn around now." My shirt is lowered over the dish towel, which is covering the poultice site. I've become a sad sandwich.

"I couldn't help but see . . ." he starts.

That I'm so averagely endowed?

When I don't fill in the blank, he finally says, "Your scar."

Oh, that old thing? That's just something I threw on when everything else was in the wash.

"I didn't mean to make you self-conscious," he says. And then he tugs the collar of his T-shirt down, way down, and reveals his own body's record of trauma. Tree-branch scars across the sky of his chest.

"My God," I say, "what happened?" And then I regret asking, because he didn't demand the etiology of my scar, after all. My face gets hot. "Sorry. You don't have to say."

"I got mauled by a dog. Years ago."

"But . . . but you're a dog walker."

"Animal exerciser, actually." He smiles.

I want to frost my next cake with that smile.

"I wouldn't be able to go near a dog if one of them did that to me."

"I was a little kid. I wanted to hand feed this beagle that was already eating, so I reached into his bowl to grab some kibble . . . well, the rest is graphic."

"I'm so sorry."

"You're probably thinking, 'How does one get mauled by a beagle?' So can we pretend it was a Rotty, or at least a Mastiff?"

I laugh. "A pack of feral Rotties. With a wolf thrown in."

There's that buttercream smile again. He walks across the room, erasing the distance between us.

"How old were you?" I ask.

"Five."

"That must've been terrifying."

He sits on the ottoman beside me. It feels like he's closer than he was before, now that we've shown our scars.

"I had a heart transplant," I blurt, immediately regretting it.

I watch his gray suede eyes. I'm on the lookout for repulsion. Horror. Or what would be the worst of all: pity. I don't pick up any of that. Quite the contrary. If I spot anything other than the same guy who was poulticing me a few minutes ago, it's admiration.

"Life has tested you," he says.

"I never thought of it that way." I reach under my shirt and slide the dish towel out. Hopefully discreetly.

"Linnea." He takes my hand. "Don't freak out." His fingers are slender but strong, even warmer than when they were on my leg. "Are you freaked out?"

"Nope." I'm liquid.

"I know we haven't known each other all that long," he says, "but experts say that saving someone's life is a bonding experience. Like it really, really accelerates the getting-to-know-you process."

"Hmm. Experts." There's a warm humming in my chest. I like it.

"Hey, you don't currently have a boyfriend, do you?"

"Nope." I hope he doesn't ask for my romance résumé. As in the never-had part.

"Good. Because if you did, I'd tell you that you should dump his ass."

"Why's that?" I never would've believed that a flawless diamond of a moment could follow a moment of partial-frontal-nudity mortification, but here it is, dazzling my vision.

"A good boyfriend never would've let wasps build a nest on your house."

"Ah. Yes. There's so much pressure on boyfriends these days."

"Do you think we could see each other again?" he says. "Like, plan it?"

"You mean not just when you stumble upon my lifeless, swollen body?"

He grins. "Exactly."

"Making plans without the wasps' permission," I say. "Seems kinda daring."

"I think we're up for it. We're Texans, after all. There's no tellin' what we're fixin' to do."

I can't hold back the smile that probably—and regrettably—makes my puffed cheeks more prominent. "Then let's."

MAXINE

I stare at the screen even as my vision turns furry around the edges. This little corner nook feels too dark, cramped, and isolated to offer me courage. My clammy palm slides off the mouse. I haven't gotten a Harper e-mail in a long time. The cops declared her death "accidental death by drowning" and closed the case. True, they found booze and pot in her blood, but the way that girl swam made fish jealous. So Ezra and I set up a website last year for any leads about that night. We even offered a nebulous "reward," though neither of our families has chunks of cash. "We'll figure that out when we need to," Ezra said, always logical. "Rewards aren't only money."

Maybe I should call Ezra. Maybe I should forward the e-mail to him without actually reading it. Maybe, maybe, maybe. No. I have to get Ezra out of my head. Out of my heart.

I hover the cursor over the e-mail and click. This might be the clue we've been waiting for.

From: goodsamaritan77@yahoo.com
To: Trethewaymax@gmail.com
Subject: your sister's death

Dear Miss Tretheway,

I am so sorry for your loss. Your family is living through the worst kind of pain.

I'm also sorry for my tardy note. I have been in Europe most of the year, and so I wasn't aware of what happened till I returned, through a neighbor of mine. And I also heard that you're actively searching for information about your sister's death, even though the police have declared the tragedy an accident.

I can't say I know what you're going through, not exactly, because of course grief is more personal than any other emotion, and therefore we each have to bear it alone. But I have a vague idea, perhaps more than the average person offering you their condolences.

You see, I too lost a sibling to mysterious circumstances. Many years ago. My younger brother, when I was twenty-one and he was eighteen. He had deferred college to backpack across Europe. I was in my final year of business school. Stephen was with a group when he fell, though I was positive he'd been pushed. He was too agile, too careful, to have merely fallen. I refused to accept it. Especially because there weren't actual witnesses to his fall. Or at least none that had come forward.

The determination to find out which of the group hated him enough to kill him—and why—was what got me up in the morning during that first awful year. Maybe I needed that hatred, even if I didn't have a specific person to pin it on.

But maybe, if I'd continued to hold onto it, it would've held me back.

I finally realized that I may never know exactly what happened, but knowing wouldn't bring Stephen back anyhow. And that maybe I could honor him best by living my life fully. Not with hate in my heart, but with acceptance.

I hope this helps you, even if in a very small way. And I hope you take no offense at my reaching out in this manner.

Kind regards,
Jonathan

I reread the e-mail, thinking there must be some embedded clue, but all I can see is Harper's picture on the website, the photo Ezra took of her when we were all jogging around Town Lake the day after they both got their UT acceptances. Harper was ahead of us on the trail, of course, with as much energy as if she'd slept overnight. She looked back over her shoulder to encourage us to speed up. The previous night they'd invited me to a show at Emo's followed by breakfast in the wee hours at 24 Diner.

By the third read I have to admit there's nothing hidden, no message to decipher.

I hit reply and stare at the flashing cursor. Why is it so hard for me to remember—and to admit—she smoked and drank before she died? The cops aren't stupid. Why am I so afraid to acknowledge that a life can be swallowed up by a random sinkhole?

"Hey, Aunt Shelby said it was my turn to pick!" Race yells from downstairs. And then what sounds like the clatter of the TV remote against the coffee table.

"You always pick!" Will fires back. "And she's not our aunt, dummy!"

And then the soft murmur of Shelby's response, something I can't make out, but I can tell it's calming to the boys all the same.

I quit my e-mail, rest my forehead on the edge of the desk, and wonder if it can hold me up for good.

LINEA

In those long post-op days in that ratty recliner, days when my lucidity rode the wave of pain meds, I read this romance novel where almost every chapter started with the heroine waking up with a smile on her face. At the time I thought about how corny that was. How unrealistic. And yet, here I am, waking up with a smile on my face.

Daniel. Baking soda bath, my bra's unexpected debut, first kiss.

I think past the pizza he brought back for us, past the part where he said he'd better get going and let me get some sleep because getting swarmed by wasps and falling off a ladder takes a lot out of a person, and he got off the sofa and I got up too and walked him to the door.

"Wanna take some dessert to go?" (That was me.)

"I'd rather have it here," he said. "Unless you're trying to tell me to get lost."

"I don't have anything thawed."

He looked at me quizzically.

"I tend to freeze things I make at home," I explained, "or I'll eat them all. So everything sweet in this house is frozen."

"Yeah, you're right: I can't wait for it to thaw."

And before I could puzzle out his sudden urgency, he leaned toward me like he was losing his balance, and kissed me, tentatively and sweetly, his feather-touch fingertips on my face the exact opposite of bee stings.

"You were wrong about one thing," he said when we separated.

"Hmm?" I was still relishing the smell of his skin (licorice).

"Not everything sweet in this house is in the freezer," he said.

I erased the space between us and brought my hands to the small of his back and *I* kissed *him*. While at first it felt like I was borrowing boldness, within seconds it felt natural. Afterward, he gave me a brilliant smile that dazzles me as much in memory as it did in reality.

Yawning, I think how nice it is to wake up without a heart-out-of-place dream in my head. As I stretch lazily in bed, I spot something on my arm. I blink fast and look closer. On the inside of my right forearm there's something scrawled in what looks like marker.

Hey its Me. You don't own me.

I slam upright in bed.

What the . . . ? Daniel? No. I said goodbye to him, I locked the door, I even double-checked when Mom texted and asked me to. Not Daniel. But it's on my right arm, and I'm right-handed.

I feel something cold against my leg and rummage in the sheets. Sure enough, an uncapped black Sharpie, bleeding into the cotton. The acrid smell fills my head.

I skim my fingertips over the letters. Starting at the inside of my elbow and ending at my wrist, they fade as they reach the final word. My pulse speeds when I touch them.

"I do own you," I whisper. "I own *it* now."

This is crazy! Who am I talking to? *What* am I talking to?

Either my vision gets blurry or the words themselves grow softer, like their edges are seeping into my skin. Suddenly I'm seeing something, but not through my eyes. There's water. A pond. No, a lake. Spread out in front of me like a rucked tablecloth, the moonlight spilling across it liquid and cloud-white. I can smell the water, the peaty earth, the gentle rot of moist leaves.

The crunch of footsteps drowns out water lapping at the shore. A shadow eclipses the moon. A fear grenade explodes in my belly and my throat turns airless. I'm facedown in the wet dirt, and there's pressure on the back of my neck that keeps me from turning my head, and all I can think about is—

I refocus my vision with a squint, and the letters appear sharp again. I lay my whole palm against the scrawled-upon skin, and my arm and hand grow warmer. I force breath into my lungs over and over, quickly, until I feel light-headed. I'm back. I'm back to seeing what's really in front of me. My legs under the sheets. The ACL poster on my wall. The stack of folded clean clothes on my dresser. My work schedule push-pinned to my bulletin board. The *Don't Californicate Austin!* bumper sticker on my mirror.

I swing my shaky legs around to the floor and stand up.

"You're right," I whisper into the empty, crowded room. "I don't own you."

Four hours later. I've managed to calm myself down. The image of the water's edge, no matter how vivid, was just that: an image. I'm safe. And the scrawl on my arm?

That's harder to shove aside since I can still see faint traces of it, despite scrubbing with a soapy loofah 'til my skin turned raw.

"Okay, woman," Alma says to me as I throw my backpack into the back seat of her Jetta, "you know I don't do well with cryptic texts. Start spilling."

When Daniel left last night, it was late. I didn't want to text Jules and Alma. Or maybe I didn't want to reduce the magic of the night to a teensy box on a tiny screen. Or maybe I wanted to have it all to myself for a little longer. But this morning, I couldn't resist texting something when Alma asked what I did last night. *Oh, the usual. Chatted up the dog walker.*

I buckle my seat belt and drop my water bottle into the empty cup holder.

"You seem different." She grabs my arm. "Oh my God. You had sex, didn't you?"

"What? No!" I swat at her arm to release her clutch on the sting sites.

"Wait, what happened to your face?"

"Gee, nice to see you, too." I flip down the visor and flip up the mirror cover. Last I checked, I thought I looked almost normal. The swelling is pretty much gone, and I've got concealer over the few stings on my face. I punch the visor back up and, because he can't glower back, I glower at the Mozart air freshener dangling from the rearview mirror. (Before Alma corrected me, I thought it was Einstein with tidy hair.)

"I don't mean it in a bad way . . . you just look . . . puffy around the eyes. Wait, were you crying?"

I reassure her with a smile and a pat on her hand. "Isn't Fina waiting to interview me?" I ask. When she nods, I say, "Just drive. I'll tell you everything."

Alma's shaking her head as we pull into her driveway. "I can't believe he walked in at the moment you were baring your tits to the world."

I laugh. "Not to the world, exactly."

"When are you seeing him again?"

"I don't know. I hadn't thought about that," I lie.

"Did he text you this morning?" she asks as we walk around the house to go through the back.

"We didn't exchange numbers." But that doesn't mean anything . . . right? "He's a neighbor. I can yell over the hedge." I was hoping to just-happen-to-see him when Alma picked me up, but his house was quiet, his garage door shut.

"Huh. That's so old fashioned, it's cute." She tugs at my right sleeve. "So if that's not a phone number, what is it, then?"

So I didn't tell Alma *everything*. Not the parts I want to forget.

"Nothing." I yank my sleeve to my knuckles.

She bats her eyelashes at me. "Did you and Daniel give each other henna tattoos?"

I can't help but laugh at how ridiculous that is. "It's nothing. Something I scribbled when I was . . . uh . . . kind of sleepwalking."

"Oh, man. First smoking, now sleepwalking. Are you okay?" She peers into my face in such an intense, loving way that it makes me want to collapse into her. Instead, I open the back door and step into Alma's sunny mudroom, which is a picture of life being lived: bright rain slickers on hooks, kid boots tripping over themselves, a backless wooden bench with gardening gloves on one end. I'm tackled by Renata when I walk into the kitchen.

"Easy!" Alma says as her little sister hugs me. Alma's ten-year-old fraternal twin sisters are flippin' adorable. And I tell them that, often, because good thoughts are useless if the people who inspire them are in the dark. "Linnea's sore. Bee stings. Lay off."

Renata peels herself off me and assesses me with wide eyes. "If you don't bother bees, they won't bother you."

"I learned that the hard way, kiddo. Where's your sister? She's got an assignment I'm supposed to help her with."

"And you've got a piano lesson," Alma tells Renata.

Renata groans. "I had one last week."

"Exactly," Alma says, "it's been a whole week!"

Alma wants to major in music. Her parents want her to major in math and have music as a "hobby," thanks to her guidance counselor telling them how gifted she is in math, how her test scores were the best in the district, how she could get into MIT without blinking. "Music theory is mathematical," Alma told me once. "But that doesn't mean I want to devote my life to numbers." To be continued. Apparently her mom and dad aren't easing up.

Josefina pads into the kitchen on socked feet, mini tape recorder and clipboard in tow. She looks so serious. That's one of the things I find most adorable about Alma's sisters: how different they are. Fina can't wait to grow up, and Renata doesn't give a thought to tomorrow.

"Thank you for agreeing to let me interview you, Linnea," Fina says.

"You're quite welcome, Josefina."

I can tell Alma's cracking up inside but maintains a straight face as she stacks cereal bowls in the sink.

"Mommy's still on her conference call upstairs," Fina tells Alma.

She checks the wall clock. "She'll be done in one hour, fifteen minutes. She told us not to be loud."

"That means I shouldn't have a piano lesson," Renata tries.

"Negative," Alma says. "That's not the kind of loud Mom means."

Fina and I take seats at the big pine table, and Alma leads her other sister out of the kitchen and to the piano room.

"As I said in my e-mail," Fina starts as she twists the cap off her pen, "my assignment is to find someone who does a job I'd like to do someday and to interview them."

I try not to smirk at the formal summation. "I'm honored you chose me."

She smiles, and I see the little kid underneath. "Do I have your permission to record you?"

See what I mean? Adorable.

"You do," I say.

We can hear the piano in the next room. At first, it sounds like Alma is playing the song to demonstrate for Renata. And then the sound of little fingers plunking it out, starting, stopping, starting again with a wrong note.

Fina clicks the recorder on and glances at her clipboard. "So my first question is: what is the best part of being a pastry chef?"

"Making people happy. It's hard to stay in a bad mood if you're eating a really great cupcake."

She nods. "And what's the hardest part of your job?"

"Hmm. On a good day, the hardest part is stopping myself from eating too much. But on not-as-good days, the hardest part is making something that you know isn't your best. Putting in lots of time and ingredients and ending up with something that doesn't taste quite right or look quite right." I've had more than my share of those days over the last couple of weeks.

The music stops. I hear Alma's voice rise, but I can't hear what she says. Renata hurtles into the kitchen and throws herself onto the chair next to me. "Alma is so mean!" Her eyes pool with tears.

Sighing, Josefina clicks off the recorder. "I'm doing an interview here."

"You're lucky," Renata says.

"I take lessons too," Fina points out.

Fina is a much more compliant student, Alma says.

Alma's in the kitchen now too. "Renata, I need to speak with you, please."

"I'm doing the interview too," Renata mumbles.

"You are not!" Alma and Fina say in unison.

Even though part of her looks like she wants to strangle Renata, Alma kisses the top of her head. "We need to let Fina and Linnea work in here, but you and I need to recalibrate in the family room, okay? Nowhere near the piano for a few minutes. I promise."

Alma leads her sister out of the kitchen again, but it's hard for me to reengage in Fina's interview. The silence from the piano room is too distracting. It taunts me. It dares me.

"Fina," I say, "I need to use the bathroom, okay?"

She sighs again, probably thinking about how off-task everyone around her is, but she pauses the recorder.

I go straight for the piano. It's a baby grand, polished to a high gloss. Other than the piano, the room's only furnished with two straight-backed leather chairs, a bookshelf, and two standing lamps.

Alma has tried to teach me to play (many times) and concluded it was hopeless. "You're tone deaf," she announced sadly. "Make your music in the kitchen."

But today, I sit at the piano anyway. I get a strange feeling in my chest. A sudden tightness followed by a quick looseness. An expansiveness that makes me feel like my lungs can handle triple the amount of oxygen. I push my sleeves up higher on my forearms, the message's scrubbed-faint residue looking on.

Renata's level one music book rests on the stand above the keys; this is the same book Alma tried to teach me from, but I couldn't ever see the notes as anything other than blobs of ink. I close the book and set it aside.

Flipping through the sheet music stacked on the edge of the piano, I choose a book that looks as far from level one as you can get. I open it to a page filled with tiny notes and sharps and flats. I prop it up and stretch my fingers wide.

And suddenly the squiggles and circles and lines on the sheet music become clear, transforming themselves to instructions that somehow translate perfectly to my knowing fingers, and I recognize more than middle C and I play and play.

I'm making music. Making *music*. Music that sounds good. It's impossible. Am I the only one hearing it? I come to the end of the song on the page, but I'm playing another song now, one I don't need sheet music for. It's not a song my ears recognize, yet it's a song I know by heart. My fingers keep moving, the piano keeps spilling the notes into the thirsty air, my heart keeps beating faster and louder.

Alma is standing in the doorway. Staring at me. An astonished, wordless stare that grips me by the collar and yells *WTF?*

I drop my hands into my lap. I look at them like they're not mine.

"Linnea," Alma breathes. "*Linnea?*"

Whoever just did that, she wasn't Linnea.

MAXINE

The next morning the boys are eating breakfast in the kitchen and I'm packing their backpacks for day camp when the doorbell rings. I feel that same blip of dread I always do at the sound of the bell. I open the door slowly. Ezra. Also known as Harper's boyfriend. I assume someday he'll go on to become someone else's boyfriend. But to me, he'll always be Harper's. I want to tell him to go, and I want to pull him into the house and beg him to never leave.

"I got a call," he says. He holds his phone up like he needs a prop. He's beautiful, Ezra is. I wouldn't tell him that, but Harper has. And Harper reported that he'd laughed at that and said someone once told him he had the kind of face a sketch artist would draw if the witness was unsure whether the dude was white or black. Harper told me she loved his face of contradictions: sleepy lids hooding bright, watchful eyes; sharp cheekbones and full, rounded lips; a smile that's tentative when it starts but certain when it stays.

Race comes barreling out of the kitchen and hurls himself at Ezra. "You're here!" Ezra torpedo-catches Race and flings him over his shoulder like he's a bag of rice. Ezra's over six feet tall, so that's an impressive height for a five-year-old. Ezra flings Race upside down and gets a squeal out of my brother.

"Maybe keep him upright so that he won't give back his French toast sticks?" I say.

"Ooh, my favorite," Ezra says, setting Race on his feet and tickling his ribs.

"You can have the rest of mine," Race says, tugging at Ezra's loose braided hemp bracelet.

"Race," I say, hating the edge in my voice but too exhausted to file it down, "you need to finish your breakfast."

Ezra squeezes Race's upper arm and scowls. "That feels like a one-French-toast-stick muscle. You can do better than that."

Race strongman poses, maple-syrup-dotted shirt and all, and runs back toward the kitchen, the swinging door swallowing him up.

"Hey," I say, "I'm sorry."

"What for?"

"I told the boys to quit calling you."

Ezra winces softly. "They didn't."

"Oh. Shit." Then it was Mom. Calling from Harper's cell. Imagine seeing your dead girlfriend's number and forgetting reality for a fraction of a second. I tried to cancel Harper's line, but my mother forbade me. I worried she'd slide even farther into the crazy pit if I did it anyway.

"Sorry," I say. A small word that can't possibly capture everything it needs to.

He reaches for my hand and threads his long slim fingers through mine. We're entwined for a moment—a beautiful, horrible moment—before I yank my hand back.

"Max, we should talk."

"Agreed. I need to tell you about an e-mail I got," I say. He looks disappointed.

"About Harper."

His face opens expectantly. "A lead?" he says, his voice taut.

"Kind of the opposite. But maybe it's okay."

There's a crash from the kitchen. Followed by a yelp. I practically trip over myself to get there, visualizing one of the boys burned or choking. But I'm only greeted with a mess. The foil-lined cookie sheet with the French toast sticks on it has been upended, the food scattered on the floor. Shelby is squatting over it, scooping up the battered chunks.

"Okay, what happened?" I ask all three of them, over Will's and Race's insistence that they didn't do it.

"Sorry . . . hip-checked it. Accidentally." She pats her hip. "These things get me in enough trouble, but maybe someday they'll make child-birth a snap. Hey, Ezra."

He says hi and moves to the table to sit between the boys. Will reads Ezra's T-shirt aloud: "If you can read this, you're too close." Clearly Will doesn't get it, but he laughs anyway.

"When'd you get here?" I whisper to Shelby.

"Two minutes ago." She glances behind me toward Ezra. "I peeked in the living room, but it looked like you guys were having a *discussion*."

I help Shelby clean up while Ezra tries to convince the boys to appreciate their apple slices.

Shelby whispers, "What happened out there?" but I shake my head. I'm not talking about Ezra in front of him. Besides, there's nothing to talk about. He was Harper's. He *is* Harper's. And she didn't give him up willingly. Even if she had grown sort of bored.

Meal over, Shelby offers to take the boys to camp. Once they leave, Ezra goes up to check on Mom. I follow.

He knocks. "Mrs. T.? It's Ezra."

I lean against the wall, prepared to wait. But the door opens immediately.

Her eyes are glazed, fevered. Her hair hangs in lanky, greasy strands. Her robe is ratty and stained. I fight back a wave of embarrass-ment. I don't want Ezra to see her like that.

"How you doing?" he says. Like talking to her is the easiest thing in the world. Not an ounce of judgment. Not an ounce of shame. Not even an ounce of pity.

"Oh, Ezra," she says, her voice raspy from underuse. She sags onto the bed. "Ezra. You're here now."

I follow him into the room even though she doesn't seem to notice me. My phone buzzes from inside my pocket. I ignore it.

"It's almost a year," Mom says. "Tomorrow."

"I know." Ezra sits on the bed beside Mom. I'm about to tell him to get up, but wonder of wonders, instead of flipping out like she did yesterday, she just leans over and plucks a puff of lint off the knee of his jeans.

"I shouldn't bother you," she says. "I should let you get on with your life."

"It's never a bother," Ezra says. "Honest."

His eyes cut to mine. I don't know what to do with his gaze, so I drop it. My phone starts up again. I slide it out of my pocket just enough to read the screen. Four texts from Chris. I slide it back in.

"Maxine is doing the best she can," Mom says. "But I didn't know if you were okay. I had to be sure."

"I'm okay." He reaches over and grabs Mom's hand.

She squeezes his fingers. "And I'm trying."

It's the most direct, honest, noncrazy thing she's said in weeks. And it's fitting that Ezra is the conduit for it.

"We know," he says softly. "And all you can do is try."

My damn phone again. Ezra releases me with a gesture toward the door. Mom must be especially lucid, since even she picks up on it.

"You can go, honey," she says to me. "I'm sure you have plenty to do."

"I should do the breakfast dishes." I don't add that if I want any chance of getting my diploma, I have a shitload of homework (makeup and otherwise). So long honor roll, hello academic probation. Most seniors are in the coasting stage. Not me. And I don't have college plans either. Shelby is going off to Seattle for school, a fact that makes my stomach turn over.

I slip out and sit in the hallway cubby where the desktop computer lives.

Hey, Chris texted fourteen minutes ago, *let me know you're OK pls?*

The sunlight struggling through the small window down the hall doesn't reach me here. My phone's screen is the only source of light as I hunch on the spindly wooden chair.

If you can get a sitter, Chris wrote eleven minutes ago, *lets go out tonite.*

And six minutes ago: *Or if you wanna stay in, thats fine too.*

Four minutes ago: *I know its a tough time for you.*

Three: *Hope I'm not saying the wrong thing.*

Two: *I want to help u get thru these next few days.*

He remembers. Even though I haven't talked about Harper a whole lot with him. Not because I can't talk about her, but because I don't have to. He understands, and that understanding makes words unnecessary. His brother Henry died four years ago. Technically Henry was Chris's cousin, but they were raised together most of their life because Henry's parents died in a crash when he was young.

Maybe because I know he gets how this feels, I'm grateful enough to leave it in the background and fill up the foreground with things like breakfast tacos and Esther's Follies and how easily we can embarrass the Walgreens cashier by buying condoms and KitKats.

He's my first serious boyfriend, but he's two years older than me, so I know he's had serious girlfriends, though I don't need to complicate what's uncomplicated between us. Which is why I reassured him that I didn't need any details.

I'm here, I write. *I'm OK. Sorry so quiet, stuff with Mom.*

My finger hovers over the send arrow as I try to remember why I didn't respond to his texts last night. I hear Mom's voice over Ezra's, hear my sister's name said aloud. I need uncomplicated. I need Chris. I send it.

And then another: *I want to see you tonight.*

Cool. Gotta get back to work. Be strong.

I smile at the phone. As if he can see me.

I'm downstairs washing the dishes, stacking them in the broken dishwasher to dry, when a shriek sounds from upstairs. Mom. A soapy mug slips out of my hands. It falls into the sink and cracks neatly in two. There's another yell, this time a more sustained keening wail. And then a loud thud.

I'm taking the stairs two at a time, blotting my wet hands on my shirt. Ezra's coming out of Harper's room when I get there, closing the door softly.

"What happened? She okay?"

"I think she will be. She just . . . uh . . . well . . ." His forehead, usually smooth and serene, is creased.

"What was that noise?"

"She knocked over the piano."

"Jesus!"

"She didn't get hurt though," he says. He holds several books of matches.

"Where're those from?"

"Apparently she's been collecting these. She flipped out when I found them."

"What was she—" I cut myself off. I can't go there. I can't.

As Ezra stuffs the matches in his pockets his angle shifts and I see something I'd missed.

"Oh my God," I say. There's redness on his cheekbone near his eye. I lift a hand to touch his face, but his hand finds mine. He grips it, then lets it go. "Did she *hit* you?"

He shrugs. "She didn't mean it."

"Oh, Ezra." I want to cry.

My phone is heavy in my pocket. I know I have to call her doctor. *Adults can only be institutionalized against their will if they are a demonstrable danger to themselves or others.* Check and check.

If you'd told me a year ago that I'd be on a first-name basis with my mom's psychiatrist I would've told you you're the crazy one. She didn't even *have* a psychiatrist back then. The Tretheways are sane.

Yeah, well, a year's a long time for a heart to break.

LINEA

"Fucking freezer," Nicola says when I walk into the restaurant kitchen.

It's hard to know when she wants a response. "I thought the guy was supposed to fix it today," I say, as if I really care about a broken door latch.

"He was, the moron." She pauses to plate a thick piece of sea bass. "Needs to wait for 'a part to come in.'" She spins the plate around, wipes the edge clean of the drizzled-out-of-bounds blackberry sauce, and glares at the hovering waitress to take it to the table. "Incompetence, everywhere."

Nicola owns Basement Tapes, a pretty swanky place, especially when you consider how unswanky she is. She's somewhere between thirty-five and fifty-five (she said this during an interview on KXAN-TV, wearing her usual uniform: unflatteringly tight T-shirt, mullet hairdo, enormous spacers in her earlobes). Kitchen rumors have her bouncing between prison time, rehab, and homelessness. And yet here she is with her own restaurant. She always says that: a) people can change, and b) customers don't give a shit about your past if you're filling their stomachs with something good and helping them forget about how hard life is for a while.

I like her, and like that she doesn't micromanage me. This apprenticeship could get me into the Institute of Art. I have an interview with them next month. Not one where you and the dean sit on opposite sides of the desk and blab about global issues and service projects, but instead, one where a panel of pastry chefs watch me work and then eat what I've made while I die a little inside.

An hour later, I'm in the tiny bakery, my own enclave of the former auto body shop. This space used to be the office. Bright and airy and sweet smelling, it didn't carry any of that dreary garage feng shui into its reincarnation. I'm cutting strips of dough for the top of a fruit pie. After three failed attempts at making straight, symmetrical strips, my hands ache. When the bell on the door jingles, I get a break. Maybe I can cut myself some slack considering I was getting kamikazed by bees twenty-four hours ago.

It's Leo. Ex-employee, likely drug addict, and all-around jerk. He saunters in, chains on the belt loops of his baggy black jeans jangling like enough change to choke a parking meter. The last time I saw him his short spiky hair was neon green. Now it's safety-vest orange. I feel a headache coming on.

"Ooh," Leo says in his usual smarmy way as he leans against the customer side of the pastry display. "Cherry. My favorite." Leering at me, he anchors a skinny elbow—the one with the tattooed spiderweb rippling out from it—on the counter where I'm working. "Well, if it's *your* cherry, that is." He smells like mouthwash.

"Wow, so original." My neck flushes. "Prick," I say under my breath, which is not the type of thing I say at work, even under my breath.

"That's it," he says, playing air drums. The motion makes the spider on his forearm look like its creeping. "Let go of the squeaky-clean thing. I like 'em dirty."

"Pathetic." I suddenly crave a shower.

"By the way . . ." He raises a heavily studded eyebrow toward my dough strips. "That's not lookin' like your best work, cupcake."

What do you know about pastry, twerp? "You'd better get lost before Nicola catches you in here."

The sinews in his neck popping like wire, he throws his head back and laughs. His ravaged teeth don't look like they belong in the mouth of a twenty-something. "She'd better catch me. She called me."

"What?"

He seems to roll around in my surprise.

"Once you get a taste of Leo's mad skills, yo . . ." He threads his fingers together and cracks all of his knuckles at once. "You don't forget it."

Maybe Leo is the second most talented chef in Austin (savory, not pastry), but he's a mess. In and out of prison for God knows what. Despite her soft spot for second chances, Nicola let him go months ago when he showed up for work high.

Nicola strides into the bakery and claps her hands together when she sees Leo. Not like applause, more like a drill sergeant impatient to get the grunts marching.

She's at least six inches shorter than Leo, but she grabs his chin, yanks him down to her level, and peers into his eyes. Probably checking his pupils. She sniffs. I'm not sure whether she's checking for booze or filth. Whatever the case, apparently Leo passes the sniff/stare test.

Or maybe not.

"Airplane arms," she commands.

"What?"

"Time for a pat-down."

"I'm clean, Nic." There's a little whine in his voice that makes me smile inside.

She glares, taps her foot. He grumbles but raises his arms.

I hope Nicola finds a felony-size rock in those oversized jeans. She pats. He jangles. She pats. He sighs.

"You think I'd bring *drogas* in here?" he says.

"No, I think you'd bring durian fruit you got off the back of someone's truck, or mushrooms you picked up camping, or ghost peppers hot enough to send a line cook to the ER. That was all you, remember?"

"The blank plate is my canvas. Can't blame a guy for gettin' creative."

"Tell that the Department of Public Health."

She stops frisking him. He passes again.

Another thing that pisses me off about Leo is that even though he looks like a derelict in his random chains and ridiculous T-shirt with the sleeves cut off—*You lookin' at ME?*, bloodshot cartoon eyes peering out from behind the *E*—once he's in chef's whites, he'll command a convincing chef presence.

"Okay, first we need to go over the specials," Nicola says to him. "The carne spesh: pork belly with black pudding mash and grain mustard sauce. The veg: roasted creminis with sherried shallots—"

"Uh, Nicola?" I say. "What's going on?"

"What does it look like?" she snaps. Leo grins at me over her shoulder in his pervy way, complete with darting tongue and ogling eyes. She gestures for me to hurry up and talk. Apparently her question was not the rhetorical kind.

"It looks like you're putting Leo on the line again?"

"Not quite, princess," Leo says. "I'm running the kitchen tonight."

"Hey!" Nicola barks and stomps on his toes with her waffle-soled boot. He yelps, which gives me way too much satisfaction. "Cut the cockiness, Leo. And don't make me regret calling you. I don't care how much talent you have—if you fuck up this time, I swear to God you'll never work in this town again."

Nicola catches me smirking.

"And you don't need to deal with him directly," she says. "You're bakery, he's restaurant. Beef cheeks have no business with cupcakes."

"Ha, beef cheeks," Leo repeats. "Cupcakes."

"Are you gonna be around though?" I ask Nicola. I kick myself; she hates neediness.

"I didn't think I had to get my personal time okayed by my payroll." She points at my dough. "Redo that. Looks like shit."

Leo smiles triumphantly.

The restaurant and bakery are too busy tonight for Leo to bother me, and for that I'm grateful. I've made a Texas sheet cake, three dozen profiteroles, and chocolate mousse in handmade chocolate cups.

Forty-five minutes left to closing. I'm looking forward to a quiet space where I can get the kinks out of the phyllo dough and make baklava.

The bell over the door announces another customer. I smell the woman's perfume before she makes it up to the counter.

"I need a cake."

"You're in the right place," I say. "Our cakes have won Best of ATX for four consec—"

"A birthday cake."

"Okay, do you have a flavor preference?" I ask.

"Not chocolate."

I slide open the door to the pastry case. "We have a lemon left, this one will serve eight to ten. Or a coconut-almond, which would serve twelve."

"Which would you choose?"

I used to hate coconut, thought it tasted like pencil shavings and had a less appealing texture. But tonight, with the tropical smell wafting out of the case, I want to press my face into the cake and gobble.

"Coconut," I say.

"Fine." The woman clicks open her purse. "Is it extra to write on it?"

"Not at all. What would you like it to say?"

"Happy Birthday, obviously."

"Obviously." I've had enough of her attitude. "Happy Birthday to who?"

"Sandra."

"Color preference?" Now I'm all business.

"Just not chocolate."

"Chocolate's not a color."

She snorts.

I choose green gel and start to write. But it's coming out all wrong, as if this is my first cake. Lopsided, uneven. Huh?

The woman leans over to watch me. "Now I know why it's included."

"Sorry." I grab a clean frosting scraper and wipe away the botch. I try again. This time, if at all possible, is even worse.

"Don't you work here?" she says.

"Of course I do." I hate that my voice squeaks.

"Did you just start?"

"No, ma'am."

The woman glances at her watch way too many times through my next two attempts, which end up looking like a middle schooler's home ec project. I wipe the top clean again and stare down at the blank white circle like I can psych it out. The bell rings to signal another customer. I can't deal with anyone else right now.

I look up but can't see through my bangs, which are now glued to my forehead with nervous sweat. I use my forearm to swipe them aside.

It's Daniel.

"Hey you," he says.

"W-what are you doing here?"

"Had a craving for something sweet."

My mind fills with buzzing, flying thoughts. Baking soda. Pizza. Kisses.

The customer huffs.

Oh great, now Daniel can witness my spectacular failure. My left arm tingles weirdly, not in an uncomfortable way, not like pins and needles, more like droplets of warm water beading up on the inside. Wasp venom? The sensation travels from my upper arm all the way down to my wrist, finally intensifying and ending in my palm and fingers.

I pick up the pastry bag with my left hand even though I'm right-handed.

In the time it takes for my heart to beat six times, I write *Happy Birthday, Sandra* in a beautiful, flowy script that is definitely not mine. I've tried writing with my left hand plenty of times and it always comes out looking like someone with a brain injury did it.

"Why didn't you do that in the first place?" the woman asks, pulling her wallet out of her purse.

I laugh uncomfortably. "Just messing with you." And messing with myself, apparently. My hands, the secret keepers. Playing piano, writing with the wrong hand. What's next?

I ring her up, and once she leaves, Daniel leans against the counter.

"What can I get you?" I ask.

"For starters," he says, "I wouldn't turn down a cupcake."

I'm supposed to launch into a description of today's varieties now, right? Instead, the way he looks at me shoves words out of reach. A car pulls up to the curb outside, its hazards on, the pulsing lights like cartoon heartbeats in my eyes.

"How're you feeling?" he asks.

"Good."

"You look good," he says, but with none of Leo's creep factor.

"Thanks." I expect to flush from the neck up, but I stay cool. Something in me makes me want to take off my apron and, and, and . . . My God, who am I? Suddenly I'm Leo.

"Is this you?" He points to the pastry case. There's not much left at this time of night, but what is there is pretty good-looking. The lattice-work on the cherry pie never came out the way I wanted, but it's passable. Just more on the "rustic" side.

"Mostly."

"Hey," he says, "I found my phone."

"Oh. That's good." It feels like we're looking for a way to break the ice all over again. Like last night was part dream. "Was it in my yard?"

"Yep."

"Do you really want a cupcake?" I ask.

"Absolutely." He taps the glass of the pastry case. "If you made it."

I nod. "That's devil's food cake, toasted marshmallow frosting, peanut butter filling."

He takes out his wallet. "I was sold on marshmallow."

"It's on me," I say.

"Really?"

"A cupcake for every person who saves me from a swarm of killer bees. It's, like, a policy. Besides, I forgot to send you home with dessert last night." I grab a small white paper bag to nestle the cupcake into.

"Actually," he says, "I think I'll eat it now. If that's okay with you."

"Sure." I'll just die on the spot if you hate it.

I place the cupcake on a small plate and hand it to him. He undresses it, peeling away the yellow paper liner. Did I taste that batch? I can't remember. Oh, God. He takes a huge bite that wipes out half the cupcake. He closes his eyes and chews. There's a bit of frosting at the corner of his mouth.

"Holy shit, Linnea . . . you made this?"

"Yeah." Why does his opinion matter so much?

"It's amazing."

I put down the tongs and come out from behind the counter. Something is waking up inside of me. Waking up in a new space and stretching and drawing in big pulls of air. I take the plate from him and set it down. Who am I?

"You have a little frosting," I whisper, "right there." I point to the corner of his mouth.

He lifts his hand to swipe it, but I intercept. Gripping his hand, I lean toward him until my face is inches from his. I dart my tongue out and lick the marshmallow off his lips. It's the sweetest bit of frosting I've ever sampled, and I've sampled a lot.

His hands are on my shoulders, then they're cupping the back of my head, then they're gently touching my face. For a second I lose track of my mind-of-their-own hands. Oh, here they are . . . tucked under his shirt, into the waist of his jeans, at the small of his back. His skin is oven warm beneath my palms.

A whole new recipe is revealed to me: Daniel + marshmallow = perfection.

The bell over the door dings. Damn.

I'm sure this flagrant PDA will earn a complaint to Nicola, but my fears are erased when I see the customers. A youngish couple holding hands and smirking our way.

I wait on them while Daniel drifts outside. I catch him peeking through the plate-glass window a few times.

Within a few minutes, the couple is gone (with a playful "We'll leave you two alone" tossed over their shoulders). And within two beats, Daniel's back inside.

"So you're closing soon," Daniel says, gesturing toward the wall clock with his chin.

"Half hour."

"You might be sick of sugar . . ."

"Impossible." Although I have been craving salty stuff today, and, come to think of it, I haven't taste-tested anything I've made my whole shift. (With the exception of what was on Daniel's lips.)

"I heard there's this all-night trailer that sells giant doughnuts."

"Gourdough's," I fill in. "They're fantastic. You can't be a true Austinite 'til you have one."

"Can I hang around and wait for you?"

I groan. "I can't tonight. I have to finish baking three cheesecakes and decorate four layer cakes. And make two batches of cookie dough."

"Maybe tomorrow then?" he asks.

"That works."

"Excellent." He backs toward the door. "So now I'm really looking forward to tomorrow."

"Gourdough's won't let you down."

"The doughnuts won't be the main attraction for me."

Heat licks my face. "You say that now, but when you take a bite of a Fat Elvis as big as your head, you'll say, 'Linnea? Who's Linnea?'"

MAXINE

Chris and I are in the bed of his pickup truck, leaning against the rear window, Town Lake at our backs. I locate Ursa Major in the clear dark sky, point it out to him with a finger drawing on the chalkboard of the night. He indulges me as I tell him how the light that outlines the bear burned out long ago. I can feel him looking at me the whole time. Like I'm the constellation. His feet are propped on a big metal toolbox in the bed with rust around the latch, a blue tarp folded underneath it. He's twirling a lock of my hair around his finger like spaghetti around a fork.

"No one should have to live through the day you had," he says.

I scoff. "Why not me, though? I'm not special."

"You are, though." He grabs my hand, kisses my knuckles. His palms are calloused from his work as a welder. I can't help but think about Ezra's smooth hand in mine earlier.

"Don't let me be one of those girlfriends who complains about everything, okay?"

"That's not you, Max. You don't have to worry."

"But what if I—"

"What-ifs never solved anything," he says.

"I'm officially the worst daughter ever." Trying to swallow a fresh lump in my throat, I throw back more of the peppermint schnapps he brought me. With each slug, the day gets fuzzier.

"You couldn't look the other way," he says softly. "She needs the kind of help you can't give her."

"Right. But I don't have to feel so relieved that she's not my problem for however long she's in the hospital." Shelby's with the boys tonight. She insisted I keep my plans, pointed out that more than ever

I needed some fun. She of course knows what tomorrow is. Knows how much I'm dreading it.

"You have to stop punishing yourself for being human," Chris says. There's the sound of something slipping into the water. Probably a turtle. But it makes me think of Harper going under and not coming back up. Her lungs filling with water, her limbs slowing until—

I sit straight up. "This was a bad idea."

"What was?" There's alarm in his voice.

"Coming here." I thought I could honor Harper by being where she was last. Coming to terms with the reality by coming back to the spot. What supreme bullshit those grief "experts" spout. "I know it was my idea."

"Then we'll undo the idea," he says. "You want me to take you home?"

I shake my head. "Not yet."

"What do you have in mind?" His feet come off the toolbox. He sits up straighter.

Although sex has been a guaranteed way for me to fleetingly distract myself from capital-R Reality, it feels wrong tonight. Plus, when we had sex last time (last week, in the cab of his truck, out by Lake Austin), I'm pretty sure he blurted that he loved me. I'm not ready for that.

And although Chris is my first serious boyfriend, he's not the first guy I've had sex with, even though I'm pretty sure he assumed he was when I told him I'd never had a serious boyfriend. Harmless assumption. After all, nothing about the first time will ever be repeated, and it was wrong from every angle. Not to mention über-complicated.

"You name it," he says. "Whatever you want to do, wherever you want to go."

"Ink."

"As in getting inked?"

I look at him sidelong. "Big strong man brave enough?"

"Hell, yes, my fair lady." He tips an invisible cap at me.

Either Chris or the booze (or maybe the combo) relaxes me. A white heron skates the breeze above us like a memory from a dark place.

"We'll get each other's names," he says.

I laugh. "Good one."

For a moment, he looks crestfallen. He couldn't have meant it, could he? Jesus, I'm only eighteen; he's only nineteen. The disappointment I thought I saw is replaced with a clowning cross-eyed expression. "I'm hilarious, I know." He takes a swig out of his bottle.

"Hey," he gasps, "the needles'll hurt less if we're buzzed."

"Working on it." I drain the little bottle. "I'm out, though, and you know I hate that stuff you drink." He's got some Texas whiskey that's supposed to make you grow horns or chest hair.

"Hold on a second." He climbs down off the bed and into the cab of the truck. I hear the glove compartment spring open and then click shut. He's back, with another mini schnapps for me. "But before you get too wasted, I wanted to give you something."

It's small, square, loosely wrapped in grass-green tissue paper. "Go ahead, open it." He's smiling, his teeth bone-white against the night.

"Chris . . ."

"Go on, open it. Don't say something like 'you shouldn't have.' I care about you, in case you haven't already noticed."

I cup his cheek with my palm. He turns his mouth to my hand, kisses it. I hook my fingers around the back of his neck, draw his face closer, dive into him with a hungry, searching kiss. Maybe I'm wrong about not wanting sex tonight.

"Whoa," he says, laughing, breaking off the kiss first. "You haven't even seen what it is yet."

"You're too good to me. Did I thank you for fixing the dishwasher, by the way?"

"Only about twenty-seven times."

Tonight Chris noticed it was broken, had the right tools in his truck, and had it fixed in about eighteen minutes (sans Internet), and that's even accounting for piggyback breaks he was compelled to take when Race crawled on him while he was kneeling on the floor.

"I know tomorrow is gonna be hard, Maxine. No way around it."

"Yeah. You do know." That's something that connects us, Chris and I, grief, even though he always reminds me it's the surviving it that matters, not what came before. Two months after Harper died, I started going to a bereavement support group. That's where I met Chris. He was a good listener, a good sharer, empathic. In the circle of chairs, he always took the seat next to me and floated Kleenex onto my knee at the precise moment I needed it. So when, after at least a month more of meetings, he nervously asked if I'd like to get coffee or dinner with him sometime, I was surprised to hear myself say yes.

I turn the package over, find the scotch-taped flaps, start to peel it open with care.

"Religion makes you squirmy, I realize," he says. "But this doesn't have to be like that. It's just a symbol."

I open the envelope of tissue paper. There's a small carved wooden cross on a simple brown cord. It's spare. Smooth. Beautiful. It looks hand-made. "Chris, did you—"

"When I was young I went to this religious camp. They taught us to work with our hands, to fix things, make things. They taught us to make those. After a while it was like meditating, you know? Like just seeing the block of pine and the knife could calm us down."

"I love it."

"With every flick of the blade I thought about you. I know you'll come through the worst of it. You will. I didn't think I would. I still think about Henry every day, but I'm back with the living now." He stifles the start of a sob with the back of his hand.

I scoot closer to him, press my leg against his. "Thank you, Chris." I drape the cord over my neck. "This will remind me I can hope."

"I'm lucky to have you," he says. He adjusts the cross so it lays flat over my heart. "Not a minute goes by where I forget that."

The moonlight softens his face. He's what Shelby calls "ruggedly handsome." She once found a picture of the Marlboro Man to prove her point and told me to imagine the guy twenty years younger, minus the hat and stirrups and perpetual sunlight squint. I see what she means now, something almost craggy in Chris's features. Prominent jaw. Strong brow. Slight cleft in the chin. His body, too, is the Marlboro variety: tall, broad shouldered, muscular. So different from Ezra, who is tall too, but slight and narrow.

"I don't feel like I can ever get where you are," I say.

He tilts his head questioningly. An owl complains from the far side of the lake.

"Strong," I explain. "Not consumed by the pain."

Chris nods. "You can. You will. In the meantime, borrow my strength." He opens his wide hand, offers it to me. I press my palm against his, and our fingers curl together.

"C'mon, sweetheart," he says. "If you're serious about getting inked, we'd better hit the shops before they close."

Although Chris chooses Atlas holding up the earth, I don't like any of the suggestions on the wall of the shop or in the book the artist offers me. The guy says, "Ladies first," gesturing toward the back with a sweep of his under-tattooed arm. He's paradoxically dressed in daffodil yellow but has a black dagger inked onto the side of his neck.

"Actually, could you go first?" I ask Chris. He nods, kisses his fingertips and brushes them against my cheek.

While Chris is under the whirring needle, I make use of the pad and pencil the tattoo artist gave me. Even though I'm still loopy from the booze, I am able to sketch what I want sunk into my skin.

Chris comes back to the waiting area looking queasy. There's a large gauze square taped over his bicep. "Let me see," I say, but the artist warns it should stay covered for twenty-four hours.

Wordlessly, I hand the guy my drawing, hoping I'm remembering it accurately, and he shrugs in a way that says to each his own.

"Colors?" he asks.

"Blue here," I point. "Red in the middle. And maybe both colors join and blend at the apex? Can you do that?"

"I can do anything, pretty girl. You're the one who has to live with it."

I follow him into the procedure room, a much cleaner and brighter space than promised by the waiting area. He asks me where I want it.

Where else? I nudge my jeans below my waistline and tap my hip.

Exactly where she had it.

LINNEA

The cheesecakes resting on their cooling racks look naked, so I go in search of fruit. Not berries, though. I'm tired of berries. Peaches aren't in season yet, but I know we've got some frozen. Because the restaurant's closed now, I have to leave the bakery, duck out onto the street, unlock the door, and walk through the restaurant to get to the main freezer. The kitchen is empty, the copper pots and pans clean and hanging on their hooks above the long spotless stainless steel counter that bisects the room. Leo may be a mess, but he runs a tight kitchen.

He must have left for the night. I'm not afraid of him. Not exactly. Maybe I would be if I encountered him in an alley. But he needs this job too much. Once he's on the clock, he tends to stay out of the bakery side, like he did tonight, which suits me just fine.

The stainless steel freezer door is two tons heavier than it needs to be, what I imagine the door to a bank vault would weigh. Until the inside latch gets fixed, we have to use a wooden wedge to stop the door from shutting all the way. "Do your business and get out," Nicola's been saying. "We don't need to overload the compressor while you slowpokes browse." After the heat of the kitchen and the mugginess of the Austin night creeping into the bakery, I welcome the cold against my skin. It makes me feel more awake. Sharper.

Clearly Nicola's hurry-up warning has rushed someone to dump a tray of chicken thighs on the pastry side, and the peaches are nowhere in sight. I escort the poultry to the right side and discover a tray of biscotti tossed onto a rack of lamb. I hear Leo in the kitchen, blabbing. Damn, so he is here. It's a one-sided conversation, so he must be on his cell.

"Dude, will you shut up for one fucking second? I said I would take care of it." Pause. "I won't get my overtime paycheck for like two weeks, so you have to hold tight." Pause. "That was the old me. I'll make this right, I swear." Pause. "'Course I have a key. I told you, I'm *trustworthy* now."

I creep over to the freezer door and pick up the telltale doorstop, keeping the door from latching with the toe of my steel-toed restaurant shoe. I hold my breath, not that he'd be able to hear it over the freezer's compressor. I can't deal with his crap right now.

"Yeah, yeah," Leo says. "I'll be there in a few."

I hear a pan clatter into the sink and then, a couple of seconds later, before I can really understand what's happening, the freezer door overpowers my foot. He must have checked the door and nudged it.

It's. Shut. Tight.

"Leo! I'm in here. Hello? Leo!"

Tomb silent. Does that mean he can't hear me either? Or is he already gone?

I scream and pound on the door. I scream myself hoarse.

"LEO!"

I grab the aluminum tray of chicken thighs from off the shelf, dump the contents onto the floor, and bang the tray against the door. I pause and strain to hear something out there but I can only hear my own crazy breathing. My back against the door, I slump down to the floor.

I notice the reorder clipboard, yank it off its chain, and tear off a sheet. Furiously, fingers cramping with cold, I write

on the back. Harder than I've ever tried anything ever before, I try to shove the paper through to the other side. There's no way to get it past the seal. My tears turn cold by the time they splash onto my neck.

The image of my phone behind the counter in the bakery is the cruelest thought bubble, one that gets stuck in my throat as a sob. Why didn't I tell Leo I was working late? Because I didn't want him skulking around me, that's why.

The cold is swarming around me like pissed-off bees. I rub my arms. Jump up and down. Keep my heart pumping blood.

The colder I get, the narrower the cone of my vision gets. I can only see right in front of me. And even that is a struggle, dimmer and murkier, even though the overhead bulb still burns. My neck is creaky with cold. Hard to turn.

Oh my God, did I survive having the heart I was born with lifted out of my chest—while it was beating—only to be killed by a giant box that will preserve my dead body?

Whoever invented a walk-in freezer anyway?

MAXINE

Chris and I are on Rainey Street, trying to remember where we parked. Sure, maybe we're staggering a bit (all right, all right, so *I'm* staggering), but whose business is that anyway? Besides, there are dozens of people on both sides of the street, exactly as inebriated (or more) than we are, shouting, laughing, living. Forgetting.

"Max?" the voice comes from behind me. Maybe if I ignore it, it'll go away. The skin under my tattoo hurts. My head hurts. I don't need a reproachful voice to hammer another nail into my skull.

"Maxine!" It's Ezra. Shit. I forgot he has a new job waiting tables at Emmer & Rye to help pay for school. He grabs my arm and spins me around to face him. He smells like warm bread and briny olives.

"Ow!" I yell.

"Max?" Chris calls. He's out ahead of me, in front of the Container Bar. He stops, whirls around and sees Ezra holding me. "Hey, whaddayou think you're doing?" He's in Ezra's face in a flash.

"Did you get her drunk?" Ezra spits. The shiner Mom gave him looks raw in the streetlight's sodium glare.

"I didn't 'get her' anything," Chris says. "She makes her own decisions."

"I'm not so sure about that."

"Guys! I'm right here!"

"What an asshole," Ezra says to me, then to Chris: "The last thing she needs is to get wasted."

"Ezra!" I shout. But I'm slurring, so it comes out like Ehzurahhh. "Calm down, okay?" I want to add more, like "This is Austin, remember? Rainey Street. Everyone's drunk around here." But my words are drunk too, and they've sunk into their own exhausted heap.

"Are the boys alone?"

"Of course not!" Chris says. "Jesus H."

I hold my hand up. I don't need him defending me. "Shelby's with them. Not that I owe you an explanation."

Ezra looks confused. Hurt. I want to ease the hurt away, but my head throbs.

"Aren't you out past your bedtime, little fella?" Chris says to Ezra, and somewhere in the back of my mind, a siren flicks on and starts to warm up, whirring soundlessly.

"Piss off," Ezra says.

"You need to face the fact that the Tretheways don't need you anymore," Chris says.

"What do you know about the Tretheways?"

"You couldn't protect Max's sister," Chris snaps, "so you sure as hell don't need to play the hero with Max."

The siren explodes into bright fragments of sound. I push Chris against a wall. Of course, I only push him because he lets me. Otherwise, I wouldn't be able to move that wall of body. "What are you *doing*?" I hiss.

"What the fuck did you say to me?" Ezra asks Chris.

"You heard me, frat boy."

I stretch out my arms, not sure if I'm protecting Chris or Ezra. Teetering on my unsteady feet, I try to keep myself between them. "Guys, please. Don't."

Ezra jabs a finger toward Chris. "Maybe I didn't hear you. You're not speaking clearly with all that shit in your mouth."

Ezra, put that finger away. You're not a fighter. I mean to say this, but it doesn't make it out of my brain.

Chris kind of does, though. "Take your book learnin' and git." Chris exaggerates the drawl and smirks at Ezra as if he's looking at a little boy trying to fill out his daddy's Carhartt coat.

"Being smart isn't an insult, you idiot!" Ezra says.

"Who said anything about you being smart?"

Chris tries to reach around me to jab at Ezra, but I'm still keeping him pressed against the building.

"Stop!" I say. "Both of you!"

"Maxine's not a consolation prize," Chris yells. "I've seen how you look at her. But she's with me. So get out of her life!"

I grab Chris's arm, accidentally squeezing the gauzed tattoo. He yelps as Ezra throws a roundhouse over my head into Chris's jaw.

I duck and try to scream, but it comes out sounding like a gurgle. Despite blood at the corner of his mouth, Chris is smiling a smile full of sneer.

People from across the street are whooping and hollering.

I'm on my feet again, trying to pull Ezra off Chris. Time slows down one moment, races ahead the next. I'm begging for Ezra to stop, then for Chris to stop since he's throwing punches now. And I'm worried about the fists going from Chris's direction to Ezra's.

There's a crowd building around us, people spilling out of bars nearby: Lustre Pearl, Bungalow, The Blackheart. A streetlight flickers overhead, adding to the feeling that we're on a stage.

The siren in my head is louder now, closer and sharper. Chris and Ezra drop their fists, look around, panicked. Cops.

They each grab one of my hands as if I'm a wishbone. Before I can move, I'm forced to let one hand slip away.

LINNEA

I need to conserve my energy. Holding the clipboard, I sit on the step-stool. Fingers numb with cold, hands quaking with panic, I flip another order form to the blank side and write.

I'm Linnea Schiaparelli. I'm
trapped in this freezer. I don't
see a way out

Mom, I'm sorry I wasn't a better
daughter. I spent so much time
assuming you regretted having a
defective kid that I missed
feeling grateful for how much
you loved me.

Jules, Alma, I'm sorry I wasn't
a better friend. You gave me so
much attention naturally that I
could've asked about you more
often. Your lives are no less
important because your bodies
worked the way they were
supposed to. I'm sorry for how
envious I was of what you got
to take for granted.

Daniel,

Even through the needles of cold, some part of me feels a flush of warmth, or maybe just a memory of warmth, at the thought of him. Whatever it is that's between us is too new to put in this note. Who will find it? And find me? Nicola? Leo? I keep Daniel to myself.

~~Daniel,~~

I'm sorry I wasn't a better citizen of the world. I'm sorry I said no that time I was asked to be a big sister to a kid who'd just gotten a new heart. I was afraid. Afraid to care. Afraid to have something my heart opens for, only to break in the end. If I give through this, I'll undo that selfishness. I'll mentor heart transplant kids.

My fingers are giving up. My brain is giving up. Words are stupid things. Clumsy. Cold. Empty. I fold the square of paper, wet with my tears, and shove it into my pocket. I feel my keys in there too. Talk about useless. The key to the restaurant, the key to my house. The metal zaps my fingers. I don't have any reason to believe Leo's in the kitchen, or that he can hear me if he is, but I try again. Pounding on the door. Screaming. The guy doesn't like me, but he wouldn't leave me in here, would he?

I scream until I'm sure my throat is bleeding. I batter at the door handle with the doorstop until my hands don't feel like part of me anymore. The zero-degree cold welcomes me, pulls up a chair for me, tells me to have a seat and make myself comfortable, because it is going to be my host for the foreseeable future.

First it's like there are thousands of tiny bees swarming around me, stinging me with ice.

And then the bees go away, and the cold swaps out the chair for a chaise lounge, and I'm stretched out on it, on the gritty floor, imagining I'm a cylinder of freezer cookie dough, waiting to get sliced into portions.

My breath is a jagged puff of ice. My skin is a field crunchy with frost.

My heart? What about my heart. *Her* heart. Did it travel from her to me only to end here? Like this?

Give up your fight, the cold whispers. Its breath is shards of glass against my face. *I don't need to peel your skin back to claim everything inside you—even what you've borrowed—as my own. I will take it now.*

There's nothing left to do but make peace with the cold: the icy teeth tearing at my skin, the thin air starving my lungs, the cruel chemistry slowing down my blood to a thick sludge.

The cold whispers one last time. *Hush, child. There are worse ways to die.*

II

The future's uncertain and the end is always near.
—The Doors

14

I'm floating. Dead man's float, face in water, limbs splayed. Bullet-size fish dart around beneath me, fronds of crinkle-cut pondweed stretching up from the pale sandy bottom. The water is air or the air is water and the distinction doesn't matter—I relax.

The peace bubble bursts when the fish, or the pondweed, or the grains of sand start talking. No . . . yelling.

"Why won't you wake up?"

"Is she dead?"

"Wake the fuck up!"

Something smacks my chest. Over and over and over. Squinting, I peer into the depths below me. Nothing. No mutant giant fish whacking me with a meaty fin, but the thud-thud-thudding on my sternum keeps on.

"Dude, she's a popsicle. Let's clear out."

"Are you kidding me? If Nicola finds a girl who died on my watch, I might as well be dead too."

It's one of those dreams where you know you're dreaming so who cares if it doesn't go how you want. But damn, the punching and the yelling are starting to annoy the shit out of me. I try to wake up. Fail. I try to swim away from the smacking and the voices. Fail. My arms and legs are as boneless as the pondweed. More thuds against my middle as I start to sink.

"I'm outta here. *I* don't have a record, remember?"

"Hide the stuff at least. Jesus."

The water's slick as blood. But it's gone cold. The shivering clacks the teeth in my head.

"Hide it where?"

"I don't know. Stick it in an oven for now."

"If she's dead she ain't gonna see it anyway."

I lean shoulder and hip into the water and manage to roll belly up. I'm losing breath now. Where are the hospitable dream rules? Water fills my mouth, my lungs. Thud, thud, thud.

"Will you shut *up*? I can't concentrate!"

"How do you know you're not making her more dead?"

I arch my back, tilt my chin, raise my knees. My pelvis breaks the surface first. Then my face. I gasp as water rushes out of my mouth and air rushes in. My eyes snap open.

No fish. No pondweed. No water.

A guy kneeling over me. Spiky hair, construction-cone orange. Sweating. A face full of lines and angles. Even the Adam's apple protruding from his skinny neck is sharp. The heels of his stacked hands dig into my chest. I try to scream, but it comes out soundless. A fish gasp. He cuts his bloodshot eyes to mine. Surprise sharpens his face further.

"Aw, yeah!" he yells, then leans back.

Another voice from somewhere behind me. "Props, dude."

"What the fuck?" My voice is reedy, waterlogged. I aim a fist at the guy near me. I miss by a mile. My arm is too loose.

He hops to his feet. "Whoa, take it easy! Need to come out of a trip nice 'n slow."

I curl myself away from him to protect my soft spots, my sore chest. Where the hell am I? There's another guy in the room. A big guy. "Who are you?" I finally say, but neither of them seems to hear.

"Dude," the big guy says to spiky hair. "That's some hard-core EMT shit; I thought she was a goner. Where'd you learn to do that?"

I pat my torso, my legs. I'm fully clothed. Mentally, I scan my body. Between my legs. Nothing. I'm cold as hell, but otherwise, nothing hurts. Except my chest.

"What do you want from me?" I ask. The wiry guy turns back to me. My scalp prickles, my throat goes tight.

"How about 'Thank you, Leo'?" he says.

I heave myself up onto my knees. Then my feet. Waves of dizziness almost push me back down. I clench my jaw 'til the waves smooth out. I'm clammy, nauseous as hell, wobbly, but at least I'm upright.

Where am I?

"What did you do to me?" I ask.

"I fucking saved your life," Leo says.

"What are you talking about?"

"It's not a mystery. You pass out in a freezer, you end up an ice cube." He scratches an arm sleeved in blurry tattoos.

"Freezer? Huh?"

"Is she always like this?" the bruiser asks Leo. He gropes his jean jacket, takes out a pack of cigarettes.

"You mean like an ungrateful bee-atch?" And then, in a less indignant tone, "You can't smoke in here."

My thoughts are jagged and tumbling, the inside of my head a busted kaleidoscope. I'm on my feet. I back away from Leo. I'm in a kitchen. Like an industrial kitchen with an endless shiny counter and bathtub-sized sinks and nested pots and pans hanging from the ceiling like bats in a cave. "Who the fuck are you?"

Leo tilts his head back and laughs hard. He's got awful teeth. "No kidding, huh? We're playing that game now?"

"You roofied me?"

Tossing his cigarettes up and catching them, the other dude snorts. "Don't flatter yourself."

Maybe I roofied myself. How much did I drink? How much did I smoke? Everything's murky, like a waterlogged notebook. I can see that something was written across the pages, but I can't read the words.

The last thing I remember is me and Tyler at the lake. "Where's Tyler?"

I get nothing but blank looks in return.

Tyler gave me some amazing weed. He was mad about something, though. What was it? I can picture his mouth moving, the sharp talons appearing between his brows, the anger broadening his shoulders. The memory scratches at me and scuttles away.

"Cupcake, did you have to make such a mess?" Leo says, opening the door to a giant fridge.

There's stuff strewn all over the floor in there. Breads and meats and cheeses. Broken glass.

"Hello?" he says, as if he's knocking on my head. "Why'd you have to go all Hulk on the food?"

"I did that?" I say.

"Uh, *yeah*, ya did. You were alone in there when I found you. Had to drag your sorry ass out."

"Okay, I don't know what you did to mess me up—"

"No good deed whatever whatever," the big guy says. He's leaning against a massive oven and phone-scrolling. "Told ya."

My head is killing me. I want to scream. I want to crawl out of this wormhole script I've fallen into.

Leo: Look, Linnea . . .

Me: Who the fuck is Linnea?

Bruiser: That's her name?

Leo: Yep.

Me: Not true!

Bruiser: The little lady must be trippin' on something fierce. I want me some of that.

Me: Stop talking about me like I'm not here!

I stand as straight as I can. Shove my shoulders back. "If you don't tell me what happened, I'm calling the cops."

The big guy groans. "Goddamn, Leo, I *told* you you shoulda left her in there!"

"Listen," Leo says to me. "I'm not fucking with you. You work here. At the restaurant." He pauses, searches my face. "Are you saying you don't know that?"

"You're bullshitting me."

"Christ, it's the truth. I went into the freezer and there you were. Fucking blue. No pulse. I've been around, okay, know how to try things in . . . emergencies. That's it. That's everything I know. The latch is busted. You musta got stuck in there and passed out. Or hit your head."

There's something about the pitch of his voice, about the way he doesn't break eye contact while he says all this. Something that makes me believe that he believes that's what happened. Maybe the weed was laced with something so that Tyler and I ended up in a restaurant and I ended up in a freezer?

"Amnesia," the big guy says.

"No shit," Leo says to him. And then to me: "I take it you don't remember Nicola?"

"No clue."

"So if I ask you not to mention any of this to her, mention seeing me in the kitchen with . . . uh . . . a friend after hours, you won't have a problem with that?" He bites his thumbnail. He can't stay still.

"Dude, if you really did save my life, then thank you, but I'm never gonna see you again, so not mentioning tonight'll be easy."

His bulgy eyes reveal his confusion, but then he relaxes into a shrug. "It's your life. Exit's thataway." He points over my shoulder.

My legs still shaky, adrenaline pushes me forward. I slam into the door. It's locked, throws me back. As I unlock the deadbolt I hear the friend ask Leo, in a loud whisper, if he really trusts me not to talk. Then I properly slam through to the outside. The night is still muggy and warm. But I'm freezing. I start walking. I can't explain where I woke up, but the world is the same. There's the Thirsty Nickel across the street. The Bat Bar. The Mooseknuckle Pub. The Voodoo Room. The Chuggin' Monkey. I'm on Dirty Sixth. Not the best place to be after the crowds go home. The sidewalks are nearly empty, the bars are closed. Okay, okay. Breathe. Breathe. I can fill the hole of lost time later. Maybe I *am* caught in a bad trip. I need to get home. Everything'll make sense once I get home.

I pat my pockets for my phone. Find paper (not cash). Keys. That's it. I don't remember seeing my stuff, but I'm not going back to look. They might change their minds about trusting me to keep quiet. I'm a couple of blocks away by now, my breathing a little more steady. I realize I'm wearing clothes I don't recognize. My body goes cold again. Did those guys do something? And then put me in the wrong clothes? Or did Tyler and I end up at a party like the one I went to a few months ago where we all thought it was funny to pool our clothes at the start of the night and then get randomly assigned pieces like we lived in a commune?

"Excuse me?" I say to a couple walking my way. She's smiling at something he says. They stop.

"Whassup?" the girl says.

"I had my purse stolen," I say. "My phone, my money."

"Sucks," the guy says, slurry.

"You want us to call the cops for you?" she asks.

"I just need to get home. Can I use your phone?" They don't seem ready to hand anything over. "You could call for me."

"Yeah, that's fine," the guy says, drawing his phone out of his back pocket.

"What time is it?" I ask.

He squints at his phone. "Four-oh-seven."

Shit. I can't wake Max or Mom. And it's way too far for me to walk. I can't call Ezra. I lied about where I'd be tonight.

"You okay?" the girl asks.

"Can you get me an Uber?"

The girlfriend nods. "You in Austin?" I nod. "Okay, then, it's on us," she says. The boyfriend rolls his eyes, but in the kind of way that says he goes along with her because he loves her.

"Thank you," I say. "You saved my life."

I wonder if my life's been saved for the second time tonight.

MAXINE

Miraculously, I down enough coffee to send my hangover to the time-out chair so I can get the boys up and moving.

"We're gonna make volcanoes today, Max!" Race says as I search the medicine chest for Advil. I shove aside Calamine lotion, bacitracin, Mom's one-year-old Valium prescription. One lone pill bounces around the past-expiration bottle that for some reason I can't bring myself to throw away.

"Max! We're gonna do volcanoes!"

"I know it was in here," I mutter, seeing the blue label promising pain relief only in my mind's eye.

"Max!" Race says. "How come you can't hear me?" And this time he pats me to get my attention. Right on my freshly needled hip.

"Ow!" I yelp too loudly.

He backs away. "Sorry, Max," he mumbles. "I didn't mean it." I turn to him. "Oh, honey, it's not your fault. I have a . . . bruise there. You didn't know."

"Do you need to go to the doctor?" His eyes are wide.

"No, sweetheart. It's fine, it's just a little tender."

I spot the Advil on the edge of the sink. So I can add dementia to the list.

I manage to get my brothers to science camp at the rec center then drive back to an empty, lonely house. Chris texts me. And then Ezra. Both acknowledging what day it is. That they're thinking of me. If Ezra is mad about last night, he doesn't mention it. But I didn't do anything more than make a choice.

I stack the breakfast dishes in the dishwasher, wipe down the table, find a Pop-Tart corner on the floor. A dog would take care of that. Harper was allergic. I guess we could get one now. The boys would love that, springing some silly flop-eared mutt from the shelter. I'm not sure I can be responsible for one more living thing though.

I decide to wash the kitchen floor. Maybe if I keep my body moving I can keep my thoughts quiet. I lug the bucket out from under the sink, squirt some soap in, fill it with water, plunge the mop in.

The night Harper was busy drowning at the lake, I was busy borrowing Harper's life and pretending I wouldn't have to give it back.

While I loaded the dishwasher, Ezra read the boys a bedtime story. Mom was meeting some friends from work for a late dinner and drinks. And Harper was out. She'd forgotten she and Ezra had planned to go to under-21 night at Cap City Comedy Club. She texted him a made-up story about needing to console a friend whose boyfriend had abruptly dumped her. *Take Max*, she suggested.

Take Max.

Of course I would've jumped at the chance if I hadn't promised Mom I'd babysit. And I'm sure Ezra could've found a guy friend to go with, but he said, "If it's okay with you, I'll just hang out here?" And that's when the pretending started.

"Hey," I said once I snapped the dishwasher shut and got the cycle going, "you want a Topo Chico? I think there's guac left, too. And chips."

"I know," he said, "I'll make you my famous hot cocoa."

I laughed. "It was eighty-eight degrees today."

He waved that away. "It's a myth that drinking cold stuff on a hot day cools you off.

It's the opposite."

"Well, then, I suppose I should see why your cocoa is famous."

He moved into the narrow space between the fridge and the island before I could move out. So we stood there, maybe two inches apart, in this hushed house with my sister God knows where and my heart racing. It meant nothing to him—I was just his GF's li'l sister, he'd known me for years by then—but it meant something to me.

He looked down at me. Blinked. Breathed. Neither of us said anything for a few seconds while the dishwasher sloshed in the background.

"Cocoa," he finally said, as if to remind himself.

"Yes, cocoa." *Your skin reminds me of cocoa. I wish I could touch it. Not just accidentally when I hand you a napkin or the ketchup, but I wish I could put my hand on your face and you'd want it there.*

"Sorry, Max," he said, jolting me out of my tactile fantasy, "but I'm gonna have to make a mess of your neat kitchen."

"Go for it," I said. And then, I borrowed a favorite phrase of Harper's: "The messier the life, the bigger the rewards." Of course if she were here she'd have pinched my neck and called me a hypocrite. Many times I told her that saying of hers was nothing more than an excuse for living irresponsibly.

He moved aside so I could vacate the space. I took a seat at the breakfast bar, our phones at my elbow. As I watched him pull stuff out of the fridge (milk, half-and-half, butter) and out of the pantry (cocoa powder, cinnamon, cayenne pepper, vanilla extract), a text came in from Harper. *Is Ezra pissed?* I ignored it, silenced my phone. And then another. *You goin' with him?* I flipped the phone over so I wouldn't have to see any others. When Ezra was looking the other way, I used a fingernail to discreetly silence his cell too. And then I saw a text from my sister to him. *I'll make it up to you tomorrow night xx*

Leave us alone, I thought. I turned his phone facedown, too.

"Voilà!" he said, handing me a mug with cocoa dribble down the side. "Ezra's famous hot cocoa." There were two pans on the stove, not to mention whisks and wooden spoons and measuring cups.

"Wow, all that for one mug."

"Two, actually."

"For a minute there," I said, "I thought I was on the set of *Breaking Bad.*"

"Yes! 'Say my name.'"

He was waiting for me to take a sip. "C'mon, Max, don't let me down." I felt my cheeks flush. But at least I could blame the ribbons of steam from the cocoa. "I know you have good taste."

The best.

I took a sip. I swallowed, the warmth and the spice lingering on my tongue. "Delicious." I don't think I was referring to the hot drink. He beamed as if I'd gifted him with something. And then it seemed like a thought hit him. He looked away. "I should go."

"No, plea—" I scribbled out the rest in my head. "You don't have to. Unless you want to, I mean."

He disappeared into his mug and came up with a little chocolate at the corner of his mouth. Oh, how I wanted to lick that off. Even now, knowing what I know, knowing how the night ended. What does that say about me?

"Doesn't it ever get boring?" I blurted. Harper sure thought it did.

"No, that's the point of the cayenne." He winked. "Keeps your palate on its toes." He gulped more cocoa, the Adam's apple in his slim throat surfacing more prominently. The slurping would've pissed me off in anyone else.

"No, seeing one person all the time."

He stopped then, his mug frozen halfway between his face and the counter. He spoke his answer as if he were dropping the words onto the surface of his drink. "Not when it's the right person."

"Oh, please." I rolled my eyes. "Harper's a pain in the ass." *And worse, she takes you for granted. She qualifies the "harmless" stuff she does behind your back as "expending my restlessness and therefore making me a better girlfriend."*

"Max . . ."

I hid my face in another long draw of cocoa. When I came back up, he still hadn't added words to my name. It dangled there, a lone trapeze artist after the audience had gone home. "I know I shouldn't come down on her because she's my sister and all, but Jesus, she—"

"Max." He set his mug down. Then he shook his head. "Never mind."

"No, really. Finish your thought."

But he'd already busied himself at the stove, moving the pans to the sink, filling them with water. "My dad always said honoring your commitments is the mark of a real man." His father died when he was nine. A few years ago his mom married a guy secure enough to let Ezra keep his real dad alive in a real way.

"I'll clean up," I said, slipping off the stool.

"What? No way. Heisenberg cleans up after himself."

I laughed. "Yeah, but I drank what Heisenberg cooked up."

"Ah. So you've implicated yourself." He stretched across the counter to reach his mug, his shirt rising up and revealing a band of bare skin above his jeans. My fingers flushed with heat at the thought of touching him there.

"I'll load the dishwasher," he said, passing me a sponge as our hands collided, "you tackle the stove." Maybe I was too slow to take the sponge, or maybe he was too slow to let it go. Whatever it was, my fingers flushed even hotter.

Music wrenches me out of that night. It takes me a moment to pinpoint the sound as coming from inside the house. I squint at the kitchen ceiling as if I can see through it. Upstairs. I freeze. My stomach clenches. My head feels light. I lean against the mop handle. Should I add auditory hallucinations to dementia?

It dawns on me in the next breath: the electric piano. From Harper's room. It must be fritzy after Mom toppled it. It's playing one of its preloaded songs. Ezra righted it, but he must've not unplugged it.

I let the mop fall into the bucket and trudge up the stairs, heading for the room I wanted to avoid today, the door closed tight as an ancient wound.

A different song now. The auto playlist comes complete with a hundred songs. Two Christmases ago, Harper asked Ezra to lug the piano downstairs so she could have autoplay on a continuous loop all day. Will said having the piano playing without a player was creepy. And we'd all gotten to the weary point of predicting which song came next. Harper obliged by banging out a bunch of carols (with her own improvised twists added), and then a couple of songs she composed. Ezra and Mom had been after her to record those originals onto the piano, but she refused. "My messing around doesn't deserve to sit alongside Mozart and Bach and Burt Bacharach."

"Greensleeves" is playing now. I don't really want to go in there, so I press my palm against the door like the house is on fire and I'm checking for heat. The doorknob is bone cold. Or maybe my hand is the cold thing. I heave a big breath and heave the door open.

My ears know what they're hearing, but my brain can't make sense of what my eyes report. There's someone playing the piano.

A girl, her back to me. Long sandy-blond hair. Sitting on the bench. Playing. Harper's. Piano.

Too stunned to scream, to speak, to breathe, for a long moment I can only stare.

She turns around, sees me, smiles, says, "Whoa, what happened to the knock-first rule?"

"Wha . . . Who . . . How . . . ?" Words flee. I'm reduced to tremors.

"Max, what's wrong?" the girl says. "And why are you looking at me like that?"

HARPER

Max is all bug-eyed in the doorway, her mouth flapping open and shut wordlessly. If I wasn't so hungover and bruised, not to mention sheepish about forgetting where I left the car last night, her fish face would be funny. I swivel back to the keyboard. Music's the only thing making sense. The rest is a blur. *Where's Tyler? How did I get freezer burn? Is that what a blackout feels like?*

I launch back into my makes-me-happy-to-play song, "The Entertainer," which Max calls the longest piano score ever. Well, until I tracked down the sheet music for Lynyrd Skynyrd's "Freebird" and proved there are longer. A tight bud of wistfulness opens in my throat. Was everything less complicated then, or is that one of those car salesman lies the mind likes to spin?

"Thank God for spring break, huh?" I say over my shoulder. "I can't imagine school today." I was so exhausted when I got home last night I tumbled into bed wearing my clothes (the clothes I found myself wearing, to be precise). Didn't even bother pulling back the duvet. Judging by the fact that little feet aren't pattering in through the open door, I guess Mom's left for work and the boys have been shuttled to science camp.

Max is standing by my elbow. "Who are you?" she finally blurts. Her tone is chilling. The anti-music.

I stop playing. "Point taken. You're pissed. I stayed out late last night. And the night before that I borrowed your white sweater without asking and got mustard on it. I know you're keeping score, but at least the sweater, I can fi—"

"How did you get in here?"

"Duh. How else? Laundry room window."

I never pegged Max for an actress, but man, she's hamming up the shock like she's auditioning for a horror movie.

"But who *are* you?" she says.

"Okay, you win. Apologies suck. But I guess I owe you one. Here goes." I clear my throat dramatically as my chest flares with pain. "I'm sorry, Max. I shouldn't have called you Miss Moral Majority. You were right. I've been acting out, taking Ez for granted, doing stupid shit. I need to stop."

Again, her mouth does that weird thing. Like her brain is giving her suggestions for things to say that her mouth keeps rejecting.

"Holy shit," I say, "you're shivering. What's wrong? Are you sick?" I'm off the bench. She backs away. Her hands fly out in front of her, blocking me. She's trembling so violently I can hear the click of her molars. "Max, what happened?"

"Who the fuck are you?" she screeches.

"Is this some sicko intervention you heard about, pretend you don't even know the person? I've punished myself enough, okay? You wouldn't believe the night I—"

"Answer my questions, or I'm calling the cops." She snatches the lamp from off my desk and yanks the cord out of the wall. Then she raises the lamp above her head. Like a weapon.

"What are you *doing*?" I'm on her. She screams. I wrest the lamp away from her and set it down.

"Don't you touch me!" she yells. "Don't you dare!" Something's rising in my throat. Something I can't swallow down. This weird flip-flop déjà vu. I know I hadn't ever been in the restaurant before last night, yet someone swore I had. Today, I'm swearing I'm where I've always belonged, and I'm told the opposite. What is going on?

"What is happening?" Max mutters as if she's talking herself off a ledge.

"Max," I say slowly, gulping air in big lungfuls, the scene at the restaurant making me tread carefully, "I'm Harper. You know that, right?"

Max collapses in my doorway. Her hair covers her face. She's sobbing.

"Eenie?" I creep over to her, start to squat so that I can put my arm around her. But her sobs intensify so much that they scare me. She scares me.

She lifts her head. "What did you call me?" Her voice is a fistful of dried leaves.

"Eenie," I repeat.

"How could . . . ?" She straightens.

"Jesus, I am never smoking again. This is weird on top of weirder. I know you hate that old nickname, but that doesn't mean it's forever off-limits."

Something changes in her eyes. A flicker of understanding.

"You are unspeakably cruel," she spits. She's steely now.

"*Cruel?* How?"

"So you knew Harper, and obviously you hated her or were jealous of her or maybe she hated you, and on today of all days you thought you'd get even by hurting her family. By walking in here and fucking with us." She's practically spitting. I don't think I've ever seen her this mad. She swipes the tears off her face with quick, angry strokes.

"*Knew* Harper? I *am* Harper!

"Get out of here. For real. Or I'm calling the cops."

Is this that mythical rock bottom recovering addicts are always blabbing about? The people who know you best stop knowing you?

The doorbell rings. Max whirls out of my room and flies down the stairs. I'm on her heels. She gets there first, flings open the door.

It's Ezra. "What's going on?" he says.

Thank God. Ezra. Normalcy.

My eyes feel greedy, feasting on him, and at the same time I'm ashamed about last night. Why did I ever think he wasn't enough for me?

I hope the shame doesn't show.

"You're here," I say, with relief. He glances at me like he sees right through me and reaches for Max's elbow. She steps outside. It's late, past noon, and the day is warm and the sun is out and the fact that the sun rose today means that absolutely everything can't be fucked up.

"You okay?" he asks Max. "Your mom texted while I was in class. She doesn't sound right. And she's never texted before."

What class? It's spring break. And why would Mom be texting him?

"She doesn't have the phone," Max tells Ezra. She sounds as exhausted as I feel.

"Then who?"

"Did Max tell you about last night?" I say to Ezra. "Is that why you're icing me out?"

He looks straight at me. "Excuse me. Who are you?"

I yank my hair. Frustration sends me into a 360-degree spin. I let out a short scream. "This is stopping. Now. You guys have punished me enough. Ezra, *I* texted you. Why would you think it was my mother?" I'd thought I'd lost my phone last night, but it was right there on my dresser when I got home. "I'm done with booze. With weed. With anything stronger than strawberry milk. Happy now?"

The way he's looking at me reminds me of how I looked at a lacrosse player from Cedar Park who came up to me at a party once and started talking to me like she knew me, as if we'd traded trig homework earlier that day. The whole time I was frantically trying to find the slot in my memory where she fit. Finally one of her friends found her and elbow-dragged her away, saying, "That's not Paula, duh."

Maxine is crying again, her head against Ezra's chest. "She said she's Harper," she mumbles.

"What?" he says, sizing me up like I've got explosives strapped to my chest. "*Why?*"

"I don't know if you guys are tripping or if I am, but just listen." I bound up the stairs. I fold myself onto the piano bench, shake my hands out at the wrists, and ratchet the volume knob up to full. Commanding my quaking fingers to obey my brain, I play my heart out. The songs I've composed. The ones no one else knows. I'm playing and playing. Barely breathing.

I hear a gasp. I swivel around on the bench. Max and Ezra are in the doorway, side by side. Agape.

I move toward Ezra, backing him against the door. He can't deny me now. I place my palms against his chest, soaking up his warmth through his T-shirt, inhaling his musk.

"See?" I say. "I told you. Now can we go back to being okay again?"

I want Max to leave us alone so I can kiss him, so I can skip the words and apologize with my body for going on a wicked bender and probably missing a ton of his calls, but she's not leaving, she's staring. *Why is everyone staring?* So what the hell—I deserve something that makes sense today—I lean in, my mouth an inch from his ear. I whisper, "Whatever I did to piss you off, I promise I'll make it up to you." Careful to block my hand from my sister's view, I grab his crotch. "How's that?"

And that's when he punches me.

HARPER

I can barely see through my tears. I don't pull over, though. I'll scream if I don't keep moving.

I take one hand off the wheel and scoop up the bag of peas I grabbed from the freezer before I left. Gingerly, I press it against my cheekbone. The tiny lumps of cold—more cold, I hate the cold—make it hurt more at first and then numb it, mercifully, but not long enough.

The bag crinkles in protest when I throw it onto the passenger seat. I blink fast to clear my vision. I keep driving. Max isn't my only family.

She freaked out when Ezra hit me, yelling and babbling something I couldn't decipher and Ezra told me to get out of the house and I can't remember all that I said to him, but I know it was bad. Impossible-to-rescind bad. As it should be. No one lays a fucking finger on me and gets away with it. And never in a million years would I have predicted I'd be knocked around by Ezra. *Ezra.* Ezra who teaches the boys how to scoop up bugs in the house and carefully release them outside Ezra. That Ezra. Spoiler alert: he turns out to be a prick like all the rest of 'em.

Wailing, hysterical, as if she'd been the one to get punched in the fucking face by someone she loves and trusts—*loved* and *trusted*—Max ran to her room. Ezra followed her, only after he told me yet again to leave and never come back.

"Why are you doing this to me?"

That's the only thing I kept coming up with. Like I was the piano, stuck on one measure.

Why are you doing this to me?

Stunner: I found my car in the garage. So maybe I got home before I took a freezer ride in an alternate universe? Maybe Tyler picked me up? No, I would never mix the two worlds. He doesn't even know my real name.

I'd never tell him where I live. Maybe I called Max before I waltzed into the icebox and she and Ezra picked up my car and this is why they're playing this mind-fuck game? To punish my carelessness?

I was about to go back into the house to get my spare keys when I noticed two tires were flat. Like sitting-on-the-rim flat. The whole car was shrouded in dust, which wasn't weird because I've never been meticulous about my wheels (get over yourself, it's a method of transportation, not an altar), but usually the windshield is (relatively) clean where the wipers and washer fluid swipe the gunk away. How did Max drive it back like this? It's like, zero visibility.

On the other hand, Max's car was sitting in the driveway, road-ready. The contrite side of my brain said, *If you thought she was pissed when you borrowed her sweater, try borrowing her car*. The freezer-burned side said, *Tough shit*.

I went to get the spare keys on the hook in the mudroom, the hook that Mom insisted on being way up high because one of the cases she litigated last year involved parents suing Honda for making it too easy for their ten-year-old to joyride one Saturday morning while they were asleep. She had Ezra move the hook rack way up, so there's no way the boys could reach it, not even standing on a chair. We all, however, just needed to stretch.

Except.

Except.

I couldn't reach the keys today.

I stretched—I *stretched*—I stretched 'til it hurt. I stretched 'til I swore I was nothing more than humanoid taffy with a beating heart inside. Did they move it even higher? But why?

There's nothing that kills a righteously indignant, furious exit more than needing to drag a chair up so you can palm your getaway keys.

I pull into the rec center's parking lot, my hands still shaking. When Mom went over the boys' camp schedule yesterday, I hadn't bothered to pay attention. So I don't know where in the L-shaped compound to look for my brothers. And I wouldn't dare bother Mom at work this week—big case: man suing Blue Cross because they denied his wife's brain cancer surgery and she died. Mom hasn't been a bouquet of sunshine prepping for this one. Her rule when she's litigating: unless one of the boys is bleeding, handle it.

I see Race first, on one of the outdoor playgrounds. He doesn't see me. He's nestled among a bunch of other kids at a long low water table, submerging brightly colored plastic cubes and watching them sink or float. The fact that life could ever be that simple pierces me right between the ribs.

There are two staffers, around my age, standing around. Bored as hell. I softly lift the latch and slowly open the gate. I head for the swings. I'm wondering if Mom knows how easy it is to breach the fortress of the camp she likely paid big bucks for and wondering if I should tell her. The empty swing I'm eyeing is a few footsteps away when I hear, "Excuse me, can I help you?"

I turn around and face a tired-looking girl wearing a photo lanyard and a whistle around her neck. As if I'm in the middle of a bank heist, my heart is going crazy in my chest. She's followed me over here while the other one looks on from afar. I can tell she's fazed by the shiner Ezra gave me but tries not to show it. "Excuse me, who are you?" she asks.

I'm really getting sick of that question.

"Hiya." I aim for breezy. "I'm a sophomore at UT, Early Childhood Dev."

"And?"

"The director said I can do an interview."

She relaxes. She yawns. Whatever happened to her last night, waking up in a freezer with a meth-head hovering over her is likely not part of it. She shrugs. "Okay, whaddya want to know? How much I love the little scamps?"

"My assignment is to interview the kids." Wish I'd thought to bring a notebook. A pen. Props.

"Oh. Yeah. You want one of them, two of them?" Another yawn, this one barely suppressed by the back of her hand.

"I'll get one from the water table."

"Knock yourself out."

"Thanks," I say over my shoulder. "Oh, and one part pomegranate juice to two parts Topo Chico is great for a hangover."

She laughs. "And raw beef is good for a black eye."

"Race," I whisper. I squat to his level. He smells like maple syrup. Even though there are other kids close by, they all melt away when I look at him. I'm ashamed I haven't given him more time at home.

"Yeah?" He's preoccupied with drowning a neon plastic cube that keeps trying to resurface when he lets it go.

"Can I talk to you for a minute?"

"Uh-huh."

"Let's go over there for a bit." I point to the swings, but it's a wasted gesture since he doesn't look up.

"I can hear you right here," he says. He's wearing a Longhorns shirt I've never seen. It's too big on him. I swear he looks taller than he did yesterday, but maybe that's a trick of the shirt.

"Race . . ." I sigh.

He looks up finally. "Am I in trouble? Because Jason said we were allowed to spit in the water as long as we weren't sick."

I smile, though it feels more like an exercise in facial muscle stretching than anything else. "Nobody's in trouble. It'll only be a quick second, okay?"

It's his turn to sigh. He lifts his hands out of the water gracefully, like pelicans lifting off into flight, and gives them quick hard shakes. Before I can find him something to dry his hands on, he's rubbed them on his shirt.

"Race," I say when we're out of earshot of the others. "What's going on—"

"Does it hurt?" he says.

"What?"

"Your face." He points to my cheek. "It looks like it hurts."

"Oh, that. Nah, not so much."

"Race, I need to—"

"What happened?" he asks. "To your face."

"I . . . um . . . bumped into a tree."

"Oh." He seems disappointed.

"So, buddy, what's going on at home?"

"Huh?" He looks wistfully over his shoulder at the shouts coming from the water table. "I'm gonna swing." He clambers up on one and starts to pump his legs. I walk around him to give him a push, but he says, "No! I got it!"

Sure enough, although it takes a bit of doing, he does have it. He starts soaring. I watch him, and the sun blinds me when he's at the top.

"Is Max mad at me?" I ask when he's closer.

"You know Max too?"

Something cold and slippery twines itself around me, starting at my ankles and snaking up*upup* till it seizes my throat. "Know Max? Of course I do." My voice is so shrill it's breakable.

When he sails near me, I catch the swing, stop it. I hook an arm around his waist so that the abrupt halt doesn't tumble him off the seat.

"Hey! No fair!" He climbs off and glares at me. The sun is behind him, lighting up his head like a fiery mane.

"I'm sorry." I take a deep breath. "But I really need your help, Mr. Hops-a-lot."

He brightens. "Hey! Harper used to call me that!"

The cold and slippery thing is squeezing itself around my heart now.

"Race. Who do you think I am?"

His little shoulders hike and sag in a shrug. There's a collective whoop from the water table. He looks back at it with longing. "No way!" one of the boys yells.

"Racey, over here. Who am I?"

"I dunno," he mumbles, looking at his feet. I'm scaring him. He's going inward. "A new teacher?"

The one thing tethering me to the world snaps. I can't control the violent quaking that starts at my core and sends aftershocks through me. "Race. Listen to me. I'm Harper, buddy. *Harper.*"

He's beaming now. "I knew you'd come back! Me and Will said you would, but Max said it was *im*possible."

He faces a little palm out toward me. It takes me a second to realize he's waiting for a high-five. Reflexively, through my brokenness, I give him what he wants.

He leans into me, sniffs. "You smell like Harper. But why do you look so different?"

"Different how?"

"Everything," he says matter-of-factly. "You have yellow hair now. You're supposed to have brown hair. And you're short. How'd you get short?"

I saw myself in the mirror this morning when I scraped my hair back into a ponytail and brushed my teeth (with a brand new toothbrush I got from the medicine chest when I couldn't find mine). My same face. Dark hair.

And yet. I have an image of my stretched fingers nowhere near the car keys hanging on their hook.

"Where were you?" he asks.

"I was out, buddy, but only for the night."

He shakes his head. "You were gone for a whole year. You missed my birthday and everything. I had a fire truck cake. Shelby got it. But Mommy was too sad to sing."

"A year?"

"Why didn't you come back sooner?" His brow is deeply furrowed.

"Race, I don't . . ."

"Maxine said dead people can't come back, but me and Will knew you would. It's in the Bible."

"Dead?"

"Maybe when dead people come back," Race says, his eyes shining, "they come back different."

"*Dead*?" I clasp myself in a hug. I'm all there. "Who said I died?"

"Everybody."

"Everything okay over here?" Sleepy calls from the water table.

Keep yourself together. Breathe.

"F-fine," I manage. "Everything's fine."

You're dead. How can you be fine when you're dead?

"My sister came back!" Race volunteers. I don't think she hears.

"Buddy, you can't say anything to anyone about this, okay? I mean, not here at camp."

He nods with seriousness. Sleepy starts walking toward us.

"I have to go now," I say. I don't know where. I just know I can't lose my shit in front of him.

He throws his arms around my neck. "You can't go! I'm scared you won't come back again."

"I'll see you at home. Okay?" I breathe him in. Maple syrup. Baby shampoo. Hope.

"Promise?" His voice teeters.

"Promise." My voice teeters too.

HARPER

I'm sitting in Maxine's car in the rec center parking lot. I may be sitting, but I'm slightly out of breath from pawing through the goddamned glove box and finally scooping every last thing in it out onto the crumby floor mat. Not one lone cigarette. Max, of course, cares about her lung tissue too much to smoke.

I really could use something to calm me down. A food truck pulls up near me, *Street Food Is Not a Crime* painted on it, unfurled handcuffs beneath the slogan. The guy gets out, props up a sandwich board describing tacos al carbon and tacos al pastor. He waves at me. I'm dead, don't you know? What are you doing waving to dead people?

I move the car to an empty part of the lot. As I take my foot off the brake, I feel the paper in my pocket, sharp against my leg. I fish it out. It's a note.

> I'm Linnea Schiaparelli.
> I'm trapped in this freezd.
> I don't see a way out...

Not my handwriting. I stare at it until my eyes water. Linnea Schiaparelli? Didn't the guy from the restaurant call me Linnea?

Shouldn't that name be like fingers snapping me out of this nightmare?

I google Linnea Schiaparelli. The closest I get is a whitepages listing for an E. Schiaparelli in Hyde Park.

My brain is a long hallway, restless thoughts pacing behind a bank of doors, threatening to elbow into the space.

Mr. Leo restarts my heart, swearing I'm someone I've never heard of.

Slam

My sister and boyfriend don't know me.

Slam

My guileless little brother says I died a year ago.

Slam

I check the date on my phone—not the home screen square that only tells me it's the third of April. I open the calendar app and hunt down the year. My God. I lost a year somewhere.

Slam slam slam.

That's how you deal with the impossible to reconcile. You shut it out. Even in the absence of an explanation for the otherwise inexplicable. And yet. Aren't I the one open to something beyond what meets the eye? The one to say humans would be a sorry bunch if this is all there is? Even when Mom and Max roll their eyes, isn't it me who says there's got to be more to our existence than what the brain can comprehend?

The phone is heavy in my hands. I've never felt more divided. One half of me intensely wants me to do what I'm thinking of doing, the other half is scream-begging me not to.

The first thought wins out and kicks the doors open.

Ignoring the batch of new texts from Max and Ezra demanding I bring the car back or they'll report it stolen, I open a new browser window . . . and google myself.

Teenager Found Unconscious in Town Lake; Police Ask for Information

A jogger called 911 after pulling the lifeless body of a teenage girl out of Town Lake last night. Harper Tretheway, eighteen, is a senior at Stephen Austin High School. She remains in Seton Hospital's ICU without regaining consciousness. Police are not commenting on whether they suspect foul play, but they are asking those who may have been in the vicinity after midnight to come forward.

There has not been a drowning fatality in the city's beloved site (known to the locals as Lady Bird Lake) in more than four years.

I'm alive in that article. Unconscious, but alive.

But then I thumb back to the search results.

Teen Dies

Harper Tretheway, eighteen, has died as a result of her injuries at Town Lake earlier this week.

Originally from Burlington, Vermont, Tretheway is survived by her mother, Beatrice, an Austin attorney, a younger sister, and two younger brothers. She is predeceased by her father, James, of Roanoke, Virginia.

Services are private.

And six months later, without a lead, the cops folded the investigation up in the "accidental" locker. Case closed. Have a nice death.

Because the Internet is one never-ending comma, I can't stick a period in my search. I fall into the trapdoor of the *Harper Tretheway, in memoriam* Facebook page.

The worst is seeing comments from people who I know hated my guts, like Trish Parette (*RIP, girl. Will miss you always xx*) and Joella Bryant (*Prom won't be the same without you. We voted you queen, BTW. Wherever you are, hope you're dancing*).

No, the worst is seeing the comment from Ezra, who I happen to know is super-private about his emotions. My bruised cheekbone throbs as I read. I try to soothe it with the bag of peas, but it's thawed by now and makes a *sploosh* when I toss it aside.

Harper, as long as I live, I know I'll never meet anyone like you. I'll watch over your family.

I have to close the window before reading what Max said.

There're only so many times one person can die.

"Hello?" I say as I unlock the back door with the key I found in my pocket. I creep inside. Mudroom. Laundry room. And then louder, less tentatively. "Hello!"

The kitchen is sunny. Airy. Neat. It takes me a few moments to stop tiptoeing like a cartoon burglar. There's a calendar on the fridge. An arrow runs through this week, *Mom away* written above it. This must be the mom from the note. There was no dad mentioned.

Convinced I'm really alone, I relax into a self-guided tour of the house (mostly tasteful and understated except for a hideous recliner that looks ripe for the curb). Heading down the hallway, my fingertips skim framed portrait photos of the same girl, chronologically arranged. She's pretty, not beautiful, her thick, wavy sandy-blond hair her most memorable feature. The older she gets, the more delicate she appears, the less convincing her smile, like she's been siphoning off her energy and diverting it elsewhere.

Vicious hunger pangs distract me. I can't remember the last time I ate. Which is ironic, when you consider I woke up surrounded by food. The last thing I remember eating: P. Terry's cheeseburgers at the lake with Tyler.

Why can I remember that and not what happened to me? Did Tyler take off, and I decided to go for a swim? Why didn't I make it out?

Raiding the kitchen for food yields nothing but frustration. There's one whole cupboard devoted to different-size aluminum muffin tins and cookie sheets. Another for glass pie dishes. Another for cake pans, dark, light, rubber, springform. "Really?" I say out loud. Even the pantry is stupid that way, its shelves stocked with lots of useless ingredients in too many varieties. Flour, for example. Why you'd need more than all-purpose, I have no idea, but there's cake, coconut, almond, teff (*teff*?). Same for sugar. You'd think brown and white would be enough. But there's granulated, super-fine confectioner's, turbinado, raw.

The fridge has similarly been hijacked by sweets, and I'm more of a savory girl. The freezer is stacked with neat rows of desserts, wax-papered and Ziploc-ed. Not a Hot Pocket or Pizza Roll in sight.

"Jesus, how loudly do you have to rattle your ghost chains to get a sandwich around here?"

I'm hungry, and I don't want to get back in the car, so I drag the pastries out of their comfy freezer hidey-hole and dump them on the counter. I start on the cupcakes with bouffant hairdos. I throw a couple in the microwave and nuke them for a minute. The frosting ends up as a foamy puddle on the glass tray. I take a bite anyway. The outside is scalding hot, the center cold. I abandon it. Next: a fat brownie studded with nuts and chunks of white chocolate. I unwrap it and send it to the hotbox too, and though it fares better after the atomic apocalypse, it's so sweet that it makes my teeth curl. Casualty number two.

And it goes on and on, through some things I can name—tart cheesecake, blueberry scone, peanut butter cookie—and some I can't—something grainy, shaped like a pyramid, that crumbles into dust after its rude nuke-thawing—me peeling these items out of their wrappers as if I'm shucking corn and taking bites that get increasingly messy and unsatisfying.

I get nauseous, not full, the sugar making me feel fizzy. The kitchen island looks like a patisserie crime scene, frosting-smeared scraps of wax paper lying around like evidence, toothed leftovers sacked out like corpses.

There's a knock at the back door.

"Go away," I say. Wait, what if it's Max? What if she's found me here and is planning to beg me to come home, to tell me we can figure everything out together?

I open the door. Not Max. A guy. Cute. Not my type, but cute.

He's holding a plated cupcake that looks like it was made by a toddler. "You inspired me," he says. He's smiling. Until he sees my face. Then his smile slides off like nuked frosting. He sucks in his breath.

"What happened to your eye?" he says.

"Look, I'm gonna skip the part where you mistake me for someone else. I'm not her."

I don't have the heart to shut the door on him and his obvious confusion.

"This is the part where you say something," I say.

"I don't understand," he says. "Are you okay?"

"Other than being stuck in an episode of *Black Mirror*, yeah. Just peachy."

"Linnea, are you trying to get rid of me?"

"Well, that's the first bullet point. I'm not Linnea."

He looks past me as if expecting an explanatory cue card to walk out. I sigh. "Shit, you might as well come in."

In the kitchen, he says, "Did I say something that upset you?"

"Okay, what's your name?"

"This isn't funny. If you want me to go away, I will. But—"

"Listen, sweetheart, I don't know jack shit. If you can't tell me your name, I'll show you the fucking door."

He looks horrified. Or maybe that's too strong a word. Maybe just devastated. "Daniel," he finally says, his voice barely above a whisper.

"Daniel. Thank you. I know this is weird for you. I'm only here because of a note in my pocket. And a key. And because my own family doesn't recognize me. Worse, they swear I died." I don't know exactly at which point in my explanation the tears start, but by the time I reach *died*, they've overtaken me. I'm sobbing. I'm leaning against the messy, sickly-sweet-smelling counter.

"Do you want to sit down?" he says softly, holding the back of a chair. I nod.

I'm in the bathroom with the door shut and locked. My fingers are hooked in the neckline of my shirt. I'm ready to tug it down. Ready to confirm or reject all that Daniel told me.

I complete the tug.

I peer into the mirror. All I see under the bright pendant lights is Harper. Not the girl on the wall along the staircase. Harper. No scar.

I'm flooded with so much relief I nearly have to sit down.

So it's a mistake. I can't be her. Somehow, my scarless chest is a check mark in the things'll-be-all-right column. Right?

I whip my shirt off. I face the mirror again. Just me. A heart surgery scar wouldn't be subtle, right? I reach for the shirt again and happen to catch something in my periphery. On me.

Cold creeps into my fingers, cinches my neck like a scarf. There's a ribbon of pink on my skin, on my sternum, traveling downward, nearly bisecting me. What the *fuck*? I claw at it. It's there. It's not ink. It's part of my skin. It looks like . . . like . . . a *scar*. I stand in front of the mirror again. And when I look into the glass, the scar is gone. How? How is this possible? The lights are too hot. I'm clammy but overheating.

Wait . . . there's something else. Another kind of reversal. There's something missing on me when I look at my body with my naked eyes, but when I look through the mirror, it's there: the heart tattoo on my left hip.

My head snaps back and forth between the mirrored me and the me I see unassisted, as if trying to catch some trickster in the act, and each time, it's the same: my tattoo is all there in the mirror, is all gone when I turn and look down.

I release my hair from its ponytail. I watch myself do it. My hands quake. In the mirror, my hair is dark. Walnut brown. Like always.

But when I turn away from the mirror, and when I get a hank of it between my fingers, and when I draw it up to my line of sight . . . my hair is sandy-blond.

How many not-possibles can one brain take in before shorting out? I collapse to the edge of the tub, a twist of pale hair in the palm of my hand, my forehead leaning against it. My heart keeps right on beating, my lungs keep right on sucking in air. What in God's name is happening?

I slip into my shirt to hide the nightmare I'm wearing on my flesh and go out to the kitchen to look for Daniel—so I can demand he explain it again as if this is all his fault—when the back door opens and two girls step inside. "There you are!" one says, the taller, prettier girl.

"We've been texting you all day," the shorter, less pretty (aka, not-so-pretty) one says.

The pretty one's gaze skitters to the mess on the counter. "Holy shit. Were you vandalized?"

"Oh my God, what happened to your *face*?"

"I can't do this again." I feel the stupid, useless tears threatening a come-back. They don't fall, though. Maybe because I'm too woozy to spare them. Daniel walks into the kitchen.

"Oh, *hel*lo," the pretty girl says, I'm not sure to me or Daniel or the situation she believes she's walked into. "We didn't know you had . . . *company*."

"Aren't you gonna introduce us?" the glasses-wearing girl asks me with a smirk.

Both girls look at me expectantly.

"Can't," I say, the room dimming. "I don't know who the fuck you people are."

And then I fall to the floor.

I wake up on the couch, a cool washcloth folded on my forehead. Daniel's in the hideous recliner, the girls are on the sofa opposite it. The pretty girl is crying.

"You told them?" I ask him.

He nods.

The one wearing glasses elbows her friend and hisses, "Alma, that's not what she needs right now."

"So sue me!" Alma snaps, still crying. "I'm not a robot. She doesn't even *know* us!"

"She's just forgotten."

"Julie," Daniel says to four-eyes, "maybe you should tell Lin—um . . . *her* your theory."

"I wasn't going to say this before," Julie says to me, heaving a big breath, "when you were . . . uh . . . doing things that Linnea wouldn't, but now I guess there's no point not to."

I prop myself up on an elbow. The washcloth—monogrammed with a curly capital *S*—slides off my head and into my lap. "Spit it out."

"Cellular memory," Julie says. With gravitas.

"If that's supposed to mean something, it doesn't."

"Though it's controversial," she says without irony, as if she's chatting it up for documentary cameras, "there's quite a bit of anecdotal evidence. I mean, I've never heard of it being so dramatic, so complete, you know. Like a total eclipse of the original persona. Usually it's partial. A thing here or there. A preference. A bunch of memories. An allergy."

"But what *is* it?"

She pushes her glasses up high on the bridge of her nose. "The heart donor's personality overrides the patient's."

Daniel makes a sound in his throat. Stands up. Paces in front of the hideous recliner.

"Okay." I clear my throat. "If no one else is going to say it, I will. That's fucking absurd."

"How do you explain that you look like Linnea to us, you're in her house, and yet you think you're somebody else?"

Personalities aren't planes. You can't just hijack them. "Where are you getting this?"

"My brother's in med school. He's talked about it before."

"We should call her mom," Alma says.

"Her mom would freak," Daniel says.

Julie eyes him suspiciously. "You've known Linnea for like fifteen minutes, how do you know that?"

"She begged me not to call after she got stung by bees," he says.

I fall back against the cushions and throw the washcloth over my eyes.

"So let's ask your brother what to do," Alma says to Julie.

"This isn't the kind of thing you do something about," Julie says. "There aren't smelling salts for it."

"What good is knowing about it then?" Alma balls up a tissue and tosses it onto the coffee table.

"What she probably doesn't need," Daniel says, "is the two of you fighting about it."

"Fighting?" Alma says. "Who's fighting?"

Julie says, "Yeah. This is called *concern*. Maybe you should stay out of it."

I get up, start to head away from them. Daniel reaches out to grab my arm and questions me with his eyes.

"I'm fine," I say. "Need to pee. The girl y'all are talking about pees occasionally, right?" Julie shoots me a look and goes on lecturing about bogus science. Nobody notices when I slip out the back.

MAXINE

I lose count of how many times I have to circle the parking lot and loop through the underground garage before I find a cramped space next to a cement post. Mom's car is bigger than mine, and I've misjudged the park—the door scrapes nastily when I open it. A woman in blue scrubs walks by and says, "Eesh." There was a time when getting Mom's car fixed before she noticed would be my problem of the year.

Once the girl who swore she was Harper—the piano-playing psycho who'd slept in Harper's bed and groped Ezra—had taken off, he nailed the window with the broken latch shut. I had to talk him down from calling the cops and reporting my car stolen.

"Let's give her time to bring it back," I said, not knowing exactly why, except maybe when someone calls you the nickname no one else ever used, not even your mother, you default to leniency. He asked me if I had any idea who she was or why she would play this cruel trick on us on the cruelest day of the year.

"No idea," I half-lied.

My shadowy, flickery idea was too crazy to say out loud, and anyway, he doesn't know about Harper's heart (only Shelby does). I wasn't about to choose today to tell him.

Once Ezra reluctantly left for campus, I called Shelby and asked her to take the boys for a few days. That was harder than it sounds. I can't shake the feeling that asking for help equals failing. Plus I feel more like myself with the boys around. Still, I don't want them to be at the house if the girl comes back and tries to claim her room. Or them.

When Shelby and I went to camp to pick them up, before I could surprise them with the news about a spring break slumber party at my friend's, they surprised me.

"Harper came back!" they said in stereo.

"She looks totally different," Race said breathlessly, "but it was her."

"I didn't get to see her!" Will whined.

"But she's gonna come back," Race said. "She promised."

Want a guaranteed way to turn a horrible day to hellish? Try explaining to your little brothers that their dead sister did not resurrect after all. That your family isn't whole once more. That things won't go right back to the way they were before the cops showed up at your front door.

And to think I felt bad for her when Ezra clocked her. Now I wish my knuckles were the ones that had collided with her face.

It takes a special kind of fortitude to not let the smell of a hospital drag you down, and I don't have it today. In a fraction of the time it took me to find a parking space, I find out that the nurse I'm here to see moved to Tulsa last month. The nurse who convinced me forging some papers in order to save a life was courageous. The nurse I sought out six months ago when I thought the whole thing had been for nothing and she told me just the opposite, that my decision had saved a girl's life. "But don't ask me who she is, okay?" she added when I was about to ask exactly that. "That wouldn't be good for anyone, Maxine."

The smell of cleaning solution and fear comes at me sharper as my devastation sinks in. "Is there something I can help you with?" the messenger nurse asks, head cocked, one hand on the receiver of a ringing phone. Her name tag says *Tina, caring since 1997.*

"Cansomeonewithahearttransplant"—I gulp a big breath and then let all the rest of the words go on the exhale— "starttothinkthey'rethedonor?"

She puts on a pair of glasses. The better to see me with. "Someone you know?"

"Um . . . school assignment." An orderly chauffeuring a weepy patient in a wheelchair passes by at a glacial pace.

Tina waits for them to move past before speaking. "Young lady, a heart transplant is one of the most major surgeries there is, so someone who's worried about complications should consult their doctor."

"It's not me." I'm five again, caught chocolate-handed after Harper discovered her birthday cake had been ransacked. "Really."

"Well, speaking hypothetically, which is the most I can do because we don't dispense medical advice to people who aren't patients, it's highly unlikely."

"Oh. Okay." I understand slamming doors when I hear them. I turn away.

She lifts a hand to keep me there. "Have you met Florabelle?"

"Who?"

"In the gift shop. She sometimes talks to people about transplants. Unofficially, mind you." She looks at me down the bridge of her nose, over the top of her glasses. "Not about anything you should be talking to your doctor about."

"It's not for me," I insist. I'm about to lower my shirt enough that she'll see I don't have a scar, but the phone rings. *Tina, caring since 1997*, snatches it up and waves goodbye to me.

As much time as I've spent in this hospital, I've never been in the gift shop before.

There's a whole wall of stuffed animals in an array of sizes and species, some wearing sweaters saying *Get Well Beary Soon!* and *I Love You Beary Much!*, some clutching heart-shaped boxes of candy swaddled in cellophane, some gripping mini-Bibles despite wearing irreverent expressions. There's a corner of prefilled restless Mylar balloons converging on the air vent in the ceiling, incrementally shifting and jostling each other like passengers in an overstuffed elevator. And there are two walls of flowers arranged like a bleachered stadium crowd, filling the air with a riot of scent instead of sound.

A middle-aged black woman I guess to be Florabelle (judging by the flowers adorning her head, a cross between a headband and a tiara) is signing for a UPS delivery. The driver laughs at something she says. "I'll remember that," he says, all teeth. "See you tomorrow."

"Have a peaceful day," she tells him.

I feel itchy. Who says that? Peaceful? This isn't where I want to be, not today. I start to back out.

Florabelle lassoes me with her voice. "You look like you need help."

I blurt, "You know something about heart transplants?"

She places one palm on her chest, raises the other in my direction. "'There is a window from one heart to another,'" she says through a smile that makes her look younger than she did a minute ago.

"Uh . . ."

Florabelle smiles more broadly. "That's Rumi."

"Oh, that's pretty."

She gestures for me to come closer and her bracelets jangle. "My daughter had a heart transplant many years ago." She smiles at me, waiting. I guess the tiara doesn't allow her to read minds.

"I . . . um . . . nurse Tina said I should see you. I'm wondering if someone who gets a heart transplant can start to have memories that belonged to the . . . you know, the person whose heart it was." I swerve around the word *donor* like it's roadkill.

"You look tired," she says.

I have that complicated feeling in my chest, the one where you're surprised someone zeroes in on something you thought you were hiding. I slump against the front counter, trusting it to hold me up.

"Tired," she repeats, "but healthy. You're not the patient. Am I right?"

The flower lady gets what the nurse didn't. Life is like that sometimes. I nod.

Florabelle moves to a tall stool behind the register and rearranges her long batik skirt so she can sit. "The heart holds secrets. Scientists think who we are comes from the brain, but I think there's more to it."

"Can you forget who you were, though?"

She blinks fast. "Come again?"

I feel sheepish as I say it. "As in, you think you're the person who the heart used to belong to, instead of the person you've always been."

Knitting her brow, she adjusts her crown of petals. She looks thoughtful, but confused. "I don't think identity is a straight path to a known destination."

"What about memories? Can those stay with the heart? Even . . . even after . . . ?"

Florabelle grabs scissors on the counter in front of her, gets busy snipping the stems of a bunch of red carnations. I hate carnations. Funeral flowers.

"You came in here for answers," she says. "But I'm afraid all I have are questions of my own."

"That's okay."

She shakes her head. "You don't have to pretend. It's someone you love?"

"Yes. She is . . . she was . . . my sister. She's gone now. But someone else thinks . . ." My throat closes over the rest of the words. They pile up like pebbles in a tube.

"Everybody's different," Florabelle says, "but my daughter used to hate cantaloupe. After the surgery she loved it, couldn't get enough of it. So which was truer, that she hated it or that she loved it? And does the difference matter?"

A dull throb knocks at my temples. I wonder if it's from lack of caffeine or the strain of trying to track Florabelle.

"Closer to what you're getting at," she says, "one time after the operation my girl got the strongest feeling of déjà vu when we were driving past the LBJ library, and I knew for a fact she'd never gone there. We had to go in. And she stood in the lobby, right beside that big ole black limousine, and she remembered being there when she was just a pipsqueak wanting to put handprints all over the shiny paint. Was it the same kind of déjà vu we all get from time to time, or was it her heart talking to her?"

"'Was'?" I say. "Does that mean it stopped happening to her at some point?"

"She died."

"Oh, I'm so sorry."

Florabelle speaks softly, but her affect doesn't change. She's careful, not somber. "Not everyone can make room for a new heart. And not every heart can be content in a new home. One in four patients die. My sweet Pamela made it ten months. But she knew she wouldn't be long for this world. I was the one in denial."

I don't know what to say. I sweep the cut stems into the palm of my hand, let them fall into the small trash can near my feet.

"I'm Florabelle," she says.

I nod.

"What's your name?" she prompts.

"Max," I rasp.

She smiles. "That's a good strong name."

There's that complicated feeling again, spreading through my chest like spilled paint.

"I'm standing way out here on the shore, Max." Her voice is round and soft. "And you're the one in the water, but maybe, just maybe, your work is to accept that your sister is gone? That her life was precious, but that now it's your life you need to be in?"

I can't stop the tears from welling; I open wide without blinking to try to keep them from spilling.

She reaches under the counter, draws out a deep purple flower with petals like soft butterfly wings. "Iris," she says, presenting me the single stem. "A symbol of hope."

"Thank you."

When I turn to leave, she says, "'Wherever you go, go with your heart.'"

I turn back. "Rumi?"

"Confucius, dear."

"What does it mean?"

"Maybe it's time to be tender to your own heart now."

The iris on the seat beside me, I drive around, going way out of the city limits into Dripping Springs in order to stay away from home and remind myself there's still a world out here, with roads and trees and houses.

I end up back in town. At the cemetery.

A caretaker's on a riding mower a couple of acres away. I brush loose grass off the edge of Harper's gravestone. I remember some long, rambling poem we studied in sophomore English. Something about grass being the uncut hair of graves. I test the ground with my foot. Solid. What did I expect? Sod rumpled like a slept-in bed?

"I miss you," I whisper.

I see her in black skinny jeans and her ash-gray three-quarter-sleeve sweater and her engine-red cowgirl boots. New guy, she says. Just for kicks. She tells me to cover for her with Mom. She checks her hair in the bathroom mirror, winks at me, and grabs her keys.

"I really miss you."

I lower myself to the ground. The smell of green lining my nostrils, I lean against the back of the stone.

Maybe Florabelle is right. It's time to accept. Accept that reality is reality, whether or not I like it. I set the iris down.

The lawn mower engine stops. There are footsteps at my back. The crazy girl stands above me. "I need answers," she says.

I spring to my feet. *She* needs answers? How can the boys heal if she peels back the scab?

I slap her across the face.

She presses her palm against her cheek. Looks at it and me. I've shocked both of us. "What the fuck is wrong with you?"

"You had no right to involve my brothers. You've messed them both up now."

She raises a hand. I flinch. But her hand doesn't come toward me. Instead, she grasps the collar of her shirt and tugs down. "How could Mom let them give up on me? Let them cut me open?"

I flinch again. I look away, but not before I see the scar in the same place nurse Tina wouldn't have seen one on me.

"Max?" she says. Her voice seems very far away all of a sudden. "Max? Did *you* . . . ?"

I don't say anything. But, apparently, that's enough.

"You had no right," she keeps saying to me, over and over. Pacing. Pacing that unsettles my stomach. "You had no right."

"Don't you remember?" I'm sitting again, because I'm sure my legs won't work if I try to use them. "We talked about it. Remember?" I'm asking a girl who looks nothing like Harper to sift through Harper's memories. Now who's the crazy one?

"I was *thirteen*, Max. I was a kid. You can't hold me to a childhood fantasy."

"But you said—"

"I know what I said! I said if I died, I wouldn't want my heart thrown away."

That's exactly what she said. So is this Harper I'm talking to? Or have I officially lost my mind?

She finally stops pacing, but she's staring at me with such ferocity I wish she'd go back to churning up the lawn. "That's the kind of thing a dreamy girl says to her sister when she's painting their toenails. It's not a *directive*."

Bingo again. Glittery purple nail polish. Harper got some on my lemon yellow duvet and I lost my shit.

"What gave you the right to pull the plug on me?" she spits.

"It wasn't like that," I say.

"I was alive one minute, then I wasn't. You tell me what that's like."

She's trembling. The lilt of her voice is familiar, yet the sound of it is not. She's unknown to me, and yet she knows. About us. About the most painful decision I've ever made.

"I thought it was the right thing," I say. "My sister was gone. Her brain was gone. But I thought if she couldn't be here, she'd want someone else to have a chance."

She sobs. "That's not the issue, Max. I wasn't dead. I was in a *coma*. I read the news, so don't try to deny it. People come out of comas. Sometimes it takes years, sure, but not everyone stays that way!" She's moving again. Her energy is frenetic. Although this girl is petite, the way she's pacing makes her seem much taller.

"The doctors—"

"Fuck them. It wasn't their sister."

"I can't change the past," I whisper.

She scoffs, kicks the edge of the headstone. "That's for shit sure."

"I'm sorry." I am. So sorry. But who am I saying sorry to? This doesn't make any sense.

Out of my periphery, I see two old people a few rows over cradling potted plants in bloom. I hear birdsong and try to use it to pry the lid off this nightmare. "You're not even real," I say to the girl. "I'm probably hallucinating you."

She scoffs. "So you're talking to an apparition?" She's loud. The couple turns. "See, they hear me."

"This is insane."

"You basically murdered me, Max. And I'm supposed to thank you?"

"Murder? No. *No.*" I'm outside, and yet it feels like walls are closing in on me, trapping me in an airless place. "They said you—they said *my sister* had no brain activity. They showed me all the scans. She was brain-dead, okay? She'd never ever wake up! That's not having a life." I can feel the couple staring at us.

She's biting her thumbnail, piercing me with her gaze. "Save the sentimental bullshit for the documentary," she says. Which is something Harper used to say.

And then she stalks away.

I have to pull over after only a mile because I can't see through the tears. Once I'm all cried out, I pick up my phone. I'm about to text Ezra, ask if he can come over. If we can process this. I dread being in the empty house as much as I dread the thought of the girl showing up there again.

My thumb zags away from him. I don't need to process. I need to get on with my life.

Harper's gone. All of her. I can't explain the girl, but that doesn't change what I know about my sister, about me. And I am not a murderer.

I text Chris instead.

Can you get away for a bit?

He responds within seconds. *This weekend?*

Now, I write. *Shelby's got the boys.*

I think I can use my vaca time.

For what feels like the first time today, I exhale without any pain.

Good. I need to unwind.

I'm your man, he writes. And then he sends ☺

I feel better already.

I want to rewrite my heart and let the future in.

—Miike Snow

MAXINE

My arm dangles out of the open passenger window of Chris's truck. The rush of hot asphalt air in my face steals the breath from my mouth, and I can imagine it stealing the thoughts from my head, too. Where we're going doesn't matter so much as the fact that we're going. When Chris asked me to name a destination, I answered, "Away."

He slides his hand over to my side and spiders his fingers around mine.

"Hey," he says, "you forgive me?"

"For what?"

The late afternoon sun slants in his window, shading his edges like melted crayons. His eyes are locked on the road, a muscle jumps along his jaw. Have I really looked at him before? I mean, really looked, without distraction? I'm seeing a picture I've always known, but it's just been set into a new frame. I squeeze his hand, squeeze back the lump of gratitude in my throat.

"You know," he says softly, "for what happened on Rainey Street. With Ezra."

I roll up my window to shut out the road noise. "Of course I forgive you. Not that there's anything to forgive. I'm not a ref between you guys."

He smiles small. "That's a good way of putting it." He raises our clasped hands to his mouth, kisses the back of mine. That heat on my skin stirs up heat in me. I bring our hands to my lap and trace the ridge of his knuckles, red and chafed from the fight.

"Was your boss okay with you taking time off?" I ask.

"Things'll be there when I get back. It's welding, not brain surgery."

Three deer appear at the grassy edge of the road up ahead. They seem indecisive about whether to dart back into the thicket or brave the blacktop. He checks his rearview mirror, slows down, pulls over. "Pretty beasts."

"They are." No antlers, so they're female. They're looking at us in that dark-eyed, nose-quivering way of theirs. Then one breaks the stillness of our locked stares and dashes out onto the pavement. The others follow her to the opposite side of the 195. I watch the trees swallow them up.

He's inching the truck back up to speed. "Good thing I stopped."

"For sure." I try not to visualize what the deer would look like if the truck plowed into one of them. And there it is anyway.

"I just finished paying off this baby." He pats the Ford symbol in the bullseye of the steering wheel.

"Oh. Yeah. That."

"You never told me why you wanted to get away all of a sudden."

"Can't a girl be spontaneous?"

He shrugs. "Sure, a girl can. But it's not your M.O."

"Geez, way to make me sound boring."

"Nah, not boring. Reliable. That's a good thing." He pauses, squints softly as if he's assessing his words before he says them. He flicks the wipers on and adds a swoosh of cleaning fluid to the dusty windshield. "So what was my unboring girl escaping when she texted SOS?"

"Not an escape," I fib. "I wanted to spend time with you." Now that I'm with him I realize I was missing what was in front of me the whole time.

"Everything okay at home?"

"Yeah, you know . . ." I picture the raging girl with Harper's borrowed memory, Harper's borrowed outrage. Talking about that whole impossible-to-believe mess will only prolong it. I'm with Chris to get past it. I grab the last stick of gum from the cup holder, tear it in half, put a piece up to his lips. He draws it in with his teeth.

After a few chews, he says, "Isn't the girl supposed to be the one to drag stuff out of the dude?"

"It's the same old grind, you know. And today was shitty because it was the one-year mark. But you've been through all that." That's one thing that makes me feel safest around Chris. Right with him. What he's been through. I wouldn't tell him that, though, because I worry that might make him feel used. "You get it."

"It gets easier," he says. "You never forget the pain, but it gets to a size where you can carry it."

There's a long pause, the kind that's content to stay unfilled.

We pass the exits for Killeen and Harker Heights, a sign promising food gas lodging, a sign announcing Temple 25 miles farther.

"You need a pit stop?" he asks.

"I'm good." I want to mean that in all ways. A few minutes ago Shelby sent a video of the boys in their jammies, saying good night to me. They looked clean and happy. I responded with every grinning emoji there is. So for now, I'm good there.

I watch the landscape blur by. I want to imagine pain as a thing left behind. Just a few days of amnesia. "You know, speaking of welding . . . I've never seen you in your welder's uniform. I bet you look hot."

"The protective eyewear is a real chick magnet."

I unbuckle my seat belt, scooch over to his side, thrust my tongue in his ear.

He laughs, and then: "Max! I'm weak, but you know how I feel about—"

"Seat belts," I finish petulantly. "I know." I slide back over and buckle up. He's sensitive to that. No wonder: his aunt and uncle were killed in a car crash when he was a little kid, which is how Henry ended up being raised by Chris's parents. And then a few years ago Henry was riding his bike when he was struck by a drunk driver. He died before the ambulance got there.

I tiptoe my fingers to Chris's jaw, rough from a couple days without a shave, to his neck, to the ear I just licked. Sex has been a way to press the pause button on the reality that is my life, at least while my body is occupied.

"Hey," I murmur as seductively as one can in a vehicle hurtling down the freeway, "how about before we reach wherever you're sweeping me off to, you park this paid-off truck?"

He blushes. God, that's a good look for him. "Damn, girl! You horny or what?"

We're stretched out on the bed of his pickup, side by side on top of one of the sleeping bags we hastily unrolled before we did the deed, under the blue tarp stretched over the bed. It's warm and humid under here. In a good way, though, not in the way that makes you wonder how long it takes for a human to suffocate under a wet blanket. Our jeans are by our feet somewhere. We're in only our shirts. I'm content and peaceful. Like a lazy cat.

"Let's get some fresh air," Chris says, reaching above us to peel back a wet corner of our crinkly sky. It had rained lightly while we were covered, the *tatt-a-tatt-tatt* against the tarp percussive reminders of how safe and dry I was beneath.

When his arm comes back down his elbow brushes against my ribs, tickling me. I giggle. That makes him laugh, and before I know it, he's on top of me again, laughter turning pensive. He presses his face between my chin and collarbone and inhales deeply. And then again, more deeply still.

"It's like you're trying to steal me into your lungs," I say.

"And keep you forever."

"This moment is good," I say. "Right here, right now."

"It's special because it'll grow into more moments. You'll see." He winks. "Gotta pee."

He rolls off me and hops out of the truck, leaving me at the mercy of my thoughts. I wonder how long it'll be before sex can keep me in my body and in the present instead of sending me back to the past.

Two months after Harper's death, Ezra and I had gone to a grief support group together, the one where I met Chris.

"I'm scared," Ezra had said after that meeting.

We were back at home. Shelby, who'd been sitting for the boys because my mother was in no shape, had only reluctantly gone home after we told her we were okay.

"Scared of what?" I said, though I was scared too. What if the worst thing that could happen happened again, this time to Will and Race?

"Scared that it'll never get any better," he said.

I was worried about that too, but it was further down on the list. "It has to."

"Do you mean that?"

"I do." I didn't. But he needed to hear it.

"We're only a few months out," he said. "And those people at the group . . . they're years into this, and they're still a mess."

"But we aren't seeing them day to day," I pointed out. "The group is a place where they can vent. It doesn't mean they're going through their lives crying."

"You think so?" he asked. And he broke my heart with the way he looked at me, like whatever I said next would make him sink or swim.

"Yeah, Ezra, I think so."

And I crossed the room to hug him, and he hugged me back, and I'm not sure if I noticed that my own breathing had sped up first, or if I noticed his breath on my neck, quick and furtive, but soon we were kissing, his tears in my mouth, mine in his, and only breath and bodies mattered, the stuff reserved for the living, and we let ourselves become bodies—only bodies, not broken hearts—and our two bodies urgently, hungrily came together in the way I had dreamed of when I was watching him with her, the way he looked at her, when I was imagining his electric touch lighting up my skin. We were reduced to hands, fingers, lips, skin—so much skin—the sharpness of want. It was my first time; I don't know if Ezra knew that. He pressed through my body's resistance. I swallowed down the initial pain. How could a first time feel so inevitable and yet so surreal? And so right in one heartbeat and wrong in the next? *Wrong*wrong, as if Harper had been in the corner of my bedroom, sitting on the floor with her knees tucked under her chin, scowling at both of us. That kind of wrong. How could the people who loved her most so thoroughly betray her at the same time they were grieving her?

Ezra never went back to the support group. Maybe it was because he feared another collision between us. There was no chance of that—I knew it was wrong. And judging by the way he never spoke of it again, he did too.

He didn't get specific when I asked about the group, he just said, "It's not for me."

But it was for me, like a dark pull. Like I was a moth circling a burned-out bulb that I knew would shine again someday.

Chris climbs back into the bed of the truck, muttering about how it's not a good idea to take a leak barefoot and pantsless right after a rain and how he needs me to warm him up. He rests his weight on me again and Ezra disappears. I have to press my tailbone against the bed in order to breathe. He makes his hands a bowl and cups the back of my head. Kissing my chin, his fingers play at the nape of my neck. They slow, searching for something.

"Hope we didn't break the cord." He sounds dismayed.

"What cord?"

"The cross," he says. "The cord must've snapped."

It takes me a few beats to realize he's talking about the necklace he gave me. "Don't worry, it's safe."

"In your bag?" he asks.

"At home."

His fingers on my shoulders turn rigid. He sucks in a sharp breath.

At first I think something hurt him. Like a snakebite or bee sting. "Chris?"

He rolls off me, sits up in the night air with the tarp around his shoulders. "Forget it."

But his voice carries an ache. I sit up too. I reach for his hand but he moves it out of the way, pulls his jeans on instead. I grope in the dark for my underwear, my jeans. He's rolling up the tarp while I pull on my clothes. We're tucked into the trees, well off the dirt road that led us here, but still, an engine I hear in the distance makes me get dressed faster. Chris is all business.

"Did I do something wrong?" I ask.

He shakes his head. "I thought it meant more to you than that."

"The cross?" When Shelby saw it, she said, "Huh. Cute." I caught her eye roll. Maybe that's why it's sitting on my dresser.

"You don't have to pretend it matters to you." There's a hitch in his voice.

"It does matter to me! I just forgot it," I lie. "I was in such a hurry to leave. That's all."

"I shared a piece of my past with you."

"And I'm grateful."

"I don't like to complain," he says, and I murmur in agreement, because I don't think I've ever heard him complain, "but it was a fucking hard thing, me growing up." He seems to choke on the words. "Really hard, Max."

"Do you want to talk about it?" I realize I don't know much about that part of his life. I had assumed everything was fine until Henry was killed.

"I *did* talk about it," he says, exasperated. "At least I was trying, when I made you the cross that you left at home."

"We're hours away by now," I say, trying to hide the annoyance building in me, "but if it would make you feel better, let's go back so I can grab it."

He scoffs. "Don't protest too much."

That's the thing about Chris. He makes jokes about being "just" a welder, but he's smart as hell. Intuitive, too.

His broad shoulders sag. He's hurt. I did that. My annoyance crumbles. Harper had told me once there was power in being able to hurt someone. She liked it, she said. I decide I don't.

"Chris, I'm sorry."

"Max." His voice goes misty. He looks up at the stars. "I know it's just a thing."

"No, it's more than that." I climb out of the truck to stretch. "I should've remembered it." Arching my back, I catch sight of a large shape gathered in the branches above. I think it's an owl, though it's hard to make out in the layered darkness. I don't believe in superstitious bullshit, but owl sightings are supposed to be bad luck. So I hope I'm wrong. The gravelly foghorn call gives her away. A great horned owl. I hear her chiding me for forgetting the cross.

I need to make it right. He's always asking me to tell him what's really going on with me. Why am I only ever telling Ezra the whole of it? That has to stop. I clear my throat. "So I got this e-mail."

I don't know why I don't tell him about the girl. I just know that I don't. I sit on the edge of the truck bed. I tell him about the cyber Good Samaritan. He listens. He takes my hand when he knows what it's about. I know it sounds cliché, but I feel lighter for the telling.

"Hey," I say, after the owl hurls herself into the night sky, "do you ever catch yourself thinking about what Henry would be doing?"

"Who?"

"Henry," I say.

The name swings on a trapeze between us. He's looking at me with part blankness, part waiting-for-more.

"*Your* Henry." I can feel the confusion rearranging my face.

"Oh. Sure, sure. I didn't hear you, is all. Yeah, of course I think about that. Who wouldn't?" And then, almost sternly, "You should listen to Jonathan, Max. It sounds like he knows what he's talking about."

"Yeah. I guess you're right."

It's only much later, in the motel shower, when something that only tapped at me before pelts me like shards of ice:

I never said the Good Samaritan's name.

HARPER

It's past midnight. I'm tired, but good luck convincing my brain to shut the hell up and sleep already.

I try sleeping in the room that's obviously hers. Linnea's. I dab the name on like perfume at a department store counter. Something I can wash off later.

I can't do it, though. I can't sleep here. Everything feels wrong. The smell of her shampoo on the pillowcase. The extra-firm pillow severe under my head. The sheets a Hallmark channel mauve I'd never allow in my own room. Next I try her mother's bedroom. IKEA nondescript. This should work. Especially because I know the mother isn't coming home until next week. Nope, not even a lousy yawn.

When I got back here from my fight with Max hours ago, Alma and Julie showed up. The way they crept up to me, brimming with expectancy, told me they hoped Linnea had returned. They must be close friends to know from just a word. Just a hey. I envy that. I've had lots of friends, but none that close. And once Ezra and I got serious, I stopped investing time in friends altogether. Many times I envied Max her friendship with Shel.

I did not invite them in. I was too tired to be around people who so clearly were rooting for me not to be around.

"So we figured we should go to the restaurant and give Nicola some excuse for you,"

Alma explained.

"Nicola?"

"Your boss," Julie said.

"Linnea's boss," I corrected.

Julie pushed her glasses up. They caught the sunlight so that bright prisms danced over her eyes. "Yeah, right. We told her that you . . . I mean *Linnea* wasn't feeling well."

"Okay . . ." I'm living through something that even science can't wrap its head around, and they expected me to be worried about some after-school job? "Thanks?"

"She said to tell you she hopes you feel better," Alma said.

I started to close the door.

"Wait," Julie said. "We got your . . . uh . . . the purse and phone."

"There are like a million texts and missed calls from Linnea's mom," Alma said.

"But it hasn't even been a full day," I said.

"She's a worrier," Julie said.

"If you don't respond," Alma said, with the knowing, patient tone of a hostage negotiator, "she'll come home."

That's exactly the last thing I needed, so they coached me in how to calm her down.

Mom! So sorry I missed your calls! Left my cell in freezer at work, can ya believe it? Apple Store geniuses finally thawed it. All is well here. ☺ ☺ ☺

Working double shift so can't talk. Miss you lots. But feel great!!

Love you to pieces! Xxoo L

"Can you take it from here?" I said, holding the phone out to Julie.

"You mean . . . ?"

I nodded. "Take the phone. Keep up the illusion, at least for now. It feels wrong for me to pretend."

"But we'd be pretending too," Alma said.

"True, but you're way closer to the gir—to *Linnea* than I am, so it's more sincere coming from you."

Reluctantly, Julie pocketed it. "She'll want to hear your voice at some point."

"Say I woke up with laryngitis."

They shared a panicked look.

"Look," I said, "I know this sucks for you."

Alma nodded. And then got teary. She pressed her fingers against her mouth as if she was holding back a sob. Julie put an arm around her.

"It has to be a million times worse for you," Julie said to me.

I half-wished she'd put her arm around me.

Although the mother's room isn't decked out in dreamy colors I wouldn't pick, I can't sleep there, either, because the nightstand is crowded with pictures of Linnea. From baby right on up. Birthday hats, goofy grins, pensive looks, golden autumn leaves, vibrant wildflowers, fake swirly studio backgrounds.

"Jesus," I grumble. "She's right down the hall."

I put them facedown and roll over. No go. I stash them inside the nightstand drawer and try again. I don't even get my eyes shut. It's like the photos are accreting strength in their prison. I set them free, rearranging them as before. They almost give off their own light in the dim room, a glow that draws my eyes to it as it dulls everything else. I have to work hard to wrest my gaze out of the picture montage, like I'm heaving a leg out of quicksand.

Shaking off the weird photo hold, I head downstairs. On the way, I'm careful to avoid mirrors. They're cruel because they conspire with my brain to show me what I want to see, not what is. I stretch out on the sofa, blanket myself with a soft throw draped over the back. I wouldn't say I'm comfortable (which I guess means I'm not Goldilocks), but at least here I feel less like a sneaky borrower and more like a *hey-can-I-crash?* guest.

It's too quiet in here. I reach for my phone and open Pandora. God knows where my charger is, but I've got enough battery for now. I try a "music for relaxation" station instead of my usual alt indie stuff.

The thought that music can't drown out, the thought that has trailed behind me from room to room, bed to bed: Max had no right to give something away that wasn't hers to give.

No right.

If Mom were here, she'd tell me to go easy on Max. "You're the strong one, Harper," she'd said to me once. "Max is steady, true, but that's hiding a fragility underneath."

The walls of my throat constrict. Mom isn't anywhere near here. I heard Max and Ezra talking: Mom's in the hospital. With a broken heart.

I sit up, pain splitting my own chest. *Mom.* I have to see her. Will she know it's me? Will she recognize her firstborn even in this unrecognizable body? And if she does, will that be worse for her? And worse for me? Still, I have to see her.

I grab the phone. Nearly 1:00 a.m. Okay. Tomorrow, tomorrow.

Linnea's purse catches my eye. It feels wrong to rummage in it, more of an invasion than being in her house, but I do it anyway.

As purses go, it's ordinary as hell. Compact, lip gloss, brush, hair elastics, stray earring, takeout menu, wallet, tissues. I don't know what I'm looking for. I open her wallet and slide her driver's license out. Happiest freaking license photo I've ever seen. Like *Whoo-hoo! I'm road legal!* I scowl at it at first, until I feel my lips turn up at the corners in spite of myself. I prop it up against a candle on the coffee table so that the pic is facing me. As I go back into her bag, my palms start to itch and feel peppered with little dots of heat. There's a paycheck in there, the stub attached.

She worked thirty-seven hours last week. And I don't remember a single one of them.

"Who *are* you?" I say to the DMV photo. "Who am *I*?"

Finally, a yawn. I sense grease slicking the gears of sleep. But a surge of dread in my belly warns me to resist going under. Maybe the real problem with falling asleep is wondering who I'll be when I wake.

MAXINE

"Max? You okay?" Chris knocks, then tries the bathroom door. It's locked.

"Fine." I try to make my voice sail over to him on a reassuring breeze.

"You've been in there a long time."

"Just real dirty," I call out, and dip back under the spray.

So maybe I *had* said Jonathan's name when I told Chris about the e-mail. It's possible, really. Maybe even likely. Did I? I'm so tired.

There's a pause. "Okay, then," he says. Another pause. "I'm gonna get some ice. You want anything?"

"Diet Coke?"

"I gotcha, babe."

I grimace at "babe," a bite of food I thought would be delicious but now wish I could spit out.

Once I hear the heavy room door open and close, I kick the faucet off with my heel. I twist my wet hair into one of the pitifully thin, nubby towels they warn you not to steal. Wrapping another around my torso, I have to hike it up to my pits and squeeze it to stay in place. It covers up my new tattoo, which is still deeply pink around the edges.

What if I hadn't mentioned Jonathan's name? What if Chris only knows it because he knows Jonathan and knew he sent the e-mail?

The towel slides off my body.

Or . . . What if there *is* no Jonathan? What if Chris sent that e-mail? And, beyond the fact that Chris was lying to me (at best) and manipulating me (at worst), what would that prove? I wipe a circle of condensation off the mirror and my own face floats up at me, weirdly surprising me for a second. I stare into my tired, tired eyes, as if the answer will float up too. The e-mail was helpful. Maybe he was only trying to help.

I shiver. I grab the towel and wrap it around me again. I pull on sweatpants and the *Y'all* tee Shelby gave me a couple of years ago. I don't notice I'm chewing on the inside of my cheek until it hurts. Damn. Where's Ez?

I untwist my hair and let the sodden towel splat to the floor. As I'm roaming the loud-as-hell dryer all around my head, I remember something else. Something I can't splat to the floor like a used-up towel.

"Who?" That's what Chris said when I mentioned Henry. *Who?* I try to imagine an instance when someone would say Harper's name and I'd respond with "Who?"

I can't.

Chris said he hadn't heard me. He heard enough to know I was talking about a someone, though. And we weren't on the noisy road when it happened, we were in a quiet, grassy field under the stars.

Is Chris a liar?

And so what if he is?

I flick off the hair dryer and try to jam it into its slot on the wall. It keeps falling back into my hand, and I don't have the fucking patience for this right now. It's those stupid little things that make you lose your shit, and before I know it I'm crying and I slam the goddamned thing on the counter and its shell cracks and I hear the door open and Chris yell, "Miss me, baby?"

Using the mirror to make sure it's on straight, I put on my best smile. I fling open the bathroom door. "'Course I did, handsome."

HARPER

There's a door. At least I think it's a door. It's shiny, it reflects my face, but distorted, like a funhouse mirror. I'm pounding on it, screaming.

Help! Help me!

My hands are cramping. Not only from the impact of fists on metal, but from extreme cold. My lipseyelashesnostrils are ice fossils. I'm crying, but within seconds of shedding, the tears turn to skin-frost.

I'm in here!

I grab a plastic tub of some frozen liquid—sauce or soup, who cares—and smash it against the door handle, over and over and over. But nothing gives, nothing breaks, except, eventually, the tub itself.

I'm slowing down. I crumple to the floor.

That's when the bees come. Not regular bees. These are made of ice. Silver and shimmery, their wings carve chinks into the polar air. They buzz near my ear, until they're in my ear. Boring straight in and into my brain.

I scream.

"Whaaa?" I'm sitting up on the couch I fell asleep on, cold and yet slicked with sweat. I still hear the buzzing. I swat at my ears.

It's my phone, spinning and vibrating on the coffee table.

"Hullo?" Icicles cling to my voice.

"Is this Harper's phone?"

"Yeah," I say.

"This is Shelby. Max's friend."

"I know who you are. Why are you calling me?" Linnea's driver's license is right where I left it, her happy pic a bizarre juxtaposition to the dream.

"Is Max with you?"

I feel the cemetery slap all over again. "Why would she be with me? She hates me."

Shelby's all business. "Look, she's not answering her phone. She ignored texts about the boys, and she'd never do that."

"What's wrong with the boys?" I throw off the blanket and swing my feet to the floor.

"Nothing. I mean, Will woke up with a sore throat and a little fever. I called to ask her if I should take him to the doctor, in case it's strep, and I got her voicemail and—"

"Wait a minute, why isn't she with the boys?"

"That's not the point," Shelby snips. "I'm worried about her."

"I'm sure she's okay," I say. "I can take Will to the doc—"

"Can you meet me at the house?"

Someone nailed the laundry room window shut since I last crawled in. Thanks a fucking lot. So I'm sitting on the front steps fingering the red streaks on my arm.

When I was in the bathroom at Linnea's house, splashing cold water on my face, I noticed writing on the inside of my left forearm, on the pale thin skin. Yesterday I'd noticed something faded on the other one, indiscernible beyond a few curves and loops. But this one was fresh. And wasn't there last night.

I was loved

Even though skin and paper aren't equal mediums, I can tell the writing is a match to the note Linnea wrote from the freezer. You'd think with all I've had to accept over the last day, mysterious writing on my body (not in my handwriting and yet not attributable to anyone but me) wouldn't warrant a second glance. But, to put it mildly, it freaked me out.

It was in ballpoint ink, so I was able to wash it off. Even if I felt a weird kind of throat-squeeze when *loved* disappeared.

Shelby pulls up and hops out of her car. "You must be . . ." she says, gawping from Max's car in the driveway to me.

I have no patience for unnecessary introductions. "Where are the boys?"

She unlocks the front door and steps inside. "With my mom."

I follow her. "So what am I doing here?"

She drops the keys on the mail table in the small foyer. They land on a stack of sale circulars and coupons. "I'm really worried about Max," she says. "What if they had an accident?"

"They?"

"Her and her boyfriend."

"Where'd they go?"

"Not sure."

"Why didn't she tell you?" I ask.

"It's not like that. She needed a few days away. She's been under a lot of stress, you know. That's why I took her brothers."

"Her" brothers. Not "your" brothers. "So maybe she wants you to deal with everything. She's never micromanaged the boys before."

"You really don't know what's happened in the last year, do you?" She shakes her head. "She's different now. The boys are everything to her."

The front door opens. Ezra bounds inside, out of breath. "I can't reach her," he says, as if he's been part of the conversation the whole time.

"What's he doing here?" I say to Shelby.

"I called him."

"What's next?" I say to him. "The other eye?"

"You did that to her?" Shelby sucks in her breath. "Shit, Max left that part out."

He doesn't even look at me. "We don't have time for petty bullshit," he says to Shelby. I'm sure I'm the petty bullshit.

"Maybe she's in a dead zone," I try.

"For hours?"

"Maybe her phone lost its charge. Or broke or something."

"She'd find a phone," Ezra says, "to let us know that."

"Max has always been responsible," I say, "but that's a little extreme."

Ezra reduces himself to looking at me. "Will and Race," he starts, "are ev—"

"I got it. I'll check her room. Maybe there's something in there."

Something wordless passes between Shelby and Ezra. Maybe they're weighing whether they should let me in Maxine's room. Whatever it is, it doesn't make it into words, and I don't let it slow me down.

Max's room is nothing like I remember it. I used to make fun of her for keeping such a neat space. As if she expected *Southern Home* to bust in at any minute for a photo shoot. Her bed's unmade. The sheets look stale. There are clothes strewn on the floor. I open her closet. Above the jumble of shoes and bags and notebooks on the floor hang three items on the rod. Only three. All mine. A nubby black sweater that I loved beyond reason ($23 at Target), a navy blue tunic with half moon buttons up the front that I'd wear with leggings in winter and alone in summer, and a pair of the softest cream sweatpants with a red stripe up one leg and *As if* across the tush. It's like a closet altar. The sweater is even on a puffy padded hanger so the shoulders don't get pointy.

I suck in my breath and knuckle the tears off my face. I back out of the closet. I shut the door, hollow sadness spreading through my belly. She loves me. *Loved* me.

"So?" Shelby stands in the doorway, hand on hip.

What am I looking for? A map? A phone bill? A ransom note? I start to feel ridiculous, poking around all Nancy Drew. Any second Max'll call Shel or Ezra and the mystery will be solved.

Ezra pats down the surface of her dresser, jostling earrings, receipts, change. "There's nothing here that says anything." He and Shelby leave the room, but I'm drawn to the dresser. Tangled up with hair ties and a chiffon scarf is a wooden cross on a leather cord. My palm goes itchy and hot as I touch it.

I pick up the cross. It's not heavy, but holding it, I have to sag onto Max's bed. A bird wheels past outside, causing the sunlight coming through the window to flicker. And I am there. The cab of Tyler's pickup, Lady Bird Lake glittering through the windshield.

"I'm not the most religious girl, you might've noticed," I say, "but this is kinda cool." I tap the cross hanging from the rearview mirror. It spins ever-so-slightly.

He laughs. "I'm not religious either, but I like the symbols. So I borrow them."

I lift it off the mirror. The back of the cross is smooth as ice, but warm. The front has roses carved in relief on the vertical axis, pale pink sparingly daubed on them, the only bit of color.

"I made that," he says.

"For real?"

"For real." He smiles. His teeth glow like they're borrowing the moonlight.

I whistle. "Shit, dude, I'm impressed. This is special."

"When I was a kid, I got sent to this camp where idle hands were the devil's workshop."

"Doesn't sound like regular summer camp." I hang the cross back up, reluctant to pull my fingers away from it.

"It was after my parents died. My aunt and uncle didn't appreciate having a little kid around after theirs were grown, so they came up with reasons to call me 'troubled.'"

"Jesus, Tyler, I'm so sorry. How old were you?"

"My parents died in the wreck when I was five. But it wasn't 'til I was ten that my aunt was looking for somewhere to ship me off to. So every summer after that I got sent there. Until the funding was pulled and the camp closed."

I let my breath out slowly. I feel like shit. Here he is, telling me all this, and I'm just messin' with him. I don't think I told him one true thing about myself. Other than I like live music.

"Hey, don't look so sad," he says, gently tapping my chin. "I'm stronger now because of what I survived."

I watch the cross sway gently in the current my breath makes. There's so much suffering in the world. I decide I'll work with kids. Maybe become a social worker. Mom will be glad to hear I'm forming that "life plan" she's been after me about.

"There's so much I don't know," I say, more to myself than him.

"I want to tell you everything about me," Tyler says.

Oops. Musing misinterpreted.

"What about you? How'd Emily get to be Emily?" He presses himself closer to me. This is the third time we've been together. And we've only fooled around. Not as in sex, but just making out, smoking weed, getting buzzed. No biggie. Despite how pay-her-parking-tickets Maxine wants to blow it out of proportion, I have never cheated on Ezra. I would never hurt him like that. Fooling around like this is not cheating. Not when you don't give your body or your heart.

Tyler's kissing me now, and I'm sort of kissing him back, except my eyes are open and I can see the cross hanging there, pale but with the illusion it's glowing, as if it's been rinsed with moonlight.

Tyler deserves better than this. Better than what I'm not giving him. I pull away.

"Oh, sorry," he says. "Did I hurt you?"

"No, no. It's just . . . well, Tyler, I think we're looking for two different things here."

He waits. I've never thought I'd use "with bated breath" to describe something, but that's how he waits.

"I . . . uh . . ." I clear my throat. "I have a boyfriend."

His brows shoot up. "You mean an *ex*-boyfriend?"

"No. I'm sorry."

He pulls away from me. He grips the steering wheel as if it needs to keep him from shattering. "Shit! I really liked you, Emily."

No point in making him feel worse by fessing up to the whole alias thing.

"And I liked you, Tyler. But I'm not looking for something serious."

He twists in his seat and looks out the window. I wonder what he sees. His breath gets choppy. Is he crying?

"Tyler, I'm really sor—"

"God*damn*, when am I gonna *learn*?" His voice sounds strangled. "You're just like everyone else. No matter how hard I try, they disappoint me."

"I didn't mean to give you the wrong impression." I have my hand on the door handle.

"Wait," Tyler says. "Don't leave like this. Maybe we can be friends."

"Sure." Not likely.

"One more drink for the road?" He's looking at me now. His expression is so earnest, so open, that I can't help but think of the little kid carving crosses summer after summer, his next of kin glad to be rid of him.

"Why not?" I say.

I find Shelby in the kitchen. She's calling hospitals.

"Where did this come from?" I practically shriek, dangling the cross by the cord like a dead rat by the tail.

Ezra shrugs. Shelby lowers her phone and says, "Max's boyfriend gave it to her."

"The boyfriend she's with?"

"Yeah, why are you freaking?" She sets her phone down.

"She's in trouble."

MAXINE

Chris's arm is a boa constrictor sunning itself on my neck, his fingers spider legs aimlessly playing on my arm. We're sitting on the stiff, scratchy couch in this cheap room, a nature show on TV, volume low. He kisses my ear and breathes into my hair. "I like the way the shampoo smells on you," he says.

"Motel 6 sulfate," I say. "It's all the rage."

I take a swig of Diet Coke. He throws back his head, finishes another beer.

"You know I hate drinking alone." He pouts.

"I woke up with such a bad hangover this morning," I say. "I'm on the wagon tonight." I drain the last of my soda.

"We're celebrating, though."

"We are?"

"*I* am," he says.

"You win a scratch-off or something?"

"Duh. Max. Our first overnight together. Our first time in a hotel room."

"Motel room." This place is right on the frontage road so the freeway traffic feels like it's aiming straight for your head. The king bed has a sad depression in the middle, like a caved chest. There's a Rorschach stain on the rug that looks like longhorns from one angle, crossed rifles from another.

"We need to have a toast," he says. "I guess yours'll be with Coke."

I move to get up and fetch another can. He gestures for me to relax.

"Let me." He fishes a soda can from the cooler of watery ice. Because the first one sprayed all over me when I popped the tab, I opened the others over the bathroom sink. He does that now. "You know what?" he says over his shoulder.

"Hmm?" There's a close-up of the insides of a rhinoceros's mouth on the screen. Apparently there's a microcosm of teeming life in there.

"We should have our toast like grown-ups. In glasses." I hear him unwrap the plastic cups in the bathroom, hear the cascade of bubbles.

The same old Chris. A nice guy, just not the guy for me. He's in love and I'm not, and my sneaky brain doesn't know what to do with that so it picks everything apart.

"That's better," he says, handing me my "glass" of Coke. He's holding one filled with beer. He sits beside me and squeezes my knee.

"Ready?" he says, raising his cup.

Pushing through my exhaustion, I mirror his movement and raise mine.

"To us," he says.

"To us."

We clink cups. We drink. He kisses me on the cheek, lets his lips wander to my mouth. He tastes like the same old Chris too.

"So there's something you should see," he says after a bit. "Since you'll see it sooner or later anyway."

My eyes flit back to the TV. "You mean other than a giant plant eating a bird?"

He hikes the sleeve of his shirt way up onto his shoulder, revealing his bicep. His new tattoo. Since the only light comes from the TV and the short desk lamp in the corner, the room is dim. Which is why it takes me longer than it should to figure it out: the predesigned art he picked out at the inkstand is not what's on his skin.

It's: M♥xine.

"Like it?" He's smiling. His teeth are too white against the backdrop of this grimy room.

"Oh. Wow."

He lets his sleeve drop. I convince myself I can still breathe.

"Is wow good?" he asks.

"Of course! I mean, I thought we weren't gonna do the names . . ."

"You weren't ready," he says, "and that's fine. But that doesn't mean I couldn't wear my heart on my skin."

"Ha. Right. I get it."

"Are you trying to make me feel like I made a mistake?"

"No," I say hastily. "Of course not. I'm . . . flattered. That's sweet."

"It's sweet?" His eyes cut to mine, coolly linger there. This time, with his teeth hidden, his face is dark. "Sweet is something you say to a prom date who brings you a flower."

"I'm tired, is all. Don't focus on my word choice."

He cups my jaw in his palm, lets my damp hair spill over his knuckles. "You seem jumpy."

"Huh? Maybe the caffeine's getting to me."

He squints at me.

"Truth?" I say.

"Of course. Always."

"I guess it's harder to be away from the boys than I thought it would."

He relaxes. "That's natural. You've been a real mother to them this year. I think you're amazing."

"I'm sorry, Chris, I need to get home."

"What?"

"I've never left them overnight before. I guess I'm not ready."

He sets his jaw. His eyes get hooded. He's breathing through flared nostrils, and it sounds weird. Choppy. "You asked me for this getaway, remember?"

"Of course. It's just that I fig—"

"Do you have any idea what it took for me to get a few days off?"

"You said it was no big deal." I sit up straighter, drawing my body into me.

"I didn't want you to worry. I know you have a lot to worry about already. But it wasn't easy. And now you want to chuck it?"

"I'm just anxious about them, is all."

"Maybe if you had a fucking drink you'd loosen up." He accordion-crushes an empty beer can between his palms and sends it to the floor. "You worried Shelby'll hurt those kids?"

"No, of course not."

"Well, then, maybe you should think it through before you get all, 'ooh, be my knight in shining armor and take me away.'"

I do a slow blink, bite the inside of my cheek, try to keep it all inside. I'll wait 'til he's asleep, slip out then, avoid confrontation. Even though my body is stiff with anger, I do my best to sink into the couch like this is exactly where I want to be.

"You're right," I say, "that was inconsiderate of me. And it's just normal jitters. I'll get over it."

He assesses me with a long look. He must be convinced by what he sees, because he grabs my hand and kisses the back of it. "Atta girl. This'll be good for you. And for them. You'll see."

"I should check whether Shelby texted at least."

I get up. He stretches out on the couch, annexing the cushion I vacated. I can't find my phone. It was on the dresser next to the room key before I got in the shower. Wasn't it?

"Chris?"

"Hmm?" He turns the TV volume up. The nature show narrator is talking about how patient lions are, how they "lie in wait until the ideal moment to pounce and kill."

"Did you see my phone?"

"No, babe. Not since you were watching the kids' video in the truck."

"Oh, it must be in there. I'm gonna get it."

"Don't be ridiculous. It's past midnight. And the parking lot is dark as hell, full of potholes. We'll get it in the morning."

Chris's truck keys are right there on the dresser alongside the room key. Once he falls asleep I can grab them, get the hell out of here.

"C'mon," he says, "let's go to bed." He aims the remote at the TV and shoots it dead. He cracks the knuckles on one hand, then on the other. Harper used to do that, even though I told her it gave me the heebies. Twisting around on the sofa so he can see me, he smiles. "What'ya say, beautiful? Hit the hay with me? I'm beat."

"Me too." And that's the truth, I realize as I pull back the covers. I'm so tired that now I'm wobbly. But I can stay awake. I keep my sweats and T-shirt on so I'll be ready to fly later.

"Our first time sleeping together," he says, all gooey. "Right." I've never been to his place in the city. He told me it was all he could afford for now, and he was embarrassed by it. "It's not good enough for you," he said once.

"You sleep in your clothes?" He strips to his boxers, tosses his clothes onto the couch.

"Yep." Stay awake. Stay. Awake. As Harper used to say, there'll be plenty of time to sleep when we're in nursing homes.

MAXINE

There are hands on my face, on my neck. Caressing hands. Hands that spread warmth around my skin. I move my face into that touch. Then there's a voice, a man's voice, calling my name. Softly. Imploringly. *Maxine. Max. Max.*

The voice is a bucket on a rope, and I'm the water in the well that has been down here for too long. It heaves me up and out. I know that voice. But when I try to shape my mouth around the name, my tongue won't cooperate. It's too thick, too dry, too stuck. As the hands keep caressing my neck, I keep working my mouth, and finally it's moistened enough.

"Ezra," I say. "Ezra."

The hands change. They stiffen. But just for a moment. Now they're smoothing my hair back from my forehead.

It takes several tries to get my eyes open. And then a moment to sharpen my bleary vision.

No. *No.* It's Chris.

"Hey, beautiful," he says. "Not who you expected, huh?"

A nameless dread floods me, drowns me. My brain is stuck like my tongue and eyelids were. Until it's not. My eyes widen.

"You . . ." I say. "You . . ."

"That's right, baby," he says. "It's me."

You killed her.

I moan.

You'll kill me too.

I'm on a narrow bed. He sits beside me, leaning on an elbow. His face is inches from mine. My eyes roam the ceiling. Rough-hewn wood. Like logs. Thick canopies of cobwebs. Wait, this isn't the motel.

My body. What's wrong with my body? It feels like it's nowhere near me. I try to shift, but Chris's forearm is now anchored on the spill of my hair over the pillow, so my scalp screams. He gets up and releases my hair. He paces, shakes his head. But he's wearing this smile that doesn't fit, so the effect is chilling. "I was a fool, Max. I really was."

I lift my neck off the pillow as best as I can—the movement sends pain searing down my spine—to look around me. This is barely more than a shed. He must've drugged me. Like he drugged her.

"Somethin' feel off about this, darlin'?" he says. His voice is thick with a Southern drawl I hadn't heard from him before. "I sink your name into like ten fucking layers of my skin so you'll always be part of me, and you wake up with another guy's name on your lips. Sound fair to you?"

Appease him. Hide what you've figured out. "I didn't mean it. I didn't know I was saying his name."

"That's what worries me. That his name was on the tip of your tongue."

"*Please*, Chris."

He sits back down on the bed again, his expression soft. "Please what?"

"Please don't hurt me." I can't help it. I start to cry.

"See, that's part of the problem, sweetheart. Why would you think I'd hurt you? Haven't I only been good to you?"

I manage a small nod.

"That's better." He traces the outline of my jaw with a fingertip. My chin. Then up along my cheekbone. My brow.

"Where are we?"

He laughs. "You said you wanted to get away for a while. 'Far away from Travis County,' you said. Don't I give you what you want?"

I start to sit up, barely hiking myself up on my elbows despite the mad spinning in my skull. With one quick thrust against my shoulder, he pushes me down.

At first he looks surprised he did that. Then he seems to stretch into it. Own it.

"Seems like you were busy makin' your bed for a while," he spits. "First you pretended you didn't hear me when I told you I loved you, then you laughed at me—fucking *laughed*—when I suggested we get tatts of each other's name, and then, the thing that's worse than both of those combined, you say his name in your sleep. While you smile."

I squeeze my eyes shut against the sting of tears. There's only one image in my head. My brothers. They can't lose me too. I let out a sob.

"Max, Max, don't cry." His voice is gentle again. He grabs my hand, gives it a squeeze. "I only want to make you happy."

I open my eyes. Oh my God, he's fucking crazy. He's looking at me like I'm his whole world. Like he hadn't drugged me so deeply he was able to carry me from one place to another without me knowing.

"You do," I say, forcing my words like I've never had to force anything before. "You do make me happy."

He's beaming at me. He's clear-eyed. It's the same Chris I've always known. How is this possible? Am I the crazy one? Is this just a nightmare?

Oh please, please let it be that. Let me wake up.

I smack my parched lips together. "Can I get some water?"

"Sure, sure." He moves to the other side of the hut. Scoops a Gatorade bottle up off the dirty wooden floorboards.

I take this moment to scan myself. I'm still wearing clothes. My body feels impossibly heavy, but I don't feel . . . *Don't feel* what? *Raped? He killed Harper, he'll kill—*

"You need to stay hydrated," he says. He's standing in front of me again. He twists the lid off the bottle and wipes the rim with his shirt.

"I'm gonna throw up," I say, holding my hand up against the drink. "Where's the bathroom?"

"'Bathroom'? We're camping out." He recaps the bottle and sets it on the floor.

Gingerly, which is the only way I can move, I slowly swing my legs to the side of the cot, my calves cold against the iron bedrail. The scratchy army-green blanket bunches under me. "I don't want to hurl in here, though."

"Hold on." He takes a knee and at first I think he's going to propose but then I see what he's going for. He's got one of my shoes in the palm of his hand. "You don't want to be barefoot out there. Snakes around here. And scorpions."

"Where are we?"

"Don't worry, we haven't crossed state lines."

He's loosened the laces on my shoe, pulled the tongue out. He tenderly bracelets my ankle with his fingers as if it's precious to him. He slides my foot into the shoe as if the act is a prayer. And then the other. Inside, I'm howling.

I plant both soles onto the floor as dirt puffs around my non-princess ankles.

"Take it slow, baby. You really tied one on last night."

You fucking liar. I know what I had.

He plants one hand on the small of my back, another on my elbow. Every nerve ending in me is screaming to buck him off. *Play his game.*

"Thank you," I say.

"'Course. We'll get you feeling better in no time."

I'm standing. *What did you use to poison me?* I want to scream as I tear out his eyes, his heart. But then I think of what drowning would feel like. Of how the strongest person I've ever known drowned at his hands, the hands that are helping me now, and I know I wouldn't stand a chance.

The numb heaviness is starting to shake out of my limbs, but the inside of my head is still a mess. And so is my balance. I'm forced to grip his forearm to avoid falling.

"That's it," he practically purrs. "Lean on me."

I concentrate through the dizziness until I can stand on my own. "I got it."

"Hey, maybe you're pregnant," he says brightly.

"Wha . . . ?"

"Maybe that's why you have to puke."

"I don't think so."

"Would that be such a bad thing?" he asks. "You and me and a little one?"

My thoughts swim. *Didn't we always use condoms? There was that one time, but . . . no, no you drugged me with God knows what. That's what's going on here.*

"Sure, we're young," he says, "but I don't get all these people waiting 'til they're so old they can't play catch with the kid or go for a lousy swim. Selfish, if you ask me." He's traipsing off into his own fantasy. "We could be totally self-sufficient. Grow our own food. We don't need to poison the kid with artificial shit. And we don't need to poison their heads with school either. You can teach him. Teach *them*. We'll have lots. I've watched you with those boys, Max. You're the best, most patient mother. Any kid would be lucky to have a mother like you."

Thoseboysthoseboysthoseboys. I have to get back to them.

We're at the door, which is as crude as everything else, not plumb or pretty, but which looks heavy. There's a faded cross painted on the wood, roses on the vertical piece instead of a body.

"Is this the camp?" I ask. "The one where you went as a kid?"

He pulls me close and kisses my neck. Inside, I'm wailing.

"You remembered." He flings the door open and there's the sound of metal on metal. "Fresh air'll do you good, Max."

I try to believe that. Less dizzy now, I draw in big mouthfuls of air. It's a sunny day, stupid with pleasantness. Birdspeak. The drone of fat bees. The air smells of spring waking and spring rot. There's a carpet of fallen leaves under my feet, damp and spongy. If Will were here, he'd be sneezing from the spores.

Trying to get my bearings, I squint into the sun. We're at the crest of a hill. Cabins dot the surrounding hills, interspersed haphazardly.

There are lots of trees—ash, maple, mesquite—the leaves still the pale green of young growth. Everywhere I look, there are gentle hills, fallen leaves, trees in leaf. The occasional dead tree, the occasional ramshackle cabin. If you subtract the sound of nature, it's eerily silent.

"You were right," I say. "I needed fresh air."

"That's my girl." He nudges my hair over my shoulder, gathers it at the midpoint of my back, and tugs it playfully before he lets it go.

"It's pretty here."

"Well then, it suits you," he says, hooking a finger into the waistband of my sweats.

"Actually, I am thirsty. Would you mind grabbing that drink for me?"

"At your service, ma'am." He tips an imaginary cap. I force out a coquettish laugh that costs me way too much energy.

He turns to duck back inside, but before he does, he says, "I love you."

I call up Ezra in my mind so I can sound convincing. "I love you too."

The second he's out of sight, I throw everything I have into it, and I bolt.

HARPER

The city that's always felt so friendly to me feels like a mountain I can't crest. I drive down South Congress feeling less like I belong than all the visitors. There are lines of people out the door of Torchy's Tacos, Hop-doddy's Burgers, Amy's Ice Cream, Home Slice Pizza. All these tourists eating up the city, forming orderly queues before they take their bite. I drive down First Street, past the Food Trailer Park where Ezra and I had so many late-night stuffed doughnuts. Now the shiny Gourdough's trailer looks menacing as it glitters in the sun. Like a giant bullet. Downtown, in front of the Moody Theater, the Willie Nelson statue that usually makes me smile seems sharp-edged, as if it's hoarding secrets. "Where there's a Willie, there's a way," I've heard people say. Now I feel judged by his gaze and duped by his wan smile. He's let me down too.

Further down Sixth, I drive past Stubbs Barbecue, the place where I saw my last concert (A Giant Dog) in the outdoor amphitheater. Before the band even took the stage, I was a sweaty, happy mess, my bare calves breaded with dirt, buzzed on the beer a guy in a floppy-sleeved flannel shirt bought for me after I flirted with him while Ezra was in the men's room. Ezra hated that venue. He went for me.

Stupidly, I scan mile after mile of sidewalk. What do I expect, that Max and this guy will be walking down the street hand-in-hand, and she'll say, "Oh, yeah, I ignored all your frantic calls. I needed y'all out of my headspace."

I loop around the block to avoid construction on Red River Street, and I'm passing the homeless shelter now, dozens of people sitting with their backs against the building, some of them stretched out on rolled-out sleeping bags on the shaded pavement.

Something scratches at me. Something Tyler said the first time we hooked up. We were sprawled on the bed of his pickup smoking a joint (something Ezra didn't like to do) and my fingers found a fabric headband among the empties and tools. I held it up in the moonlight. He snapped it away.

He said his apartment wasn't too far from the shelter and one morning he came out to find a couple sleeping in the bed of the truck in their two-man sleeping bag. The headband must've been the missus's.

"What'd you do?" I'd asked.

"I started the truck. That woke 'em up."

He lives near the shelter. At least he did when I knew him. That's something. Blue pickup. That's all I remember. And of course once I set my radar to blue pickup truck, I see them everywhere. This is Texas. Pickup trucks are like the weather: look out the window and you'll see 'em.

I slow the car down around apartment complexes, cruising past street parking and lot parking, looking looking looking. Other drivers, annoyed by my rubbernecking, lay on their horns.

Hoofing it has to be better than this aimless, fruitless motor tour of the city. I find a spot on the curb. I don't have money to feed the meter, but I don't care. A parking ticket is the last thing on my mind.

The sun on my head like a warning or a promise, I walk.

And walk.

And walk.

And walk.

It's hot. Upper eighties, likely. And the sun is relentless. But still I walk, hoping for a shred of a clue, some scrap that can point the way to Max.

I lose track of how long I've been searching. Hours, for sure. The light has softened, the sidewalk shadows have lengthened, the air is a notch less hot. I'm exhausted. Heatstroked, maybe. Hungry, but the hunger is reduced to a dull ache, as if my body knows it's not the priority. My phone's officially dead.

I also lose track of how many people I've asked—homeless and non-homeless alike—whether they've seen anyone who looks like Max, like Tyler/Chris, like his truck (some people flat-out laugh when I ask about a blue pickup; no, I don't know the make/model/plate number, and no, I can't recall any distinguishing features). No one had any information, but one homeless guy looked me up and down and tried to give me a crushed package of peanut butter crackers (I wouldn't let him). If you don't count my death, that's a personal low point, someone who hasn't had a shower in a month taking pity on me. One woman promised to pray for me.

I've given up. Now the only car I'm looking for is mine. Well, Max's, technically. I'm just trying to remember where the hell I parked. And because I have Max's car on the brain, I almost trudge right past it. In a parking lot that I've scoped before.

At first I'm sure it's a mirage.

No. It's real. He's real.

I stop dead. You don't forget the last face you saw alive.

I don't have to duck out of sight. He doesn't know me. Not on the outside.

He's putting a box in the bed of his blue pickup truck underneath a blue tarp. I watch. Frozen in fear and hope. He slams the tailgate and climbs the steps to an apartment on the second floor. He goes in but doesn't shut the door all the way.

"Max," I whisper, the people, traffic, sunlight blurring away and leaving only Max in my mind.

Tyler/Chris/whoever this sociopath is comes out a minute later with another box. While he's coming down one outdoor stairway, I go up another. I'm in.

"Max?" I whisper. Fiercely. The apartment is tiny. Broken mini-blinds on the windows. A trash bag overflowing with pizza boxes and paper plates. Keys on the counter. Otherwise empty. I want to cry. But I don't have the time.

"Who the hell are you?" he says, stepping back in.

And just like that, I'm face to face with my death.

"Oh, s-s-sorry," I say, struggling to keep my face above water. "I saw the door open. I'm thinking of moving into the complex."

"This ain't the leasing office."

I gulp. "I wanted to see what people thought who lived here. You moving in?"

"Out."

"Did you like it here?" I ask.

His back to me, he opens a drawer in the kitchen, grabs something, puts it in his pocket or under his shirt. "'S fine," he mutters.

"Where you moving to?" I try.

"Look around if you want." He snatches the keys off the counter. "Shut the door on your way out."

I stand at the window and peek through the missing teeth of the blinds. I see him cross the parking lot, toss the trash bag in the Dumpster, enter the leasing office. The farthest point from his truck.

My heart crazy in my throat, I run down to the parking lot and race to his truck. I unhook an eyelet of the tarp, peel back one corner of it and crawl in among the boxes. I contort myself to fit and refasten the tarp. And then I hold my breath. I hope he's not the type to recheck his stuff before he takes off.

Hot, dark minutes pass. Finally, my lungs burning from this stingy bit of air, I feel the shift in the truck that signals someone getting in. The engine starts. And then we're moving.

I've never been a God person, but in this moment I pray that wherever this truck takes me, Max will be there.

Alive.

HARPER

Tongues of wind lick the edges of the tarp and slip underneath so that the rippling material over my head competes with the hum of the tires beneath me. With my eyes closed I can almost imagine there's a sail above me, scooping big fistfuls of air and steering me while I'm blind and cramped down here. I'm curled small, my hands clasped at my chest because there's nowhere else for them to go. As if they're frozen in prayer.

After a while music wafts back here. And the man Max knows as Chris and I know as Tyler is singing along, humming when he doesn't know the words. I can't make out the song. But I don't want to know it.

Max. You have to be there at the end of this. You have to.

I'm on the verge of throwing up. And I'm probably dehydrated. When was my last sip of water?

Max. I'll save you. What I couldn't do for myself.

The truck swerves sharply, and then dips hard, as if into a pothole. The impact presses my fists against my chest—a quick, hard punch aimed at my heart—and a toolbox skids toward my head.

I'm writing on a birthday cake at Basement Tapes with green gel, I'm presenting Daniel with a cupcake and watching the admiration in his eyes. Then I'm stealing a sugary kiss from him, but it's not a theft for long, because he starts returning it right away. My heart beats hard, on the cusp of pain. My hands pulse with heat, and Daniel disappears.

I go searching for him, in the pastry case, in the flour bin, under an opaque cake dome. I only find pieces of him: a lone Converse with frayed laces, a Longhorns cap (L+D inked into the bill), an EpiPen with the safety on.

I laugh. Of course only pieces of him can fit in those places. Not his whole self. I go in the back, open the fridge. The light that spills out is too bright, the cold too cold. He's not in there. Stacks of egg cartons (four-dozen size) take up one shelf, the lid removed from the top one so that the blank eggshells seem to taunt me with my own failure. I smash them with a fist, all forty-eight, the whites running out like tears, the yolks melting out like dying sunlight. My hands, slick with the blood of all those wasted eggs, are cold now, too cold.

I move to the giant freezer in the restaurant kitchen, certain Daniel will be in there. He's not. But I am.

Me coated in frost so white it looks like sugar crystals. We stand eye to eye. Freezer me blinks at searching me as flakes of frost flutter off my lashes and onto my cheeks. She pulls me into the freezer with her, slams the door shut behind us.

"Make yourself comfortable," she says, her breath an icy blast against my face. "You're gonna be here awhile."

I'm swimming up, heaving myself out. Head's killing me. There's light in my eyes now. I'm too cramped to use a hand to shield them. My vision is blurry.

"What the fuck?" a voice says. "What. The. Fuck?"

My vision sharpens.

Chris/Tyler shoves boxes aside and drags me by the ankle through the aisle and out of the truck. "What the fuck is this?" he says. His voice is a growl. I'm the *this*.

He grips my upper arm, shakes me.

"Talk!" he commands.

"I'm sorry," I say. *Sorry I ever laid eyes on you. Sorry I didn't drown you that night.* "I have nowhere to go. I just wanted to get out of town."

"So you used my truck?" His hand falls away from me.

I back up and clutch the tailgate, rub the side of my head where a biscuit-size lump has risen. "I didn't hurt anything."

"You have no idea what you did. You stupid bitch."

"I'll leave then." I take a step and stop. What is this place? Trees. Dirt. Some sort of camp. A few scattered cabins. A bigger one, ramshackle like the rest, at the top of a hill, its few steps crooked and unwelcoming. This spot feels especially lonely in the twilight. The truck is the only vehicle in sight.

"I can't catch a fucking *break*!" The tremor in his voice is the one I heard at the lake that night. After I told him we didn't have capital-R relationship potential. "I needed to be alone with her. Alone."

Max.

"Alone with who?" I ask.

"My fiancée."

"I'll leave you alone. I swear." I want to sense her, not that I would've believed that was possible in my past life. But I only sense my own raw adrenaline.

"You ruined everything!" He gropes me roughly, his shovel-size hands slowing around my hips. I yell out.

"Shut the fuck up," he says. He rips my cell out of my pocket. "Who'd you call?" His eyes are wild, darting.

"No one. It's dead."

He tries to power it on. When he can't, he seems satisfied. But he doesn't hand it back to me. Instead, he tosses it onto the ground and smashes it with his heel.

He lunges at me, and I'm too unsteady on my feet to move aside. He gets into my other pocket, comes out with Max's keys on a photo key chain, Will and Race in miniature, smiling giddily.

"Holy shit," he breathes. "These are hers."

He assesses me in a new way. Like a butcher deciding where to make the first cut. "They sent you!" He looks beyond me, to the dirt road unpopulated save for the birds and the trees. He grabs me by the shoulders, the keys digging into my flesh along with his fingers. "Who sent you?"

"No one." Was that the right answer? The wrong one?

"Why do you have these then?" He shakes the keys by my ear.

"They were in the truck. I just grabbed them. Didn't think. I didn't know whose they were."

He's not so much convinced as he is thrown off. He pockets them.

"They're your fiancée's?" I ask.

"I have to figure out what the hell to do with you now." He's pacing, churning up clouds of dirt as the sun gathers its remaining light and fades away.

"I'll stay out of your way. I promise."

"She's not well," he says, seemingly to himself. "She needs some time. That's all. Time away from the rest of the world. She'll be fine then." "Max?" I blurt. *Shit.*

His feet stop short. "You know her?" The stench of paranoia rolls off him again, hits me square in the face.

"You said her name," I lie. "Before."

I can't tell whether he believes me. *Max. Show me Max.*

Sighing, he rakes his fingers through his hair. I see a sheathed knife at his hip.

It's all too much. I can't keep the roiling in my stomach down. I throw up.

He jumps out of the way. "You're fucking disgusting!"

"Sorry," I gasp. I'm bent over. If not for my hands on my knees, I'd be facedown in the dirt. Everything sour in me is in my throat, on my lips, on my shirt. I spit the last of it out and wipe my bottom lip with the back of my hand. "I can help Max. You said she's sick. I have medical training."

He snorts. "You can't even help yourself."

"It was the ride in the truck that did it. I'm okay. But if Max is sick and you're way out here . . ." The desolation of the place tries to fill in its own unhappy ending. I have to pick new words to have any hope. "I can help."

"And if you can't?"

"I can. I will." Can I though? It all feels like too much. The knife in the sheath. No sign of my sister. My sour insides soaking into the earth. "She's alive," I breathe, my fists pressed against my mouth, "isn't she?"

"Of course she is." He hawks and spits. "Who do you think I am?"

A monster. A fucking monster. I will destroy you.

"Where is she?" My eyes dart all around, landing on nothing that says *Max*.

"She doesn't need you bothering her. You're a mess."

"*Please*." I don't mean it to come out that way, but there it is. Clearly the level of my pleading puzzles him. "I'll prove myself to you," I try to explain. "I can see you're in love."

"What do you know about love?" he says.

"I know it's precious and rare. If she's feeling sick, you want her to get better, don't you?"

"Obviously. I don't want to be engaged to a dead girl." The way he says *dead girl*, like the words are heavy chess pieces he's slamming down on the board, chills me.

"Where is she?" I say.

"For a nothing little stowaway, you sure are nosy."

"Just let me see her."

He spits at my feet. "She's not some carny freak you can gawk at."

"I swear to God, if you've hurt her . . . " I start, hearing my mistake in real time. I back away.

"Then what?" he snarls. "Then *what*?"

He lunges toward me and I launch into a run, aiming for the nearest building, but he's on me, yanking me by my hair. He tugs my head back so hard that I feel a snap in my neck. I claw at his hand. I wing my elbows behind me, hope to slam into his face.

Still clutching my hair, he hooks an arm under mine and anchors his palm to the back of my head.

"If I let you live," he says into my hair, "you don't get to make the threats."

He twists my arm so far back I'm sure something's broken. I'm on the verge of blacking out when he releases my wrist, my hair. My face is drenched in eye-watering pain. I fall to my knees.

"I could kill you in a second," he says.

You already did. I won't let you do it again.

"Maxine!" I scream. "Where are you?"

He's laughing. "Go ahead. Yell your head off. Nobody's gonna hear you but the birds."

I lurch away, my legs pumping with blood, and run. I crest the dusty hill and stumble onto a creaky porch. My right leg breaks through a rotting floorboard. The wood splinters and bites and claws my leg, swallowing it past the knee.

He just laughs and laughs. "Maybe getting rid of you won't be as complicated as I thought. You've been here five minutes and already you're puking up your guts and burying yourself."

I anchor my hands on the stronger edges of the porch and heave my trapped leg out of the hole. I hear something scuttle away in the dirt below the porch. My leg weeps blood from several places but I push on. More carefully now, I get to the door of the cabin and shove it open.

"Max?" I call.

Nothing but a faint rustling that might be the sound of the wind through the trees outside. The cabin is dark and close. I can make out a cot in the corner, a trunk at the foot of it.

"Maxine!" I say, hoping against hope for her voice in return.

I push deeper into the cabin. My footsteps creak the wooden plank floor and send up clouds of dust. Something in the corner squeaks and then flies at me. I scream and duck and cover my head. A bat. It wriggles through a crack in the wall, flapping its way outside. My heart beats faster than those furry translucent wings. Blood throbs in my throat.

He's in the doorway, blocking the light. "Real tough, huh?"

"Just let me see her," I whisper. As if taking my voice any louder will elicit sobs. "I've got medical training."

"Bullshit. If you don't tell me why you're really here, I'll get rid of you before you can say a prayer."

I want to cry. But I have to play this game. One move at a time. "I saw you in the parking lot. At your place. The way you were putting the boxes in your truck . . . and then when I talked to you . . . I don't know . . . you seem confident about who you are. About what you want out of life. I wanted to borrow some of that. I've got nowhere to go. Nothing to lose. No one to care that I'm gone. Just tryin' to survive."

Now he's grinning like he's watching a sitcom. "Shit, you're plum crazy."

"Let me stay. I can be useful."

"Get on your knees."

"What?"

"You heard me. Get on your fucking knees."

My lips clamp together. I can't do this. I shake my head, the motion churning my stomach again, making the lump on my temple throb more painfully. "I don't want to do that," I say. My throat tightens.

He makes a sound halfway between a belly laugh and a roar. "You think what you want matters? You shoulda hitched a ride with somebody else then."

I can't get to Max if he kills me.

His big hands on each of my shoulders, he shoves me down hard, forcing my knees to buckle. As my kneecaps hit the dusty floorboards, sending currents of pain through my legs, he grunts. The next sounds I hear will be his belt unbuckling, his jeans unzipping.

Max. I'll do whatever I have to for you.

"Now," he says, "pray for mercy."

My throat relaxes.

"Don't tell me you don't know God."

"It's not that," I say.

"Then let me hear you pray. Let me hear you beg for your sad little life."

And I do it, for the first time in my life, there in that broken-down, abandoned cabin that even flying rodents see fit to escape. I pray. Keeping my eyes downcast—the warped floor, a beetle scuttling past, my linked hands hanging down in front of me like afterthoughts—I pray.

After a while of my looping, rambling pleas—to an omnipresent power or to this sick man, I'm not sure which, and I'm not even sure of the difference in this moment—he silences me with a finger to my lips.

"Aw," he says, almost tenderly, stroking the curve of my jaw and ending at the tip of my chin, his fingers rough and calloused, "you're just a little ole fly. And I'm gonna love pulling off your wings."

HARPER

He tells me his name is Chris. I tell him I'm Linnea. He leads me along a hard-packed dirt trail—narrowed by encroaching prickly pear cactus and rosinweed—to a cabin on the other side of the hill. Our steps scare a cottontail out from a mesquite bush. It darts behind the cabin fast. Every cell in my body is telling me the last thing I should do is duck into another building with this man, but my brain keeps saying *Max*.

It's dark in here. He goes to the corner, stoops to light a rusty lantern, and holds it up so it throws off its watery light.

I gasp. Max is stretched out on a low, narrow cot, an itchy-looking army-green blanket bunched up at her feet. Her eyes are closed. Her chest rises and falls gently, and once I see that, I can breathe too. She's alive. That's all that matters. That's everything.

I kneel beside the cot. Her face is sweaty; damp hair clings to her forehead. She is pale, so pale. Even her lips are pale.

"Max," I whisper, patting her cheeks gently.

"Let her sleep," he says. "She needs to rest."

I find her hand—a tight fist. I unclench it enough to squeeze her fingers, to offer proof I'm here. I whisper her name once more. She turns her head as if she's seeking my voice. She whimpers softly.

He's drugged her.

"Harper?" she says, her voice a scratch in the sand. I want to say, "I'm here, I'm here!," but instead I grip her hand more tightly and murmur that she's going to be okay. She shifts her weight on the bed and something rattles. I see it then, a rusty chain locking her other arm to the bedrail.

"Oh my God," I say. "What is this?"

"She needs to stay safe." He rests his hand on the hilt of his knife. "You heard her, she's hallucinating."

"What are you talking about?" I forget who has the power. His energy shifts. A bull lured by the red cape. "I mean," I backpedal, "I don't think that's necessary."

"Harper," Max says, her eyes still closed, her voice still weak. "Where were you?"

"She keeps asking for her sister," he says with dismay. "Her dead sister."

"She needs a doctor," I say.

He makes a noise in his throat. "I thought *you* were the doctor."

"She may be severely dehydrated. I can't give her IV fluids."

"She'll be fine. This place is good for girls. Especially ones with fucked-up families. The clean air, the quiet. It brings them back." He skims his knuckles over her cheekbone. I don't want him touching her. I glance at the knife at his hip. I imagine grabbing it, sinking the blade into his neck.

"Ezra?" she mumbles.

"Ah, see?" He snatches his hand away from Max and kicks the nearest wall. Sawdust and dried insects crumble down from the rafters. "How are we gonna make a new life together, Max," he screams, "if you won't leave the old one behind? How can our love survive that?" And then he turns to me. "You see that? That's what she's sick with! Not something an IV'll fix. *That.*"

"What?" I ask.

"She asks for *him.*" Now he's pacing the short length of the cabin as if he's caged. I'm worried he'll mistake one of us for his jailer.

"That's only because you've frightened her. Unchain her. Let me help her and she'll forget all about him." I swallow hard and add, "Whoever Ezra is."

There's a chillingly long moment in which he seems to think. Then he mutters something about this day needing to end already.

"You smell like puke." He hurls a shirt at my face. "Put this on."

I hesitate.

He laughs. "You waiting for me to turn around? Fine. There ya go." I swap shirts fast. He grabs mine, tosses it outside. The peasant blouse he gives me—elastic neckline broken off one shoulder—smells stale. Like this place. If it was Max's, I don't recognize it.

Next he hurls a musty sleeping bag at me that I don't bother unrolling. I'm wrecked with fatigue, but I sit up, spine against the crude tongue-and-groove wall, and watch Maxine breathe. On a cot at the other end of the cabin, Chris sleeps in snatches. Every time I move, he wakes. Exhaustion or no, it's not like I'd be able to let my guard down enough to sleep with the dragon curled under the same roof.

As I hold vigil over my sister, I assess my own body: the arm he twisted doesn't seem broken, just bruised and sore. I can't feel hunger anymore, so that's a plus. I'm thirsty, but he made me take a few sips of water before he turned in, so I suppose dehydration isn't imminent. I'm weak, of course, but how much of that is thanks to this impossible day, this impossible situation, or . . . Linnea's friends had warned me that I needed to take "my" (her?) meds or I'd get sick.

"It's been a whole year," I'd pointed out.

"Forever," Julie had said. "That's how long a heart transplant patient has to stay on the anti-rejection meds. Every day of forever."

The morning when Shelby called me, panicked about Max (my God, was that only *yesterday*?), before I drove to the house, I had grabbed a carton of OJ from the fridge—didn't bother looking for a glass—and swallowed one pill from each plastic prescription container, just like Alma showed me ("Make sure you take all three," she stressed). More out of scratching a better-safe-than-sorry itch than anything else. I hadn't taken the pills with me. I'd thought I'd be back.

Every day of forever.

I want my forever back. I'm sick of this tour through someone else's.

All night while I watch my sister breathe I spin vivid fantasies of getting Chris's knife and plunging it into his chest, even though when I try to imagine what that might feel like, to send a blade through someone's heart, what kind of force it would require—physical and mental—I doubt I'll be able to follow through. One blip of hesitation, and I'd be the dead one.

Even if I could be quick enough and ruthless enough to murder him in cold blood, I wouldn't have gotten the chance anyway. Before he settled in, he pulled the knife off his belt and slid it under the mattress.

Somehow, the sun rises in the morning, feeble early rays setting light to the window quilted in cobwebs.

Somehow, we have all survived the night.

HARPER

"Chris," I say, "she doesn't need to be chained like that." *You do, though.*

He's trying to loosen a bolt at the base of a water pump at the bottom of the hill. The wrench keeps slipping. "She was getting up. Sleepwalking," he says. "It's so she'll be safe. There's snakes out there, you know."

"I'm here now. I'll watch her."

"Oh, sure, now I suddenly trust you. Like magic."

I guess I'm the naive one, thinking he'd let down his guard after I sobbed and prayed at his feet. "There's no reason not to trust me."

"Mind your own fucking business, how about that?" He progresses to slamming the wrench against the bolt.

"She knows how to avoid snakes. And if it's sleepwalking you're worried about, there are ways to prevent that."

"Like what?" He squints up at me from where he squats. The sun is in his eyes. I picture slamming his face against the pipe, over and over and over, until Max and I are free. But I know I'd only get one chance, and that wouldn't kill him—would only enrage him—and then he'd be on his feet and there'd be no amount of praying that could earn me mercy.

"You can lock the cabin at night," I suggest.

"Good idea."

"Great," I say, forcing cheer. "So where's the key? I'll unlock her now."

He's back to work, grunting at the plumbing. "Never said that." I want to scream. I shift my weight. "But it doesn't make sense—"

He throws the wrench down. I wince, thinking it's coming at me. He takes his knife out, sends the tip of the blade into the gummed-up crevices around the bolt. "Like I said, not that it's any of your business, but Max needs to get her old life out of her system. It's a disease. An addiction. It's hurting her. She needs to ride it out, 'til she realizes where she belongs."

"She's not a horse you can break!"

He stands up. We're eye to eye. His voice is quiet. "She's not a horse, no, but 'breaking' is exactly what she needs. And I've broken enough horses to know how to do it."

He kicks the stem of the pump with the heel of his cowboy boot. One, two, three times. Then he ratchets up the lever and pumps. Water starts gushing out, brown at first, then clear. "There we go," he says to himself. He cups some of it with the hand that's not operating the pump, laps it, splashes it onto his face. He's grinning. For one moment—one confusing moment—with the morning sun on his face, witnessing his sheer joy at striking water—I can see the boy he must have been.

I look away. "Okay, fine," I say. "Why not chain me up instead?"

He squats to pick up his tools. He sends me a look of pure bafflement. "Because I don't care about *you*."

Maxine and I are alone. Finally.

He unlocked her and allowed me to take her to the outhouse. More evidence that wherever the hell we are is not in use: the outhouse didn't even smell bad. It only smelled like earth.

He reshackled her right after, though he did it with this weird tenderness, almost reverence. Watching him murmur something to her while he brushed her hair off her forehead with his palm, only to have him chain her to the cot again, was the eeriest thing I've ever seen.

And then he made a big show of adding a latch and a hasp to the outside of the cabin and grabbing a padlock from his truck—the keys always hooked to his belt—and locking the door to this prison. From the outside.

"I've got some hunting to do," he said. "Don't want you ladies to get hurt by a stray bullet."

I'm slumped on the floor by Max's cot. She's more alert. Her face is still a study in defeat—mouth turned down, eyes empty—but at least she's fully awake.

She sits up as much as the chain will allow. "When are they coming for me?"

I tell her to keep her voice down. I'm not convinced our captor isn't eavesdropping from the outside. I don't have the heart to tell her that no one knows where we are.

"Are they looking for me?" she asks.

"Of course," I whisper. "Like crazy. Shelby knew there was something wrong the first time you didn't answer her."

A wan smile. But it's quickly replaced by panic. "The boys. Are they okay?"

"They're fine. It's a big adventure for them. Shelby won't worry them."

"What about Ezra?"

"Thanks to Ezra," I say, "your face is probably on every electric pole in Austin by now."

She starts to cry.

"Max," I whisper, "you have to pretend."

"Pretend what?" she says with surprise, her eyes glassy.

"Pretend . . . pretend you . . . you like him."

The tears stop. She sets her jaw, a gesture I know so well. "Never."

"That's the only way we can get out of here," I say.

She turns to look at me, a movement that appears painful. "You know we're never getting out of here, right?"

"You can't say that!" I forget the need for quiet. I go on, more subdued. "You can't give up hope."

Her listless gaze swings to the far wall, to the wooden peg where three carved wooden crosses hang on cords. What I hoped she hasn't seen, what used to be mounded on the floor directly under the hanging crosses, what I shoved beneath the cot while she slept, were a pair of lilac

Skechers—one minus its laces—that I know aren't hers (two sizes too small); a tiny beaded purse (empty except for a desiccated tube of Burt's Bees pink grapefruit lip balm); and neon green earbuds knotted in several places. I assume the shirt I'm wearing used to live there too.

"You signed your death sentence when you showed up," Max says.

Am I fated to get murdered by Tyler all over again?

She frowns. "Remind me, what's your name?"

"Max, it's me, Harper."

She shakes her head fiercely. "You're not. You can't be. I won't let you be."

She rolls onto her side and closes her eyes.

And because we're alone and because I haven't slept in what feels like three lifetimes, I heave my body onto the other cot and do the same.

When I wake up, my palms are strangely hot, as if I had been holding them over a campfire. Max is sleeping. We're still alone. Judging by the diffuse light at the lone window, it's late afternoon. I sit up, groggy, achy, heartsick and headsick.

Other than the soft sound of my sister breathing, the cabin is quiet. I don't even hear birds out there. I smell cool earth, old wood, musty bedding.

Slowly, I sit up. It takes me a moment to notice that there's something strewn on the floor where there wasn't before. It's the stuff I shoved under the cot to hide from Max. The purse, the shoes, the earbuds. It takes me another moment to see something on the floor along the edge of the wall where a chunk of wood planking is missing and the dirt underneath is revealed.

Letters?

I blink fast, try to clear my vision. I breathe fast, try to clear my head.

There's a scratch in the dirt after the *u*, but if it's a letter, I can't make it out. *Mu?h*. I'm guessing it's trying to be a *c*. *Much*. There's a line near the *h*, which could be anything or nothing, and that's where the lip balm lies. As if it's a pen and the writer set it down to take a break.

It couldn't have been Max. She's still chained up. And I can't imagine sleeping through the beast barging in. So it had to have been me. Me, but not really.

I look at my hands, pale in the weak light except for crescents of dirt under my fingernails, shadows of dirt on my fingertips. I bring my hands up to my nose, inhale. Cool earth. The kind under my feet.

If this is a message, what am I supposed to do with it?

HARPER

"There's got to be a way," I mutter as I knock on walls, kick at the place the rough-hewn beams meet the floor, poke at the door hinges. Most of the floor, except for the part where "I" scrawled a message in the dirt, is made up of splintery warped planks. Even if my energy held out and even if he didn't catch me in the process, how could I tunnel, with my bare hands, through the hard-packed earth to the other side? But being alone with my sister emboldens me, even though every time I say "hope" aloud Maxine shoots it through with so many arrows I can't recognize what it was before the slaying.

The words from my sleeping mind are no help.

Now that water is plentiful, I drink enough of it. I force Max to drink too. Before he left to hunt, he tossed me a stale granola bar and tried to feed Max a single-serving-size applesauce, which she refused like a rebellious baby bird. I open a fresh container and get Max to eat that undefiled one. It doesn't take much convincing. Clearly she's hungry. I nibble a bite of the granola bar and put the rest aside. In case there isn't more food coming, I'll save this for my sister.

I search for a weak place in the iron bedrail or the chain tight around Max's wrist. She sighs, lolls her hand in its cruel bracelet. "You tried that already. A dozen times at least. Why don't you cut my hand off and be done with it?"

"The sharpest thing he leaves us alone with is your teeth. So unless you plan to gnaw on your own wrist . . ."

She makes a noise in her throat, a distant cousin to a laugh. I've never wanted to hug a sound before. And then the sound turns. She's crying again.

"Max, we'll get out of here."

"The boys can't grow up with a broken mother and two dead sisters."

"He's not gonna kill us." I have no doubt he'll kill me once my usefulness is over, but he prizes Max. "He thinks he loves you."

"He's batshit crazy," she says.

"Yes. Which is why we need to use that. We can't come at him with logic."

"I never thought I could kill before now," she says with a sharp inhalation. "You know?"

"Max, did he . . . did he . . ."

"Did he rape me?" she finishes.

I nod.

"No. He's probably waiting 'til we're *married*." She winces.

There's a noise at the door. Max pretends to be asleep. Sucking all the light from the room, the beast is back.

He drops a box to the floor. I don't dare point out the obvious, that he didn't manage to kill anything.

"There might be some food in there," he says.

I look through it. There's a small bag of Sun Chips, a package of three links of jalapeno beef jerky, a Chock full o'Nuts can containing a dusting of ground coffee, a few peanuts and lots of papery peanut skins.

"Not much," I say. For all the boxes he hauled in the truck . . . he's a psycho and a shitty camper. "Why don't we go on a food run?"

He snorts. "Yeah, right."

I plunk the coffee can back in the box. "This won't get us far."

"Look what I ended up with the last time I went to town." He skewers me with his stare. "Besides, they're probably looking for her by now. And that means they're looking for me."

"But if we're really caref—"

"You stuck to me like a tick."

He steps right up to me, daring me to occupy the same space. I step back. Again. And again. Until the wall has my back.

He smells of sun and sweat. His knife is out before I realize he's going for it. I squeeze myself rigid. He brings the knife up to the top of my head and parts my hair with the tip.

"And you know what you're supposed to do with a fat, happy tick," he says. "Pop it so the blood drains out."

"Leave her be." It's Max. Her raspy voice seems to surprise him. He hides his knife, turns to her.

"Hey, Maxine," he says, all syrup. "You're awake. You feelin' better?"

Her head's off the pillow, then her shoulders.

"I wasn't doing anything with her," he says. "You know I only see you."

"You're fucking sick. You won't get away with this."

I glower at Max, flash her a shut-up hand signal.

"Me?" Using the flat of his knife, he gestures toward his chest. "*I'm* fucking sick? You can't even get out of bed."

Max, I want to scream, *there are shoes under your cot and a shirt on my back that prove how dangerous he is.* I implore the crosses on the wall: help us, why don't you?

"Me," I say to him, putting my body in front of the weapon. "She's talking about me. I'm the sick one. She thinks I'm trying to come between you two. While you were gone I told her she was lucky to have you."

He's facing me, his back to Max. I can see her biting back her fury.

"Help me with the boxes," he says to me, sheathing his knife and nodding toward the door.

Once we're outside, he stops short and says, "Prove it."

"What?"

"You heard me. Prove your words."

"I don't know what you mean."

I know exactly what he means.

He punctuates his words with stages of undoing: belt unbuckling, jeans unbuttoning, fly unzipping. "You . . . think . . . Max . . . is so . . . *lucky* . . ." His hands clamp my shoulders and press down hard. My body folds, my knees slam into the earth. He's a pillar of salt looming above me, making sure the sun can't reach me here. He grunts. "Then fucking *prove* it."

The birds go right on praising the day.

His hands cup the back of my head like a preacher bestowing a blessing. Until they push.

This time, prayer is not what he wants from me.

MAXINE

Chris doesn't sleep in the cabin with us tonight. On one hand, I'm relieved. But that relief is overshadowed by the hopelessness of being locked away. What if he never comes back? Would we just starve to death? Die of thirst when our water runs out?

The girl hasn't looked so good all day. I mean, you'd think she's the one who has been chained to a bed for a couple of days. It's dark in here now, so I can't see her clearly. But I assume she still looks terrible. I hear the water in the bottle glug, hear her swallow.

"You want some?" she asks.

"No thanks."

I hear a screech owl outside. The murmur of doves in between screeches. I worry about the doves.

In the darkness, she's made of shadow and breeze. "Max, we have to learn how to manipulate him. You have to cooperate."

I scoff. "Cooperating got me chained to a cot in the middle of nowhere."

She comes closer. "We'll figure it out."

My brain feels clear, but considering the bleakness of the situation, I think I'd rather be drugged. "You know we're not getting out of here alive, right?"

"You can't say that," she says. I notice that's not exactly disagreeing.

She squeezes my shoulder. Without thinking, I stiffen. She backs away.

"I wouldn't care if it was just me," I say. I wonder if I mean that. I think I do. "I could accept that I got myself into this. But my brothers . . ."

I hear her settle on the other cot. I can smell the mustiness the movement stirs up.

"Max?"

I have to keep reminding myself of her name. Linnea. It's pretty. Prettier than mine. "Yeah?"

"Remember when Mom used to tell us the story of the Beast and the Dragon?"

"Yeah." I feel my face smile. "Until I started having nightmares."

"I was so mad at you for that," she says. There's a long pause. "I'm sorry about that."

"I was mad at myself too," I say. "Hated the nightmares, loved the story."

Mom made the whole thing up and would add to it each night, after a day working as a prosecutor and then later, a public defender, roles she said the world saw as polar opposites, but to her weren't really all that different, not where it mattered.

"The Beast and the Dragon" was the saga of creatures who loved each other but couldn't admit it. So they ended up locked in fierce competition, trying to find—and exploit—the other's weak spot. The stories grounded me and thrilled me . . . and scared me. Sometimes I'd have nightmares that were far more frightening than anything in Mom's stories, nightmares of the scaly dragon shredding the beast with his claws and then sobbing over the unrecognizable body.

The owl screeches again. He's circling.

I never told my mother what my nightmares were about when she'd rush into my room. I didn't want to give her a reason to stop spinning the stories. But she figured it out on her own. And maybe that's why she never gave the Beast and the Dragon to Race and Will. It was mine and Harper's.

"'The Beast and the Dragon hated each other for precisely four hundred lifetimes,'" Linnea says now.

"'And on the four hundred and first,'" I say, "'they realized they didn't have enough hate left to get them through four hundred more.'"

"'So the Beast gave the Dragon his thick fur and his sharp claws, and the Dragon gave the Beast his glittery scales and his fiery breath, and the Beast became the Dragon and the Dragon became the Beast.'"

I gasp. Just when I think I have no more tears left in my head, I start to cry.

"Max? What's wrong?"

What's wrong is that for a few seconds, I had forgotten that my sister was dead. I had forgotten that I don't believe the unbelievable. I had forgotten that I am the prisoner of a madman, that I am without hope, soon to be forgotten myself. And forgetting felt like home.

HARPER

"Let's go," he says, barging into the cabin.

"What?" I stand up too fast. I'm light-headed. I have to lean against the wall to get the spinning to stop. Through the open door, it looks like high noon outside. In the cabin with its one small window hazy with cobwebs and grime, it's always some version of night. "Where?"

"You and me," he says, pointing to me, "are gonna get some food."

"Take me," Max says. She's on the cot, her arm twisted so that she can be on her side.

He ignores her.

"Let me use your phone at least," she says. "Please."

"I told you, there's no signal out here."

"Then let me go with you." She flops onto her back. "*Please*. I need to call home." A small yellow butterfly wings its way through the open door, whittles a choppy circle in the air, and heads back out into the sunshine. Max watches it go.

The noise he makes in his throat says it all. I want to take his knife and carve out the noise, leave him gasping and rattling. The force of the image, the lure of it, makes me more unknown to myself than the scar down my chest.

"I'll call for you," I offer. "I'll check on the boys."

"The goddamned boys are fine!" he shouts. "You baby them too much. They're gonna grow up weak."

"They're kids!" Max says, her eyes sparking. "They lost their sister. Taking care of them isn't babying them!"

"If you're not worrying about them, you're worrying about what happened to your sister. I'm so sick of it!" He grabs a fistful of his hair. There's spittle on his bottom lip. This is what crazed looks like.

I hold my hands out like I can stay the flood. "Okay, guys, let's take it down a notch."

His voice is a wire stretched to snapping. "You stay out of this. It doesn't concern you."

Other than I'm the sister you killed, motherfucker.

"So was it all lies?" Max says. "Henry, the Jonathan e-mail?"

"A year's long enough," he says. "You needed to move on. That e-mail was the best thing for you!"

Her scowl digs in so deep it looks like stone. "You targeted me at the grief group, made up a sob story about a cousin like a brother."

"Max!" I warn.

"And so what if I did?" he says to her. "Stories never hurt anybody. Besides, there's got to be a Henry somewhere. I know what's good for you. That was good for you."

"Good for me?" she screeches. "*Good* for me? You're a mur—"

"Maxine!" I yell. What is she doing?

"All that matters is that we're together." He spits a disgusting glob of phlegm onto the floor near her cot. "We're meant to be."

Mercifully, Max has stopped talking. She uses her free hand to cover her eyes. She's crying. I want to cry, too, but I can't spare the energy. Her fingers grow taut and she claws her face with her nails.

He bounds over to her, grips her wrist. "Whoa! Why would you hurt yourself like that?"

She looks at him with such naked hatred that I'm worried he'll kill us both and be done with it. There are scratch marks around one eye and down her cheek.

"Why would *you* hurt me?" she throws back at him.

When he seems confused by that, she says, "You took me away from the boys. They need me."

"*Our* boys need you," he says.

"What boys?" she spits.

"The boys we'll have together. You'll be their real mother. Not a babysitter like you are now."

Maybe he's too delusional to see the revulsion in her eyes. He caresses the inflamed skin on her face, looks at her with tenderness. "I'm trying to make a life with you. I can't do that until you leave the old one behind."

"She wants that too," I assure him. "Give her time."

Max makes a strangled sound.

He stands up straight and speaks only to me. "Let's go."

We're deep in the woods. He's behind me, pressing a hand to my back to keep me walking. I'm trying to hide how weak I feel, trying to disguise my shortness of breath as vigor. Under our feet, the crunch of dead leaves. Above us, the fragile, feathery, pale green of new growth. Around us, the bright, soft smell of spring.

I imagine the trees swallowing me up, the roots taking my bones and the leaves taking my breath. If it were just my life at stake, it wouldn't be so tragic, dying out here. But it's Max's. And, though I don't understand it or maybe even fully believe it, it's Linnea's life, too.

He grips my shoulder. "Do you hear that?"

"Hear what?"

Birds. Bugs. Breeze.

"Is that a helicopter?" he says.

My heart leaps. Could it be . . . a rescue? Until I hear what he means. A faint flapping. The old camp flag at the main building. Maybe I should stoke his paranoia. But maybe that'd convince him to kill me now, prevent me from talking. I tell him it's the snap of flag. He seems satisfied and presses me onward.

I know there's no food run. We're going away from the truck. Away from the world.

"Stop," he says when we reach an old gnarled oak with an archery target on its trunk and a tire swing hanging from a massive branch.

"What are we doing out here?"

"Max is worse since you showed up. Crazy. Always dredging up the past."

A woodpecker jackhammers a tree nearby. There's the sawing of a cicada. And always, birds. Our father was an amateur birder. He loved to take me and Max out on watching expeditions. "The male cardinal's a very involved dad, you know," he'd whisper. "He carpools, runs to the store for milk, and sews Halloween costumes for the chicks." And we'd collapse into giggles. The memory lands in the middle of my chest, its beak and talons tearing a hole in the past and tossing me back into this day. Today could be any spring day in Texas. If I hadn't just heard my own death sentence.

"She'll be okay," I say. "She just needs more rest."

He shakes his head. "You made me cheat on Max. You're making her hate me."

"She loves you." Please God, don't strike me dead at the lie. "Besides, she doesn't even know about . . ." I can't say it, can't name what I let him do so I could stay alive. "I didn't tell her."

"She can read me," he says. "See my guilt. She's smart that way."

"She doesn't know, I swear."

"Shut up now. It's time for purification."

He grips the hilt of his knife. I run.

One, two, three tree-lengths away. My lungs crowd out my heart. A tree root trips me. I push myself up on my hands, but he grabs my hair, yanks my head back.

He's not even winded. He's laughing.

"Little bit of a thing like you," he says, his arm hooked around my throat, his pulse seeping into my skin, "trying to squirm away." He presses his lips against my ear, as if he's worried about eavesdroppers. "Haven't you figured out there's nowhere to go?"

He releases me. The truth of his words presses down on me. I collapse. I'm so tired. Tired enough to give up and give in on this mattress of leaves?

"Time to get right with your god," he says.

I'm not dead yet.

"God sent me a dream," I gasp.

"The likes of you?" He squats, jerks me up to my knees. "Your dreams aren't god-borne."

"In the dream, you're praying over a meal. A meal I cooked. You and Max are holding hands. She looks happy, serene."

"So?"

I'm facing him now, and there's the merest hint of uncertainty in his eyes that belies the *so*. And maybe there's a petal of curiosity too. For the second time, I can detect a trace of the boy before the beast.

My pulse is fast, my thoughts faster. "You can't go back into town. You said so yourself. They're looking for you. You and Max will starve before you can make your new life together."

"I can take care of us."

"I can cook. I know things." The part of me that's not me knows things. It hits me all at once, like a brain-freeze after a too-big swallow of milkshake. It wasn't *much* scrawled in the dirt. It was *mush*. As in mush-*room*. "I can forage out here, turn it into meals. I'll help you and Max be who you want to be." I pause, bite my lip. "God told me."

He scoffs. "Get God out of your filthy mouth. God didn't tell you anything." He chokeholds me again, puts the knife to my neck. The cool tip scratches my skin. He says something unintelligible. I think it's in another language. The pulse in my ears makes it hard to hear.

Something reaches up inside of me. Some last fist of strength. "God came to me in a dream! He told me about you, Tyler."

The knife falls away.

"What did you call me?"

I've either saved my life or hastened my death. Too late to back down. "Tyler."

His arm falls away next. I breathe.

I can't read all that's in his face. His eyes are moving rapidly, like he's in REM sleep.

After a long beat of silence—plenty of silence for him to reach into and slice my throat with—I say, "How would I know who you are if God didn't tell me?"

"The devil talks too," he says coolly. "You go ahead and cook for me, girl, and I'll decide which one is talking through you. God's knife of righteousness won't spare Satan's mouthpiece."

Little does he know that he may not get the pleasure of a righteous killing. This body may stop my heart before he gets the chance.

HARPER

He is at my back as I push past the wooden door's warp and step into the building that houses the cafeteria and the kitchen. Much bigger than the cabins, it sits at the top of a hill noisy with wildflowers. I scan the ceiling beams for bats. It's quiet. There's a linoleum floor in here. A sink, too, but it looks inoperable.

Three long tables fill the eating area, upside-down chairs resting on top. Even though the ceiling is higher than the cabin's and there are lots of windows, it's eerie in here. I wonder if I'll hear the silverware-clink and mealtime murmur of ghosts of campers past.

He pulls a chair down, arranges himself in it like a lizard sunning itself on a rock. Leaning back like they tell you not to do in school, he hooks his fingers behind his head and says, "Go to town."

I move to the kitchen area. He can still see me from the caf through the wall cut-out. And I can feel him watching me.

There's an avocado green fridge wedged into the corner next to a giant gas stove with eight burners and a griddle. The fridge is unplugged, the black cord snaked around to the door to keep it from shutting. I check anyway. Empty. Not even a box of baking soda or a shriveled lemon.

Although I'm exhausted and wobbly—the adrenaline chaser after being held at knifepoint—I zoom through the cupboards. Avoiding dark drifts of rodent turds, I gather up the pitiful things remaining: a half-empty (or half-full, depending on your mindset) metal canister of cornmeal, a bottle of cloudy maple syrup, three cans of beans, two of evaporated milk, one of tuna, and, way in the back next to a cheeseless, mouseless trap, a bulging can of something so old the label is worn into illegibility. I line up all the sorry spoils on the counter, not sure what to do with them other than stare. Especially since I don't find a can opener.

Now what?

"What's for dinner, honey?" he calls from his seat. As if we're playing. As if he hadn't had every intention of killing me minutes ago. I hate him so intensely that I feel light-headed. Or maybe it's me that I hate the most, for my failure to see the homicidal psychosis under his sweet, guileless Southern facade.

I remember the few nights I'd met "Tyler" to hang out, how safe I felt with him. How his slow, easy drawl relaxed me; how the way he looked at me—with interest but not intensity, not a hint of possessiveness—made me feel more my age than when I was with Ezra. Ezra, serious, responsible Ezra. With Ezra I felt thirty-eight instead of eighteen.

But I love Ezra. *Loved* Ezra. Maybe I was confused about how I felt about myself around Ezra, but I was never confused about how I felt about him.

Like an unknitted shadow determined to reattach more tightly, Chris/Tyler/Monster is standing next to me now. He rubs his hands together as if he's starting a fire. "I have no food allergies, but you should know I don't love onions."

"How about mushrooms?" I ask.

"Yeah, they're good. What're you gonna do, order a pizza?"

"Just thinking about what's out there."

He slips into an Irish brogue and says, "This is Bear Grylls, stranded in the treacherous wilds of the Texas Hill Country. Tune in to see if I find enough food to feed my obese film crew, or will they have to shred me like jerky?"

"You're in a good mood?" How can someone be on the verge of murder one moment and Mr. Fun Guy the next?

"Why wouldn't I be?" He drapes a sloppy arm around my shoulders. The weight of him nearly buckles me. "I've got nothing to lose and everything to gain."

"Okay, I'm ready to forage."

"Like a doomsday prepper?" he asks.

"Exactly like that."

Who do I think I am? I can't cook. I've never even scrambled an egg.

I hope *she* can. I hope I don't get in her way.

Somehow, I find edible things in the forest that I'm able to name only for a second, like there's a wispy bit of skywriting tugged along the horizon of my brain, there for a moment, then poofed against the sky the next. But it's enough to know which berries are edible, which leaves are tender, which shells can be bashed open with a can to yield pecan-meat.

There's no room for celebrating, though, because he is always there. Watching. Waiting. Silent. No less intense for his lack of words—perhaps even more intense, with hunger.

HARPER

Somewhere in the rest of the world, I'm pretty sure it's Friday. But here, in this ghost camp that God has forsaken, it's just the next morning. It's overcast. I'm on the trail, cardboard box in tow, foraging for grub.

He's nearby, peeling the bark off a tree, nibbling on it like a curious fool. I feel his energy, coiled, ready to strike. The fact that he can go from inconsolable to jovial without segue makes him scarier.

I pass a live oak with a trunk of mossy green. I double back and duck under its lowest boughs. At its base, congregated like gossipers, are jaunty-capped mushrooms.

My palms go crazy—itchy, prickly, burny crazy.

I stoop, I dig, I gather. I feel him watching, but I try not to care.

A few hours later and I'm gathering mushrooms again, transferring them from the cool earth to the sad box. It's even more overcast now. The kind that makes you swear the sun never was.

I move to the other side of the tree, the mossier side. When the sun's out, this is probably the shadier side. I pick up a stick and dig around at the base of the trunk. Huddled in a cul-de-sac of roots, are some paler, thinner, more densely clustered mushrooms.

As if I'm a human divining rod and these little growths are gold, my palms flush with heat.

I pull up the mushrooms and lay them in the box, being careful not to let them touch the ones I already gathered. I squat there for a minute, seeing my plan take shape.

His feet pulverize fallen leaves as he makes his way over. He stands over my shoulder. "Hurry the hell up. It looks like rain."

I straighten up. "I'm ready."

"I'm gonna get us out of here," I say to Max. *You*, I correct in my head. I'm going to get *you* out of here.

We're locked in the cabin, just the two of us, after all three of us ate sautéed mushrooms. I don't shape my plan into words, in case he lurks outside.

Maybe because he was pleased with me that I foraged and cooked, I was able to convince him to unchain her for the night. In the dark, she's poking at the walls, at the door, even though I warned her if he hears he'll shackle her to the cot again.

It's funny, but she reminds me of me now. Stubborn. Ignoring sound advice. Scoffing at reason.

"I'm sorry," she says when her feet stop moving.

"For what?"

"I've been thinking about Race, about Will, about my mom. I haven't been thinking about you. Not in the same way. It's so fucked up that you got pulled into this."

"I hitched a ride on his truck. I wouldn't exactly call it 'pulled into.'" I bite my lip, deliberate, take a deep breath for courage, and say it before I chicken out. "Besides, it's really my fault anyway."

"What? Not true."

"It is." I sob and surprise myself with it. Damn, here are the tears. Mom used to say tears were little liquid truth tellers. I try to staunch them and end up making a weird honking noise.

She sits beside me on my cot, puts an arm around me, pulls me to her. "That was the least feminine sound I've ever heard."

I laugh and surprise myself with it.

"He was crazy before you got here," she says. "You can't blame yourself for that."

"No, that's not what I mean."

"What then?" Her arm's still around me. I want to collapse into it.

"If I had listened to you," I say, "if I hadn't taken Ezra for granted, if I hadn't gone out to do some harmless 'fooling around,' I never would've met this bastard, and none of this would be happening." *At least not to us.*

And then her arm's not around me, and she's not beside me on the cot anymore, and I have nothing to collapse into other than the well of my fears and regrets.

"I can't do this," she says, on the other side of the room. "I can't go there."

"Then how do you explain it?"

"I don't know, I don't know." I feel her pacing in the dark. "But you're not Harper. I know Harper. You have a bunch of memories that were Harper's—like accessories, really—but you're not her. My eyes don't lie."

I'm tired, so tired, in my head as well as my body. I'm trying to formulate a response, but she gets there first.

"Can't you just be her?" she says. "Just be Linnea? Can't I like you for her? Can't we make that a new start?"

"Yes, we can." The part I don't say is that the end, at least for me, is almost here.

Saturday.

If this were a regular Saturday, the boys would be watching cartoons while I slept. Around noon, the smell of bacon would coax me out of bed. Mom would marvel aloud at how anyone would want to miss out on the best part of the day. Max would roll her eyes in solidarity, even though she'd have been up for hours helping Mom with brunch.

Despite his joke that he wanted eggs benedict, hollandaise on the side, there are mushrooms for lunch again, sautéed in the big heavy skillet on the big heavy gas stove that he brought to life with his lighter. My hands are doing the cooking, I guess, but they're hands that look nothing like mine (they're smaller, for one), and it's a trippy disconnect.

I only cook the mushrooms that "I" know are okay. I'm not 100 percent sure about the skinny ones. I have to be sure first. I have to do this right. I can't pull the weapon until I know it's a weapon.

Now I've got the mushrooms—routine and very much non-routine—in the kitchen, sitting on the drying rack, segregated. Part of me mistrusts the knowledge that the other part of me is sure about.

I decide to take a tiny tiny—whisper-tiny—bite of the one I'm pretty sure is poisonous. My cloudy subconscious, weighty with someone else's knowledge, knows enough to know that I can't die from a minuscule shred of it, and if it is as toxic as I think, in a few hours I should feel something.

Before I can talk myself out of it, I do it. Just the sliverest of pieces, so small I don't even have to chew. It's spongy and dry. I swallow.

Okay, and one more sliver.

I know it's too soon to feel anything physical, but I feel something else: hope. How ironic: downtrodden girl feels hope after tasting her first killer mushroom.

The door whooshes open. He's whistling. I have the irrational urge to cover up my gathered prize, but that would arouse suspicion.

He stomps up behind me. "Mushrooms again. What a surprise."

"They're plentiful around here." I force the words out. *Sound nonchalant, stupid.*

"Ready for a side of rabbit?" he asks.

"You caught one?" Opening cans without a can opener was one thing. Skinning a rabbit, quite another.

"Not yet. But I made a trap."

"Oh."

He suddenly lurches toward me. At first I have no idea what he's doing. But then I realize he's hugging me. Savagely. Maybe the only way he knows how.

He pulls back. Appraises me. His gaze lingers around my mouth.

"I feel it, you know," he says.

"Oh? What's that?"

"The heat between us."

"But I won't come between you and Maxine," I say. "She loves you. She told me so."

"She's not ready for me, though. She still needs to work through the sickness she brought with her."

I busy my hands so I don't blurt something that'll get me killed. Like: *Lay a finger on her I'll bash your brains in.*

"It's been right in front of me the whole time," he mutters. "I can't believe it took me this long to see it."

"What has?"

"Moses had three wives. King David had seven."

Before I can think, move, talk, his mouth lands on mine.

He thrusts his tongue into my mouth. Searches with it. I command myself to keep my tongue there, keep it flat, instead of giving in to the instinct to jerk it back, swallow it down, way down into my gut, choke on it, even, if that's the only way to keep it from him.

"Mmm, you taste good," he whispers, his mouth still on mine.

You like the taste of death, motherfucker?

He brings his hands up to the tangle of my hair. He pulls his lips away from mine and presses his face against my scalp, inhaling deeply. "And you smell good too."

Using dish soap I'd found in the kitchen, I washed my hair last night at the pump. I was weirdly proud of that accomplishment, of at least the outside of my head feeling more normal. I don't have a comb, so my hair's a knotty mess. I wish I had kept it dirty.

He kisses my neck. Bites my earlobe. I manage to keep my shoulders from stiffening and not knee him in the nuts.

I know that no matter how still I remain, it won't end here.

But I know I will do it.

For my sister.

HARPER

"Lunch can wait," he says, taking my hand like it's a marvel, newly discovered. He turns it over and back, then his eyes bore up my body.

"Later," I say. I try to make my voice sound promising, demure, coy. Instead of trapped. "Tonight." *After you've eaten.*

He drops my hand. Practically throws it back to my side. "I need to see you in the daylight."

"But lunch will spoil."

"Nothing here's gonna spoil." He shoves the dry faucet with the heel of his hand so that it spins around and slams into the backsplash behind it. "Yes or no?"

The girl who wore the Skechers. The girl with the little beaded purse. The girl who owned the peasant blouse. They lost. I won't lose.

My breathing labored, my steps wooden, I follow him to his cabin. It's the one closest to the road, no doubt so he can keep watch. There's a cedar hugging the building, a nest in its low branches. A mother bird feeds her noisy young. I want to know what kind of bird this is, as if my survival depends on it. My view of her isn't clear, though. Another bird swoops over and perches beside the nest. A flutter of tomato red against the tree's browns and greens. That one's easy to ID: the good dad, the male cardinal.

The monster's already in his lair. Waiting for me. Expectant.

I don't think I can step inside the cabin. It's dim in there. Birdless and treeless. *Play the game. Hide your fear.* My feet resist until I command them. *Max. This is for Max.*

I'm inside. There's not much here. A wicker chair. A sleeping bag on the dirt floor. A lantern. A milk crate holding a canteen, a couple of towels, a few blocks of partially carved wood. On one wall, a poster-size cross, crudely cut out of what looks like pine. Twenty times bigger than the necklaces in our cabin. On the opposite wall, a set of antlers, wide as wings and sharp as pain. There are two small windows, but one is boarded up. From in here, it's easy to think of the sun as small and struggling to reach the earth. The air is hot, and still, and close.

He whips the knife off his hip. I flinch. I hope he doesn't notice. That wouldn't be playing the game.

He sets his weapon on a high shelf, one I'm pretty sure I won't be able to reach. Not in the body I'm in. Not that he needs it—the way he reaches up and brings his hand back down is knifelike.

He takes off his shirt in one swift movement, tosses it on top of the crate. He's got a *M♥xine* tattoo on his arm. He touches it.

"That means forever," he says. "But Max won't care this time."

Skechers. Lip balm. Purse.

Fierce, unyielding Max. Why is she still alive? He must have something special planned for her.

I move to the window. Inside, I'm flailing. "Max is a good person."

"Her soul is immaculate. I see the way she mothers those boys."

Then why take her away from them? I want to scream. But that would be violating the rules of the game.

"What were things like for you when you were a boy?" I ask with as much gentleness as I can spare. Who hurt the child so he'd hurt us? And can knowing that help me now?

He steps forward, pressing me against the window. "Relax," he says, and reaches under my arms and lifts the pane, setting a wooden block under the sash. He places my palms on his pecs. His skin is hot and smooth. The smell of him—musk and metal—is all up in my head. Before, when I was only Harper, we saw each other three times, and we made out, fully clothed. He hadn't even tried to sneak his hands under my shirt. I thought he was such a Southern gentleman. And then, when I told him I had a boyfriend, he knocked me out and left me to drown.

He presses my hands down more firmly on him, twitches his muscles under my touch. I force my hands—mine but not mine—to behave.

"What do you see in me?" he asks.

"Ah, so many things."

"Like what?"

I open my mouth to speak but nothing comes out. The dust motes over his shoulder churn in the slant of light. I don't need to look into his face to know he's glaring.

I say, "It's just that I don't want to come between you and Max."

He rears back. "Don't bring Max into this."

"You're strong. Confident. Devout."

"What else?" A muscle jumps at his jaw. His eyes dart all around my face until they pounce on my mouth. Like he's scanning for a lie.

"Handsome, of course." I thought so when I met him at Tracey Bigelow's party, when he handed me a beer and introduced himself as Tyler.

He smiles. A smile I would've said was winning before. "'Man and woman shall cleave together and become one flesh.'"

I turn and face the window head-on. Where's the bird family? I need the babies' unbroken chorus of *cheep*s, pure and clean and innocent in this filthy room. I catch my reflection in the glass. I can almost convince myself I'm not borrowing a body.

"You're thoughtful," I say.

"How so?" He parks his hands on my hips.

"You let me and Max sleep on cots, but you only have a sleeping bag."

"I want the best for Max."

I'm still in list mode. "You're hardworking. Smart. Resourceful." *Paranoid. Damaged. Deranged.*

He spins me around and shushes me with a finger against my lips. The smell of metal is stronger in my nostrils. "You did good." He does that staring thing again, and I have to work hard to hold his gaze. "You have pretty eyes," he says. "They're the color of cornflowers."

And yours are the color of wrath. "Your eyes. That's another thing I like. They show who you are."

"The eyes don't lie." He tugs the blouse's elastic sleeves off both my shoulders at once like a magician unveiling the finale. "And now we're done with words," he says, a guttural drag in his voice. He rests his calloused palms on my shoulders for a moment, then hooks fingers under my bra straps and slides them down my arms.

Breath escapes me. I close my eyes.

"Open them," he commands. "You need to see me seeing you."

I obey.

He roughly yanks everything off, bra and blouse, and takes a step back to take me in through a wide lens. Despite the heat in this musty hut, my skin goes cold.

"What did man do to God's beautiful handiwork?" he asks. As if it's a zipper, he travels a finger up and down the scar, whistling low. "What happened to you?"

"Bad heart."

"Fuck's sake, that looks serious." He brightens. "But God chose you to survive."

I clear my throat. "I'm grateful."

"I'll bet you don't like people knowing about it."

I don't know which answer he wants to hear, so I stay quiet and cast my gaze downward. I've been standing up so long. Years, it seems. I've been told Linnea's body is small, but I am carrying so much weight. My head is too light and my body too heavy. My vision flickers.

"A flower so few get to see," he says to himself, turning to the chair. He removes his boots, jeans and boxers and faces me again.

The old Harper knew how to conceal. How to pretend. Ezra asking where I was when I didn't want him to know. Mom asking where I was when I was supposed to be at school. Harper knew how to spin stories, how to sound convincing. Why now . . . why is this the moment I'm feeling less like myself than ever? It's as if Linnea's body gives me away. Judging by her goofy friends and how they talked about her, she's never cut class, or snuck out, or smoked a joint in a boy's Mustang. Or . . .

Will her body betray me?

He's kissing me now. I try not to squeeze my eyes shut in disgust but let them flutter closed like when I kissed Ezra.

I'm kissing Ezra. *Kissing Ezra. Kissing Ezra. Kissing E—*

"I like your enthusiasm, girl."

He doesn't remember my name. Linnea. Harper. Girl with the beaded purse. *Just not Max.*

He tugs the drawstring at my waist.

If I'm the one bargaining for my life, where does that leave Linnea? Whose body is being sacrificed? She can't give consent. Whose life am I saving? Whose life am I ruining?

My pants fall to the floor when I suck in my breath. I wish I could undo the breath.

He moves his lips to my chin, to the curve of my throat. His hands are on my shoulders like he's preparing to rip me in half down the middle. He moans. I imagine having the knife in my hand, burying it into the back of his neck.

He misinterprets my shuddering. The shuddering I tried to keep inside.

"That's it," he murmurs. "It feels good, doesn't it?"

I can't stop shaking. My knees buckle.

"Whoa!" He catches me before I hit the floor. "Whoa, girl!"

He scoops me up like I'm weightless, gingerly carries this body to the sleeping bag. This body I've borrowed. He lays me down on top of the bag, the zippered flap bunched under my hip.

"Christ, are you sick?" he asks. He's on all fours above me, his fists on either side of my head.

"I need . . . I need my heart medicine." For the first time, I consider maybe it's not only that, but the sliver of mushroom already working on me.

Something flits across his eyes. Regret? Remorse? Genuine

concern? And then the something is gone. He scoffs. "You need faith."

I press my palm over my eyes. To stop the spinning. To hide the tears.

"And maybe some protein," he snaps. "I'll get the trap working, get you and Max a stupid squirrel or something."

"Thank you," I barely edge out.

He sighs. "You rest up, darlin'." He pats my leg and straightens up.

Oh, sweet Jesus, is he leaving me alone? *Oh, please, leave me alone.*

He's putting his boots on.

Wait . . . *only* his boots.

"Where are you going?" I ask.

"To Max. God wouldn't put this desire in my heart if he didn't want me to use it."

Your heart? It's in your fucking prick. Now I feel all Harper again. No muddledness. No tug of contradiction. Mind over body. Sorry, Linnea. I'm giving something of yours away. Letting it be stolen. *Forgive me. But for Max, I must.*

"No!" I say. "I'm ready. Max needs more sleep. I'm here for you."

I prop myself up on an elbow. Every muscle hurts.

He glances through the window in the direction of the cabin where Max lies. I pat the sleeping bag. He kicks off his boots and stands over me, blocking the sun.

"Max is the one," he says, flipping back the sleeping bag flap with his bare foot. "But you'll be her surrogate."

"Yes." *And after, I will kill you.*

"For whenever I need you."

"I understand." *That you're soulless and sick.*

"No matter what, you'll never be Max to me." He rips the sleeping bag flap out from under me so that the surface I'm on is wholly flat. And then he descends.

I wonder how many different ways the same person can die.

MAXINE

I'm alone. Dusk bleeds into the window, turning the light in the cabin to flame. There's faint scratching on the roof. And then the scrabbling sound speeds up. From the prison of this cot, I can see a flash of squirrel as it bolts down a tree, another at its heels.

I hear Chris's heavy footfalls on the warped steps outside. I may not know who Chris is. Who he *really* is. But I know him better than Linnea does, even if Linnea thinks she has a ribbon of Harper curled within her.

Pretending isn't going to get us anywhere but dead. And she looks half there already. The fact that pretending is the extent of her plan makes me crazy.

I close my eyes before the doorknob creaks. Not because I am pretending, but because I don't want to see his face.

He steps inside. He's probably ready to feed me more drugs, which he hasn't been able to do with Linnea around. I'll bite his fucking finger off if he tries it now.

He strokes my cheek, sweeps the hair off my forehead. He smells like rotting leaves. And campfire ashes.

"I love you," he whispers.

I work hard to keep my facial muscles slack.

"It didn't mean anything," he says softly. "It just . . . happened."

What is "it"? My God, he killed Linnea.

He sighs, gently plays his fingers over my shackled hand. "No matter what she says, you'll always be the one who has my heart. I promise."

Oh. So he didn't kill Linnea. Thank God.

I hear the jangle of his keys. Gently and slowly, like I'm made out of the thinnest glass, he adjusts my arm so he can get at the lock. I hear it snick open. Still feigning sleep, I feel him bring my hand up until it stops at his mouth. He kisses my knuckles.

And then, just as gently, he lays my arm back at my side.

I hear him walking toward the door, his heels dragging in the dirt. He stops.

"Maxine," he says, "I know you can hear me. And I want you to hear this: no matter what the girl thinks, it has to be you and me. No matter what. Alive or dead. *Us.*"

He walks out.

HARPER

I'm back in the kitchen. My body feels like an empty husk, like he scraped everything out of it but the stubbornly beating heart. And because I'm still alive, I feel something. Past the horror of what I let him do to me. Past the horror of what I let him steal from Linnea. Something else. Something physical: a numbness at the base of my skull, tiny tremors in my fingers, a feverish flush. Nothing like the weakness and shortness of breath from being without those meds Alma and Julie warned me I needed.

She didn't lie.

"Thank you," I breathe.

Fall semester of tenth grade, I was on the debate team. I soon realized that being in antagonistic roles with people I wanted to hang out with wasn't for me. One of our debates was about capital punishment.

Of course I argued against it. I used to believe—*really believe*—that every life was worth saving, no matter what. I know better now.

Before he climbed off me, he whispered that just the two of us should eat "dinner" (as if anything we do here can be given sane-world labels) in the cafeteria. "Make it special," he said, planting one last kiss on my neck.

"Let me borrow your knife," I said, "so I can make a proper meal. So I can mince and dice and chop."

"Never mind," he said with an infuriating chuckle. "It doesn't have to be *that* special." And then, his tone stripped of everything but warning: "You'd best not mistake me for stupid, girl."

And with that, he left me to clean up the blood between my legs.

I don't care where we eat, as long as he eats. And eats enough.

For once I'm glad Max is confined. That will keep her safe. She doesn't have the heart for a game. I'll be able to unlock her soon enough.

Once the poison's humming through him, I'll snag his keys, free her, and we'll use his truck to reenter the world of the living.

Judging by the sad kind of light leaking into the windows of the caf, it's late afternoon. Even on the best of days, this is my least favorite time of day. Always has been. Of course as a kid I didn't have the word for nostalgia, but I had the feeling. Daylight's low simmer, before it burned out completely, made me feel like I was missing something I couldn't quite remember, and wasting something I'd carelessly forgotten. I never grew out of that.

On this particular afternoon, as far away from the best of days as I can imagine, the wistful tone of dying sunlight triggers a whole new kind of sadness.

The world has shrunk down to something too small and at the same time too big to manage. As if Max and I are puppets in a theater, Tyler has become our world. And the world is monstrous.

Watching my hands that aren't my hands, I use a wooden spoon with gnaw marks on the handle to coax the mushrooms around the hot pan until they hiss and shrink, curling into themselves like comfort. This is my portion. In the smaller cast iron pan.

I back the pan off the flame, shroud it with a dishcloth, and set it aside.

I took my power

I add different mushrooms to the larger pan. This is his portion.

in my hand

I sauté them with sprigs of fresh dill I tore from the overgrown herb garden out back.

and went against the world.

I breathe in. The food smells good.

# MAXINE

The smell of food is a hook lodged in my hunger. It reels me in, pulls me up the hill.

All that hope Linnea's always blabbing about? Strength is what really matters. Still, there won't be any hope or strength unless I eat.

I crash the cafeteria.

"I'm starving," I say, loving the look on Linnea's face. I had already thought she was pretty, even when I assumed she was a sadist messing with my family. But shock makes her even prettier. Her big eyes even bigger. Pretty doesn't equal healthy, though. Her skin is ashen, her lips pale, her eyes glassy.

"What are you doing out of bed?" she says.

She doesn't get the chance to say more, because Chris bursts in brandishing an arrow with something furry and limp impaled on it.

"Rabbit!" he announces proudly, like we'd all been dying for one.

"Oh, Jesus," Linnea mutters, eyeing the poor dead thing. "Now?"

"Hey, Max, you're looking good," he says, winking.

I ignore him.

Chris plunks the rabbit on a butcher block. The arrow quivers.

"I thought you were making a trap," Linnea says.

He flicks the arrow with two fingers so that it trembles even more wildly. "Dead rabbit is dead rabbit. What do you care how it gets dead? I remembered we did archery here, so"—he mimes pulling back the bow and spreading his fingers—"pow!"

"Um . . . what's going on?" Linnea says, gesturing my way.

He shrugs. "I unlocked her. You only whined about it a million times. I thought you'd be glad."

"Oh, yeah," she says. "Of course. I am." Even a blind man could see she's lying. She turns to me. "You really should be in bed."

"I'm done with being in bed."

Chris takes two chairs off the tabletop and sets them on the floor with the one already there. He motions to one with a flourish. "Sit down," he says to me. "It'll be a while."

I keep standing.

"No, it won't be a while," Linnea says. "It's ready now."

"I killed a fucking rabbit," Chris says, steely, "so you're gonna cook a fucking rabbit. Wasn't that one of your selling points, that you can cook?"

"Fine," Linnea says through gritted teeth. "Good. Rabbit. But the mushrooms are ready now, so let's eat those before they get cold."

"Doesn't make sense," Chris says. "Mushrooms are a side dish tonight. They can wait."

"I've never skinned a rabbit," Linnea says. "It'll take me forever. And you heard Maxine. She's starving."

Chris laughs. "You think what happened before means I'm gonna trust you with the knife all of a sudden?"

Hand it over to me. *I'll cut you in two seconds flat.*

"What happened before?" I ask.

"Nothing," she says. And then to Chris, "It's not like the thing can wriggle out of its own skin."

"No kidding." He comes over to her, drapes his arm around her shoulders like it's a scarf and she's a coatrack. Why doesn't she push him off? Why does she just stand there?

"I'll do the skinning," he says.

The light outside is fading fast. The caf dims. Chris lights one of the lanterns and stands over it as if to guard its fragile glow.

She sighs. "Fine. But can we please eat the rest of what I cooked now?"

"Nah," he says. "Don't want to ruin my appetite. Besides, a mushroom is a mushroom is a mushroom. We've had 'em last three meals."

She sighs even harder. And then, weirdly, she bursts into tears.

"Hey, hey," Chris says, rubbing her shoulders. "What's going on?"

Her face is squinched up in tears and it's blotchy red and her eyes are already puffy. She looks even less healthy now.

Chris whispers to her, but not soft enough. "Do you get really emotional after . . . you know . . . ?"

WTF?

She shakes her head, looks at the floor. She manages to splutter through her tears. "I worked really hard on the dish and we don't have a microwave or anything and it'll be ruined if we wait." Then she looks up at him. Pleadingly. And with something else in her eyes, something I can't define. But the look makes me want to break her pretty nose. "Please, Chris. Just this once?"

Now it's his turn to sigh. "Fine." He points to one of the chairs he set up, looks my way. "You jealous, Max?"

"Jealous?" I say.

Linnea brings two plates over, sets one in front of him, one in front of me.

"Eat," he commands me.

I sit down. Not because he told me to, but because if I don't eat, I might as well stay chained up.

"Here," he says, taking a big forkful from his plate and glopping it onto mine. "Just to prove you're always my best girl, no matter what."

"No!" Linnea says.

"Whoa," Chris says. "What's your problem?"

"That was for you." She sulks. "It was just the right amount."

"What is this?" he asks. "Goldilocks and the Three Goddamn Bears? 'Just right'?"

I pick up my fork and stab a bunch of 'shrooms.

Rushing toward the table, Linnea must trip on a curled-up edge of linoleum. She falls onto me before she rights herself and my dish flies off the table and lands, food first, on the floor. My fork is jostled out of my hand too.

"Watch it!" Chris says.

"Oh, shit," she says. "Sorry."

"Good thing we have the rabbit," he says, and he pushes his plate forward. "But for now, dig in."

"No, you eat yours," she says. "Max and I will eat mine. It's on the stove."

"You're worried about us now?" I say to him.

"Maxine, *shut up*," she says.

"No, don't shut up, Maxine," Chris says, his voice icy. He drops his fork onto his plate. "What do you mean by that?" He draws his lighter out of his pocket and wakens another lantern on the table. The hollows of his eyes are dark and prominent with the watery light striking his face.

All of a sudden the gamey stink of the rabbit hits me. I gag. "I meant that we're not—"

"She didn't mean anything," Linnea interrupts, bringing over the pan with mushrooms in it, a spoon sticking out of it. "She's still delusional from being sick. Just eat, Maxine."

"I don't need you to speak for me." I stand up. "We're going to die here, and you're acting like this is *Little House on the Prairie*."

"Nobody's going to die," she says. "We're just working things out."

"What exactly are we working out?" I ask.

Linnea grabs my forearm, squeezes. "Just stop," she whispers. "You have no idea what you're doing."

"You wanted to leave home," Chris says to me, anchoring an elbow on the table, pivoting his stiffened torso so he's looking at me straight on. "There were too many *people* there." He adds a mocking whine. "Your brothers, your mother, Ezra."

"Leave my family *out* of it. You're deranged."

Linnea sets the pan down, covers my mouth with her hand. "Max, *don't*," she hisses. I shove her away. She yelps.

"Why don't you tell the truth for once?" I say to Chris. "What do you really want with me?"

"Max." He pushes his dish away, pushes away from the table. He comes toward me. "We've always been honest with each other. That's why we work. You're nothing like your sister." "I *said* leave my family out of it!"

"I'm your family now," he says.

"No!" I step back. I turn away. "Never."

"Oh Jesus," Linnea wails, hiding her face in her hands. "Maxine. You're ruining *everything*."

"Everything's already ruined!" I say. "Maybe you're too sick to see it. You can barely stand up."

Her face, when she peels her hands away, is a blotchy, creased mess. "Stop. Just stop."

"Why? To spare his feelings? He doesn't have feelings."

Chris yanks his knife out from under his shirt.

Linnea screams.

# HARPER

I scream.

I wedge myself between Max and the monster. "Shut up, Max!" I shriek, but I know that look in her eyes. The wriggling fury. Just like her big sister. She's gearing up to fight.

"You think you can hold me hostage and I'll be your little wifey?" she spits at him.

I need to silence her. To keep her safe.

"Chris," I say, "don't listen to her, she's just—"

"Let her talk," he says, sheathing his knife. "Let her hang herself. She's unspooling the rope."

I don't exist for Max in this moment. She's in his face, on her tiptoes so she's closer to meeting his eye. "You're vile," she hisses, spittle flying, fists so tight her forearms turn ropy. "You killed my—"

I grab the pan off the table and whack her on the side of the head with it.

She crumples to the floor. I cry out. I did it, but I'm in shock anyway. He yells, "What the *fuck?*"

I fall to my knees, check to be sure she's breathing. I find her pulse at her wrist. It's steady. *Oh thankgodthankgodthankgod.*

"Why in the hell'd you do that?" he says.

"She's too emotional right now. It's her time of the month. She didn't mean any of it."

Please forgive me, Max. Afterwards, you'll understand.

"She'd better be okay," he snarls.

"She's fine." There are mushrooms on her chest, on her forehead. I wipe them off. The pulse in her neck beats steadily. *Thank you, Jesus.*

I'm kneeling in mushrooms. Oh, Jesus Christ, these are the safe mushrooms. At least the important batch is on his plate, but I need a safe batch to play the game. And I've already cooked all I gathered for the day. I grab an empty plate. I scoop mushrooms from off the floor and heap them onto the dish.

He thuds into a chair. "She hates me."

"No, no. She loves you."

"Bullshit."

"Just let her sleep it off," I say. "She'll be fine when she wakes up."

"What're you doing?"

"I made a mess when I conked her out."

"You can't eat that," he says.

"It's fine."

"That's disgusting. There's rat shit and stuff on the floor."

"It's fine," I repeat. "Really."

"Just eat mine," he says. "I'm not hungry anyway."

"I worked hard on this meal. I wanted it to be special for you."

"So we'll share it," he says. He hikes me up by my elbow. "Jesus, you're bleeding."

"I am?" I press a hand against my heart.

He points to my stomach. There's blood oozing through my shirt. And now I feel the pain underneath.

"I must've . . ." I feel woozy. "I must've bumped up against the knife . . . when I got between you and Max."

"That was stupid of you."

I latch on to the table for balance. He goes to the kitchen, comes back with a roll of rough brown paper towel. He tears off a length of it and hands it to me. "'Righteous blood cries out for vengeance.'"

I apply the paper towel over my shirt; I can't get sidetracked by my wound. I have to get him to eat. That's all I'm here for.

Thinkthinkthink.

"Everything's all fucked up now." He paces a path in front of Max's splayed body. Like he's building a fence of footsteps.

"No, it'll be okay."

"How can you say that?" he practically shrieks. "Maxine and I were supposed to be together and now—"

"You're still together." The paper towel feels sticky and warm under my palm.

"She should've been over it by now," he says.

"Over what?"

"She still thinks about her sister's boyfriend."

"No, not true," I say. "She never liked him."

He does a double-take. "What the hell you know about it?"

"She told me."

He looks at her. I look at her. *Please stay knocked out a while longer.*

I take his hand, even though I'd rather pick up that poor arrow-pierced rabbit. I murmur as seductively as I can. "God wouldn't put a desire in your heart unless he wanted you to act on it. Max'll come around. But I'm here now."

He grunts a grunt that could mean anything.

I go on. "You'll see that the way I show my love is through feeding the people I care about. And right now, there's nobody I care about more than you. Let me feed you."

His eyes soften. His breath slackens. He pulls me to him. I think he's leaning in for a kiss, but he bites my bottom lip so hard I nearly yelp.

"You just made me hard," he says.

"I'm glad," I force out. "Come on, let me nourish you."

He sits at his place. He smiles at me while picking up his fork. I set his dish back in front of him, hoping the tremor in my hand doesn't show.

"Ladies first," he says.

"Oh. Sure. Thanks." I dig into the mushrooms that had been on the floor.

"Not those, I said!" He wipes out the plate with the whisk of an arm. It lands somewhere south of Max's feet, abstract mushroom art on a linoleum canvas.

Now we're down to poisonous mushrooms or no mushrooms. A seesaw I don't see a way off.

He glances at me and then back at his dinner. He narrows his eyes. "Is there something wrong with mine?"

"What?" I force out a laugh. "Of course not!"

He sends the plate over to my side of the table. "Sit."

I sit. I force myself to smile. I try to nudge my setting to autopilot: pierce food with fork, force food into mouth, chew, swallow. "Mmm, delicious." I take another bite. *Happy now?*

He watches me for a minute as if to see whether I combust.

"More," he says, his voice all edge.

"I really should get to work on the rab—"

He glowers at me. "More, I said."

I take more. He wags his finger at the plate. I take more still.

"I've eaten more than my share," I say. "And I want to take care of you. I feel like that's what I'm here for." *To take care of you once and for all.*

I smile at him. Which feels as hard to do as knowingly swallowing poison.

He drags the plate back to him and starts shoveling big forkfuls into his mouth, grunting again. There's a loud screech from outside. A bird of prey. A great horned owl? A hawk? One's a harbinger of death. That should cheer me, considering I need this man to die.

"You need to teach Maxine how to show her love," he says, his mouth full of food.

"I will, I will."

"I'm gonna show you mine." There's a piece of mushroom dangling from his lower lip. He's staring at me greedily, like he can pierce me with a fork and swallow me down. "Now," he says, "let's go back to my cabin."

He slurps up the last bit of food and eyes me like a conqueror. His expression makes me unbearably nuts, makes me want to do something stupid like pick up that skillet again. I calm myself by imagining his arrogance a riptide dragging the poison through his blood with great speed and perfect aim.

Go ahead. Leer.

I think he eats plenty.

The problem is, I have, too.

HARPER

Maxine is still out cold on the floor. She murmurs occasionally (I think I hear "Race," but I could be wrong), so maybe she's merely sleeping now and not knocked out. I want to fold up a dish towel and put it under her head, but I'm afraid to wake her. She's safer unconscious. That way her fury just maybe won't get us killed.

The rabbit's still dead on the counter above where Maxine sleeps, the arrow still burrowed into its flesh. The slash at my stomach still weeps. He swipes his finger across his plate and licks it.

I need to throw up. And fast.

"Where the hell you going?" He digs the blade of his knife into different spots on the tabletop. *Taptap*dig, *taptap*dig.

"Outhouse."

"Just piss in the grass." *Taptap*dig, *taptap*dig. "And after that . . ."

After you do the unthinkable to me all over again, you God-fearing lunatic?

"After I'm gonna teach you to skin that fucking rabbit." Digdig*dig*. "Flay the ssskin."

My heart leaps. Was that a slur? Is the poison working? He's a big guy. There's a chance he didn't eat enough to kill him or at least make him sick enough where I can get his keys.

That's if I can even lift a set of keys by then. I feel like a shadow of a shadow of a shadow. How much is it this heart being shut out by a body hostile to it, and how much the poison I've consumed, I'll never know.

"I'll only be a minute," I say. *Please don't follow me.*

"Hurry up," he calls, still at the table.

The night is cool and clear. The stars are noisy. The air is bright with cricketspeak.

I scuttle down the stairs and duck under a tree on the opposite side of the cabin. I stick my finger down my throat. Way back. My fingernail scratches the roof of my mouth. Finally, I gag. But that's all it is. A dry heave.

I try again, this time with more courage and force.

Another eye-watering dry heave, but one that comes from deeper in my gut.

I thrust my finger back there again and this time the heave pulls something up besides air: a hot splash.

Once it starts, the waves take over. My throat burns and stings. I'm left exhausted, wrung-out, terrified . . . and, something I haven't felt in days . . . hopeful.

Something grabs my hair. At first I think it's the talons of an owl, mistaking my head for a rabbit.

"What the hell you doing?" He yanks my head back. He squats beside me.

"I'm sick." Shit. Did he see me force it? He'll know. He'll do it too! He'll survive. If I hadn't retched up every drop of liquid this body carries, I'd burst into tears.

"Get up," he barks.

I try. I can't. I fall to my knees. And then I fall further still.

"What's going on?" he says. The suspicion in his voice slices my hope away.

"I'm pregnant," I blurt.

"What?" He lets himself plop onto the ground next to me. "Seriously?"

"Yeah. That has to be it. I've had morning sickness all day but I didn't want to tell you until I knew for sure. Now I know for sure. I never throw up."

His face is the brightest thing in this night, competing with the stars. He reaches out, reverently lays a flat palm on my wounded belly. "And I know it's mine, because no other man ever had you."

Keep him talking. Keep him excited. Keep him digesting.

His speech is so pressured it tilts and leans, heads for the cliff. "God wants me to people his army. He knows I am a good provider." He grips my chin, makes me hold his stare. "I'm ready for this. I told Max I was nineteen so I wouldn't creep her out, but I'm almost twenty-three." *Extra time to hone your madness. Of course.*

"What name will you choose for him?" I say.

He nods. "I'll call him Isaiah. 'Fear not, for I have redeemed you; I have called you by name, you are mine.'"

"That's beautiful." *That's insane.*

He's got a lantern in one hand, my elbow in another. "Let's go."

"Wait," I start. I need to keep him talking, need to keep him hosting the toxins. "Do you think you could baptize me?"

His eyes are eerily bright in the lantern's flickery light. "There's a crick a couple miles south of here. If there's been enough rain, there's a deep spot where I can lay you down."

Oh, that's your specialty. Taking living girls and giving them to the water.

"And the baby," I say, "he'll need baptizing."

"Isaiah."

"Isaiah," I parrot.

He must like that. He creeps a hand into my shirt, cups my shoulder with a hot palm.

"Can we just sleep now?" I ask.

"Later."

"But—"

"You don't want to be with me?" He holds the lantern up to my face as if to locate a lie.

All roads end up at the same place for this damaged creature. Devouring us, one way or another.

He moves his hand to my upper arm. He grips tighter, sending his fingers in for a twist until they feel like five arrows in my flesh. "C'mon," he grunts. "Lesss go."

He drags me down the path like a misbehaving balloon.

Please, I bargain with no one, *please don't make me go into that cabin. Not again.*

"Get inside," he says, shoving me into his cabin.

My leg muscles have been swapped with crumbling clay. I can barely lift my feet.

"What's wrong with you?" he asks, poking my spine with the lantern.

"Just tired. Pregnancy does that to women."

"Not so soon it doesn't."

Oh, so now he gets a clue about biology?

He sets the lantern down next to a cot he must've dragged in here since the last time. The sleeping bag where Linnea lost a piece of her is rolled out on top of it.

He points to the sleeping bag, bloodied from what he did to me before. "Get in."

I sit, slowly, my head a bucket of bees. My body's lurchy and uncooperative, but I'm past caring about that. I just have to see him incapacitated. Get the keys, get Max. *Just a little longer.*

He's frowning at me. "You look like shit."

Yeah, dying does that to a person.

"Not worse than the rabbit." I laugh ruefully.

He smirks. I bought myself another quarter of an hour.

"I don't think I'm gonna be able to take my shirt off," I say. The blood has dried and caused the fabric to stick to it, and if I rip it off, I'm sure the bleeding will start up again. It throbs like starlight. "I think we should leave it alone for now." *Leave this body alone for now.*

"You're healing. God won't let you die."

Without explanation, he turns and steps outside. What's he doing? I don't have to wait long to figure it out. I hear his piss hit the dirt, leaf litter, the bark of a tree. Like he's playing.

"Miss me?" He stumbles on the stairs, has to catch himself on the doorframe. "My little mama." He collapses onto the sleeping bag, and then onto me.

My face is in the crook of his neck, my nose mashed against his pulse. He pets my hair. Tells me I done good.

I want to scream and never stop screaming. I want the scream to turn to blade and cut out his heart.

The petting slows, and then it stops, and then his breathing goes deep and rhythmic.

"Hey," I whisper. "Chris?"

Nothing. Nothing but his breath.

You're still breathing, motherfucker. I haven't succeeded yet.

Ignoring the ache spreading across my chest and stomach like branches of a sun-greedy tree, I ever-so-slowly wriggle out from under him. He moves sloppily to redistribute his weight, says something unintelligible, but doesn't wake. I unhook the keys from his belt loop, careful to grip them all against my palm so they don't jingle. I tiptoe outside. Out where I can breathe.

I have the keys. I want to cry. My legs are rubbery mushroom stalks, but I can't give in now. I'm nothing if I don't have Max. Almost there.

I'm walking the narrow dirt path toward the caf where my sister sleeps when a giant snake, black as an eel and glossy as satin, darts out of the monkey grass.

"Ah!" I fall back, topple right onto my ass, the breath sliced clean out of me. The keys fly out of my hand. *Don't lose those keys.* The snake is gone. I can still see the keys in the moonlight. Until they turn into glittery scorpions and beetle off and then they're gone too.

It must've been too much mushroom. *Say it fast, ten times: too much mushroom; too mush muchroom; moo tush roommuch.* A laugh burbles up from inside me but then the laugh bubble bursts before I can cup it in my palms.

My vision is blurry, chipped, fading in and out, like I'm wearing the world's worst pair of glasses. My mouth is filled with burrs or sand or roofing nails. Too mush muchroom to throw up completely. Or else thrown up too late.

I'm cold. I'm wet laundry clinging to a clothesline under a gray sky. I'm a pincushion shot through with wriggling needles. I'm a girl who once was.

There's something I have to do. Something . . . something . . . what? The something is an itch I can't reach. I spy, with my little eye, something shiny on the ground near me. Something I'm supposed to do something with. Something. Some*one*?

I'm sitting on the ground, a tree trunk holding me up. I don't remember getting from up there to down here. I try heaving myself up onto my knees. The giant hand of gravity—hairy-knuckled and crowded with sinister rings—keeps pushing me back.

It's better to be down here anyway. Where was I trying to go? How silly to think that dragging a body—that sack of dust and water—from one place to another means getting somewhere.

I creak my neck to peer above me. Ah. My eyes work better up there. I'm not afraid anymore. There's the blue-black sky, the sharp stars spilled against the dark fabric. The tree trunk liquefies and lets me go. I fall flat to the ground. The back of my head lands on a pinecone. Something with legs crawls onto my leg, hugs it. Do snakes have legs?

I let myself melt into the ground so that it is all me and I am all it. Outside/inside the same. I am filled with dirt and sky and pinecones. I'm just fragments of atoms, wildly dancing and jittering.

The moon has slipped out of the dark sky and wants a way back up. Up past the pine tree. Up past the cold stars. Up past the horizon's shelf.

Thinking about the long journey the moon has ahead of her exhausts me. I wish I could tell her to just stay put.

This is what giving up feels like, a lonely star says to me. *Enjoy it.*

And except for the pain in my stomach—from a sharp-edged star I swallowed once, trying to break free and add its light to the sky again— I do. I open my mouth to let the glow radiate through me.

MAXINE

Straddling her body, I press down on her chest. Again. My hands are slabs of meat, stupid and clumsy. Why didn't I pay attention during mandatory first aid in swim class every summer growing up? Why was I so sure I'd never need to restart anyone's heart?

With Ursa Major looking over one shoulder, and a great horned owl looking over the other, I try to coax a life back.

One, two, three palm presses to the sternum, and then I move to her face, tilt her chin up, pinch her nostrils shut, and blow two breaths into her mouth.

I ignore the broken glass under my shins. When I found her here, in this pile of leaf litter, I dropped to my knees and set the lantern down so quickly it fell over and a panel shattered. But the wick still burns, loaning me its stingy gleam while I repeat the process all over again.

Her ribs feel so fragile. I'm afraid I'll break them.

Still no breath but mine.

How many cycles? I've lost count. The only thing I'm counting are the chest compressions and the breaths I loan her.

"Harper." I'm crying, sobbing, choking. "Harper. I know it's you in there. I was stupid to deny it. I'm sorry."

I push down on her chest harder, desperate to feel her heart's echo under my palms. I press harder and harder, not worried about her ribs anymore. Ribs can heal.

I can't lose you again.

I have no choice but to keep trying.

Finally, *finally*, when I move to her side to lend her my breath, there's a breath that meets mine. Just a small huff, but it's warm and round and all hers.

I would start to cry, but I'm already crying.

My sister! You came back to me.

She opens her eyes, rolls to her side, throws up.

I never would have thought I'd be so happy to have vomit practically land in my lap.

"Harper!" I cry. "We're gonna get out of here!"

On her back again, she wipes the corner of her mouth with her knuckles. I lay my forehead on her chest and a final flood of tears and sobs escapes me. "Harper, everything's going to be okay now. Just rest."

"Who are you?" she rasps. "And who's Harper?"

LINNEA
Three years later

Skimming along a current of air, a bee staggers into the shop through the propped-open door. I don't bother swatting it away. I even stop following it with my eyes. Should I need it, my EpiPen is in my bag behind the front counter.

Working in a dessert food truck for two years forced me to make my peace with bees. The secret, I learned, is to stop fighting them. Give them all the sugar they want outside the trailer and they won't go after the sweetness in your mixing bowl.

Tess, my seventeen-year-old apprentice, walks in, glossy auburn ponytail swinging. It still feels surreal to say that, *my apprentice*, like I'm a sorcerer or a blacksmith.

"What's bakin'?" she asks with a sunny smile. Her standard greeting. She and her mom moved to Austin from Philly before the holidays and she's Texafyin' her speech somethin' fierce. She's Nicola's niece, but that's not why I agreed to tie her to my apron strings for a few months.

Despite getting my GED and getting a letter of recommendation from Nicola that made me bawl my eyes out (especially the part where she talked about my "quiet strength and unwavering perseverance"), I didn't get into pastry school in Chicago three years ago.

I was devastated. Like huddled under an old ratty afghan without brushing my teeth or washing my face for days devastated. I'd been dreaming of it for so long. Had pinned my identity onto it. Didn't know who I was without it.

On day four of my pity party, Nicola blew into my living room with a proposal. She smelled of cilantro. I probably smelled of unwashed socks.

Nicola asked that I commit to running a dessert trailer she was eyeing for at least nine months, 'til it was time to reapply to the pastry school. And if school was still my burning desire, then she'd pay for my application. If I wanted to keep baking in Austin, though, she'd be my silent partner, let me develop my own brand, give me complete creative control, and work out an agreement that I pay her back with a share of the profits over ten years.

Mom worried about my long hours. Yes, I pushed myself harder than ever before, but for those five godforsaken campground days where absolutely no one from my life knew where I was, I'd been through something my body remembered, even if my brain hadn't. So I decided surviving that meant I was stronger than I gave myself credit for.

Plus I loved the work. Loved the fact that my busiest time was from 11:00 p.m. to 2:00 a.m. All those happy drunk people, draped all over each other and shimmering in the dark, all that messy enthusiasm when they'd take their first bite of Bailey's hot bread pudding or hazelnut flan and shout, "Holy *shit*, this is good!"

Nine months later, Nicola had to remind me application time had rolled around. Since I couldn't even imagine myself in a classroom at that point, I didn't bother applying.

Six months ago Nicola convinced me I was ready for this brick-and-mortar shop. And although I miss the dusty trailer park, the camaraderie with the other truck people, the sodium lights of the lot processing our faces like photo negatives, I know I'm where I belong. At least for now.

A middle-aged suit comes in and asks for my best-selling macaron. It's the lemon lavender, but he ends up taking the three dozen I have left, in all flavors.

The customer feeds his card to the chip reader. "I'm going to be the hero in the office tomorrow morning."

"I bet," I say. "Macarons are much sexier than bagels."

"I like bagels," Tess says. I smirk as I nest the pastel beauties in their clear clamshell case.

He laughs. I hand him the bag.

"Don't you have a tip jar?" he asks.

"Nope, I'm the owner."

His eyebrows shoot up. I get that a lot. I look younger than almost twenty-one, but even if I looked my age, that's young to run a shop off South Congress Street in Austin.

"Good for you!" he says. He gives me a backhanded wave as he walks out. "Take care, Harper."

I don't bother to correct him. I get that a lot too. People assume if there's an apostrophe-S in your business name, it's gotta be named after you.

I turn to Tess. "Nix the phone, please. Apprenticeship is starting."

"Okay, but your phone has been blowing up. You might want to check it first."

Three texts. I wouldn't call that "blowing up," but my heart quickens when I see who they're from. Daniel.

Howdy.

Just wanted to say you're on my mind.

I'm glad we reconnected.

After the campground, I retreated from everyone but Mom for a while. And from everything but baking. My body bounced back far more quickly than my mind. Which was weird because I couldn't remember any of the campground except being jolted awake in it.

But not only had I changed, like at a cellular level, someone had died there. Someone who I was assured was a killer, but still . . . someone lost his life. When it was clear my memory was a blank, Maxine told me about it. We were in the hospital then. Washed. Fed. Our wounds disinfected, stitched, and bandaged. But we were broken just the same.

"I had no choice," she'd said. She told me he had a weapon—the slash on my belly was proof of that—and we couldn't have ever overpowered him, and he'd never have let us go, and she knew about mushrooms and got him to eat some poisonous ones without him knowing.

Something about the way she told me, though, the way she looked anywhere but into my eyes as she quickly recounted events, made me wonder. Of course, I didn't know her well enough to know what she looked like when she wasn't lying, but I'll always wonder.

Daniel was kind to me back then, and patient, and he tried, but I had to keep pushing him away. Coming back from that blacked-out nightmare was no recipe for a new romance. He went off to the Peace Corps a few months later.

Over the last three years I've had a smattering of dead-end first dates and a grand total of three sort-of boyfriends, none worth talking about. Mostly, I've been content to pour myself into my cake batters and pie fillings.

But Daniel got back last month and surprised me at the door of my apartment with a plate of disastrous-looking cupcakes, a ribboned can of wasp spray, and a hopeful grin. Mom had given him my address when he showed up at the house, and she hadn't even given me a heads-up. The fink.

We've been on two dates so far and we've got a third one planned for Friday night. I can't think with Tess by my elbow, so I write *Me too* and send it.

I close the shop door since Tess and I are headed to the kitchen and need to hear customers come in.

"More cakes?" she asks, rolling up her sleeves. The stainless steel counter, the pride of my little kitchen, gleams quietly.

"Not just any cake. A wedding cake."

"Yeah, but it doesn't start off any differently."

"That's where you're wrong." I pull out eighteen eggs and nine sticks of butter from the fridge. "Haven't you ever heard that a chef's mood gets baked into her food and affects the eaters?"

She rolls her eyes, blows the bangs off her forehead with a jutted lip. "That's not real."

"What if it is, though? Do you really want to be responsible for an unhappy bride?"

I can see her gears spinning. She grabs the pad and pen I put out for her and writes something.

"So we need to be in a good mood when we bake?" she asks.

"Not only that. We need to remember what we're baking it for. Think good thoughts."

She looks at me like she can't believe I'm only three years older and not three decades.

Can I remember what I was like at seventeen? Do I want to? I see my watery reflection in the shiny stand of the cake mixer. My eyes are distorted, like I'm swimming up from something. I wonder if I'd be more like Tess if I had been born with a healthy heart.

No matter. I'm here now.

I pull myself away from my face and turn to Tess. "Girl, as we say in Texas, let's start crackin' eggs."

An hour later, the cakes are in the oven and the warm scents of butter and eggs fill the kitchen. Tess and I are working on the fondant. I want to check my phone, but it's stowed behind the register and I need to set a good example for my apprentice.

"The clients are just talking design today," I tell her.

"They already decided you're the one?"

"They have." This is my first. Not making my first wedding cake, but using it for an actual wedding. It's two months from now, the first week of June.

The bell on the door jangles. We head toward the front of the shop, but Tess uses my apron to hold me back.

"Are those the clients?" she whispers.

"What do you think?" I whisper back.

"They're holding hands," she says. "It's them."

"Why are we whispering?"

"They look like they're in love," she says. At first I think she might be saying it in an eye-rolling way, but her sincerity comes

through. "They're early. I'd show up early, too, if it was my wedding."
"Don't go all dreamy on me now." I link my arm in hers and lead her toward the front. "We're on the clock." But I'm smiling anyway.

I unwind my apron and greet our customers. "Howdy."

"Hey," they say in unison.

I introduce Tess as my "whip-smart apprentice," which makes her beam. I lead the couple to the long table tucked in a corner. The table started out as a door I found leaning against a Dumpster behind Lone Star Restaurant Supply. I stripped, sanded, and painted it and propped it on sawhorses I stenciled with bluebonnets. I urge them to dig in to the snacks Tess and I laid out. Mexican wedding cookies, apricot tarts, mini lemon Bundt cakes. They say no to coffee or tea so I bring a pitcher of lemonade to the table and Tess follows me with a tray of glasses. Everyone's sitting but me. I rarely sit when I'm working.

"First of all," Tess says to the couple, "congratulations, you guys!"
"Oh," Maxine says. "Uh . . . thanks?" She shoots me a searching look. I shrug.

"Where are you having it?" Tess asks them.

It's Ezra's turn to shrug. "Somewhere on campus, I guess."

Max turns to him, rests her forearm on his knee and leans. "Wouldn't it feel too sterile there? Institutional?"

"Well, it is relevant." He reaches up, moves a lock of hair over her shoulder.

"I was thinking we'd have it in our backyard," she says. "Will and Race don't want to go anywhere without that puppy."

"Wait," Tess says, like she just witnessed a crime and is burning to report it. "It's only two months away?"

Ezra thinks, nods. Max says, "Just about."

Tess goes on. "So you're designing the cake before you figure out where you're getting married?"

"Whoa!" Ezra jumps up from his seat as if sitting obligates him to matrimony.

Max turns the pink of frosting roses.

"Apprentices are so much fun," I say.

"Linnea!" Tess shouts. "You said they were engaged!"

"Actually, I didn't."

Max mouths *you're evil*, but her eyes are soft.

"Max, Ezra, why don't you tell my enthusiastic young protégé what brings you here today?"

Ezra takes his seat again, reaches for Max's hand. "So our families have set up the Harper Tretheway scholarship fund for a music student who's been accepted to UT."

"It's mostly funded by his family," Max whispers, as if he can't hear. "And by my friend Shelby's family, too."

"Hey, your mom's added a bunch to it ever since she started back to work," he says. "But more importantly, she chose the student. She's changed someone's life."

Max explains to Tess. "So we're throwing a little party for the pianist who's getting the scholarship. She's moving here from Nebraska in June."

"Ah," Tess says. "And you need a cake."

"Yep." Ezra finishes off a cookie and, ignoring the cloth napkins I'd set out, uses his shirt to wipe the powdered sugar off his fingers. "And we want something creative. Thoughtful."

"That's nice," Tess says. "Not as fun as a wedding, but nice." Max is finishing up architecture school and Ezra's wrapping up elementary ed student teaching. If they do have a wedding cake in their future, they probably want to get their careers off the ground first.

"Okay, everybody," I say. "Can I suggest a toast?"

We lift our lemonade glasses. Tess starts to sip prematurely, corrects her mistake.

I clear my throat. "Here's to our future, y'all. May it have more sun than rain, more forgiveness than grudges, more sweetness than bitterness."

"God, that's beautiful," Tess whispers. Ezra bites his lip, I'm guessing so he doesn't laugh at her.

We clink glasses, the little clear notes like music floating down from an icy plane, melting into us and turning round and warm.

"And guys," Max says as she looks around the table, "I think the future's already here."

ACKNOWLEDGMENTS

I owe heaps of gratitude to the people who have helped this book find a place in the world—and to the people who have helped me find mine.

For everyone at Elephant Rock Books, especially Amanda Hurley and Christopher Morris (who wears many hats, and wears them well), and an extra-special thanks to Jotham Burrello for working so closely with me to shape the draft into a book. Rewinding a little more, for the Helen Sheehan Book Prize contest readers Kathryn Fitzpatrick and Chloe Spinnanger, and judges Jennie Kendrick, Mark Pumphrey, and Suzy Takacs. And a big shout-out to Elephant Rock alum Kristin Bartley Lenz.

For readers (and encouragers) of early drafts: Susan Carlton, Jan Czech, Angela Reilly, Kate Simpson, Tess Faraci, Marianne Knowles, Lynda Mullaly Hunt, and Shannon Parker. And Larry Hayes, for connecting the book with its first official reader.

For the kidlit community in Austin, Texas—you have welcomed this newcomer so warmly and have made me feel part of that big Texas y'all: Jessica Lee Anderson, Cate Berry, Donna Janell Bowman, Lorraine Elkins, Alisha Gabriel, Bethany Hegedus, Tricia Hoover, Kat Kronenberg, Cynthia Levinson, Eileen Manes, Susan Pope, Gayleen Rabakukk, and Cynthia Leitich Smith. An extra helping of thanks to the Regional Advisor of the Austin chapter of the Society of Children's Book Writers and Illustrators, the generous and tireless Samantha Clark.

And speaking of Austin, thank you to Abby Fennewald, Meghan Dietsche Goel, Eugenia Vela, and everyone at my spectacular local bookstore BookPeople, for the way you champion words in general, and local authors in particular.

Katya de Becerra, you are a shining example of all that is good in cyberspace. Thank you for your writerly friendship and for sending so much cheer and good will into the world.

I feel grateful to have more people to thank than space allows; my original draft included a note for each of the following and what I'm thanking them for, but alas, it had to be whittled down to a mere list. (The most excruciating book cuts I've made to date!) Y'all have supported me in various ways and have made my life richer and warmer and brighter. (Long version sent on request.) Mary Harlan, Barry Ilioff, Joel Rathfon, Kathi Barit, Julie McCammon, Alexis McCammon, Annette Montgomery, Katherine Souza, Faith Souza, Jenny Kimball, Qing Liu, Cathryn Colgrove, Glenn Williams, Tanya Dawson, Lily Vincenzo, Rebecca Zambrano, Paige Britt, and Kristy Scullion.

Jen Cervantes, Marcie Ferreri, and Cindy House are writers whose talent, perseverance, and integrity I deeply admire, and whose support, feedback, and guidance I am lucky enough to rely upon.

Jen, thank you for your unshakable faith in me and for using it to lift me up when I needed it most.

Marcie, thank you for being your radiant self, for sharing that radiance with those you love, and for opening your compassionate heart to me in such a powerful way.

Cindy, thank you for so often and so strikingly intuiting what I needed long before I did, and thank you for following me into the difficult places, and then for holding on and never letting go.

For unwavering, boundless love and support, I will never have enough words to thank my brother Sal, my sister Sergina, and my daughter Sandra.

And to Rich, for everything, everything.

AUTHOR INTERVIEW

Elephant Rock's Christopher Morris discusses the writing of *Borrowed* with author Lucia DiStefano. Learn more about Lucia at www. LuciaDiStefano.com.

Christopher Morris: *Borrowed* is certainly an unusual brand of YA novel, drawing from multiple genres and keeping readers on their toes with an ever-twisting plot. How did *Borrowed*, in all its nuanced complexity, come to be? What was it that inspired you to tell this story?

Lucia DiStefano: The germ of the story infected me many years ago when I watched a young woman ahead of me in the post office queue write something in pen on the palm of her hand. Of course I would have loved to know exactly what she wrote. We've all jotted "note-to-self" reminders on ourselves when we needed to remember something in the absence of paper or device (I trust I'm not alone in that?), so it wasn't that it was strange, but rather, seeing it from the outside made it more memorable.

I started thinking about memory and how fickle and deceptive it can be, how we feel it's important to hold on to certain memories and forget others, so I began a novel about a grieving girl who writes messages on her palms in her sleep and has no memory of putting them there. I wandered, aimlessly, within that story for awhile, and it wasn't until I stumbled upon some anecdotal (but powerful) evidence for cellular memory in heart transplant patients that I landed on the missing element my protagonist needed.

CM: While I hesitate to try and define *Borrowed* as belonging to any one genre, your novel might best be described as spec lit—or speculative fiction. Spec lit tends to draw from any number of other genres, including fantasy, science fiction, horror, dystopia . . . Which genres do you see yourself *borrowing* (get it?) the most heavily from, and how did this evolve in the writing?

LD: I wish I could answer this question in an impressive way. But for me, YA is the genre I'm working in, so I didn't consciously think of sub-categories while I was writing. I thought more of where I wanted the book to fall on the light-to-dark spectrum. And because the story had a loss at its center, I knew it needed to have a darker tone. So it's cool to hear other people define it in ways I wouldn't. For instance, one of the judges called the novel a "thriller." I read that and thought, "Wow. I wrote a thriller? If you say so!"

One thing I did consciously think about in the writing and in the revision was leaving space for different readers to draw different conclusions. Because scientists can only observe the phenomenon of cellular memory (they can't exactly prove or disprove it), it lends itself to different interpretations and calls upon different sets of beliefs. I like that kind of ambiguity or elasticity. If you are a hard-core scientist, you might look at Linnea's experience through that lens (and yes, I have taken full advantage of my "rights" as a fiction writer to dramatize cellular memory and ask the reader to consider an extreme or even improbable example). And if you're thinking along more mystical lines, you might see what happens as belonging in the realm of the miraculous. Both mind-sets are equally valid. There's lots that science can't explain, but that doesn't mean that those things won't ever be explained by science . . . nor does it mean that they will.

CM: One of the most impressive things about *Borrowed* is how well it juggles three points of view—one of which is from a character who is technically, well . . . dead. Walk me through the process of developing the characters and voices of Linnea, Maxine, and Harper.

LD: Part of me believes there is no "process," at least not one that can be distilled in a neat way. Norman Mailer called writing "the spooky art," and in the sense of a writer imagining the inner workings of characters and then fixing it all on a blank page in the hopes that readers will emotionally connect, writing certainly is one of the spookier things we do as humans. I do hope the voices of the three narrators sound different to readers; I certainly aimed for that, but beyond trying to feel my way into the girls' heads and stay there as long as they would let me, I don't know exactly how I did it. And the fact that I just referred to them as hosts to my nosy writer's brain shows you how I don't really have a clue about the "process" . . . I just showed up at the desk day after day, even on the days when I knew my task was to cut all of what I'd written in the days or weeks before!

CM: You're a pretty sunny person, and yet *Borrowed* goes to some very dark places—both thematically and in terms of the violence on display during the novel's final act. How did you decide on what to include— and on how far to go—with those late-game scenes?

LD: I don't necessarily think of myself as "sunny," but you're not the first person to have called me that. (I am so not always in a good mood—my husband can attest to that.) I've always been drawn to books and movies and pieces of art that push me to the edges of my emotional limits, both the difficult emotions as well as the joyful ones. So it makes sense I'd write the type of book I like to read. In terms of how far to go, though, I needed help with that. There's an important moment in the story that I had not written but had only alluded to. Jotham, wise story visionary that he is, urged me to write it (and he knew it would be tough, so he apologized for asking). I wrote it, and I went too far.

CM: You mean the scene in part 3 between Chris and Harper in the cabin?

LD: Correct. Robert Frost said, "No tears in the writer, no tears in the reader," so once I committed to trying what Jotham suggested, I suppose I was determined not to spare myself. However, we ended up scaling it back and landing somewhere in the middle: not glossing over the event, but not narrating every moment of it either. I couldn't have gotten there on my own.

CM: *Borrowed* resonated with our judges in no small part because of how realistically it deals with grief, loss, and guilt. How did you go about portraying these powerful emotions from the points of view of teens?

LD: My mother died when I was a high school sophomore, and my father died before I turned 21. And because both succumbed to long illnesses, in a real way my teen years were shaped by grief and loss. Although Maxine's grief is obviously very different, and although her guilt also has a different source than mine (perhaps mine was more survivor's guilt), I can't help but think that my own long season of loss somehow informed Max's. Again, it wasn't something conscious I set out to do as I wrote. As a teen dealing first with the fear of my mother's death, and then struggling to cope with life without her, I took great comfort in books, especially those that had captured even a shadowy sense of what I was feeling. In that regard, fiction felt like a much more grounding, authentic part of life than "reality" did. And yet, I didn't start out by deciding to write a book about grief. Rather, since I was so profoundly moved by the novels I read as a teen that did a good job of depicting grief and loss (and I'm still moved by them), I think subconsciously I was motivated to just generally join the literary conversation.

CM: Despite their roles as supporting characters, Shelby, Alma, and Julie all play key roles in the story and in the lives of Linnea, Maxine, and Harper. Tell me about how you developed characters who, despite their relatively short "screen time," are still able to make such a profound impact.

LD: I love secondary characters—as a writer and as a reader. Unlike the main characters, who are burdened with carrying the story's through line, minor characters can have more fun, and, therefore, can be more fun to write. I am thrilled to hear you say that these characters had a strong impact on the story. Of course, despite the fact that I felt freer to let them call the shots, and therefore I enjoyed sketching them, I also did want them to move the story or assist (or foil) the characters along the way.

As far as "how" I achieved what you say I achieved, I think you'd need to ask the characters themselves, since mostly, I'm stumped. I do know that I absolutely love writing dialogue (even though my first attempts at writing fiction contained almost zero dialogue; I just meandered in my characters' heads). Many times I discover the minor characters' true "roles" when I get them talking to the protagonists. I end up having to cut lots of that explorative chatter, but for me, watching the characters interact helps me determine how they can all best add to the whole.

CM: It can be difficult to write teen characters that teen readers will find realistic and relatable. What motivated you to start writing for teens?

LD: Well, as I said, I was a serious reader as a teen, not only for the unique and lasting enjoyment that reading can bring, but to reassure myself that emotional pain didn't mean a diminished life. After all, I spent time with characters who survived painful situations and ultimately connected with aspects of life—even the smallest—that made it worth living. And most importantly, they didn't deny or overlook or turn away from their problems, but rather explored them—sometimes with trepidation, sometimes with courage. (John Dufresne calls fiction "the lie that tells a truth." I think that's exactly right.) So perhaps I've always subconsciously felt like I "owed" something to the books that buoyed my struggling teen self. And what better way to repay that than to add my voice to the conversation?

CM: And you're a former teacher, you've spent hundreds of hours with teenagers.

LD: Right. Long before I ever tried my hand at writing for teens, I taught high school English. I was lucky enough to be a student of the YA lit pioneer Dr. Don Gallo at Central Connecticut State University when I was working toward my teaching degree, and his legendary course on the YA novel deepened my passion and respect for the genre. (I read over a hundred novels that semester, and that's not hyperbole.) So when I started teaching and found out I was restricted to teaching whatever was in the book room (the most contemporary being *Fahrenheit 451*, and there was lots and lots of Charles Dickens), I decided to prove to teens that there was a rich and varied body of literature out there written with them in mind. I brought in dozens of YA novels from home and lined my classroom with them, encouraging my students to borrow them by jotting their names down on the checkout sheet I'd provided . . . but only if they'd like to. Needless to say, the books weren't flying off the shelves.

But because I was so frustrated with the school board's insistence that I stick to the "classics" and so frustrated with the result (teens thought reading was boring), I carved out ten minutes at the end of most class periods to read aloud to my students from a bona fide YA novel. They loved it. They started asking for that time and were disappointed if we didn't get to it. The book was *Up Country* by Alden R. Carter, and it dealt with serious subjects like substance addiction, dysfunctional families, criminal activity, and, because it was realistic, it included the occasional curse word. (My students were shocked when they heard me read a swear word for the first time; they thought I added it to hold their attention, and I had to show them where it appeared on the page.)

You can see where this is going, right? One of the students happened to tell her parents that her English teacher was reading something . . . um . . . colorful, and those parents went to the school board, and I was told to knock it off with the "unapproved" reading material or I'd be out of a job. The superintendent remained staunchly unmoved by my assurance that I was devoting the bulk of my classes to the required curriculum; by anecdotes of recalcitrant readers' engagement and absorption during those read-aloud segments; by how animatedly my students were talking about the characters and wondering what would happen next. (They had never given one whit about Pip or Oliver Twist.)

CM: Were you writing during this time?

LD: Literary short stories, yes. YA novels, no. I didn't consider writing my own YA until years later, when I was in graduate school. One of my assignments for my class on teaching writing was to complete one of the projects I'd assigned my freshman composition students. I opted for one of the creative, open-ended assignments, rather than the required research papers. And in my piece, I narrated from the point of view of a high school junior who was selling his prescription drugs to his classmates. Unbeknownst to me, my professor gave what I'd written to his teen son, who reportedly liked it so much that he asked his dad for the "rest of the book." My prof shared this with me (thanks, Dr. Riggio), and a goal was born.

CM: And *Borrowed* is the result of these years of writing?

LD: *Borrowed* is my first published book, but it's not even close to the first novel manuscript I've written.

CM: What was the revision process like for *Borrowed*? What did you focus on as you revised?

LD: What didn't I focus on! The revision process was intense but rewarding. I feel incredibly lucky to have worked on my first published book with Jotham Burrello (the mastermind behind Elephant Rock Books; rest assured, people, he uses his powers for good). I bet I would've been overwhelmed with the typical twelve-page, single-spaced revision letter from the editor, probably not knowing where/how to start. So I'm especially grateful for the way Jotham works: systematically, breaking things down into manageable chunks. We spoke by phone each week, and we worked on the manuscript in "passes," having a different focus each round (for instance, deepening characters and character motivations; voice; setting). One of the first things Jotham identified that I needed to zero in on was the story's time line. Basically I had such a squishy time line it was nonexistent. Because time lines feel like math, and math and I are not the best of friends, I'd been avoiding that. Before we could get down to serious story work, we needed to work out the story calendar.

CM: When did you know that the book was "capital D Done"?

LD: When Jotham told me we had to stop noodling with it! I can't stress enough how important trusted readers are to the revision process. We'll always be too close to our work to read it like an editor. Henry James was famous for that, always wanting to rewrite published work, even when he was only asked to write an introduction to a new edition. Because we're always different people when we revisit our work (even subtly different, even a few months' different), it's impossible not to see words/phrases/details we want to change, regardless of how capital D Done the work felt at the time of publication.

I've put my all into each round of edits. But I know if/when I go back for a reread, I will encounter things I wish I could change! I'll have to devise a distraction to get me through those times. Maybe I'll dust off a volume of Henry James.

QUESTIONS AND TOPICS
FOR DISCUSSION

1. Maxine is driven, perhaps above all else, by her love for her two younger brothers. What do Race and Will teach Max about love and about family?

2. The theme of knowing yourself/others runs throughout the book. Which challenges push Linnea, Max, and Harper to learn more about themselves and what they're capable of? And how do the assumptions they make about the people in their lives hold up along the way?

3. Despite its hopeful message and optimistic ending, *Borrowed* travels to some very dark places. How does the novel balance competing tones of hope and hopelessness during its final act?

4. On more than one occasion, Harper feels that she can see past Chris's monstrousness to the boy he used to be. Why do you think Harper is the only one who seems able to see this side of Chris?

5. Max feels an immense amount of guilt over Harper's death. How does Max wrestle with this guilt throughout the novel? Do you think it's justified?

6. One of the major themes of the novel's final act is healing. Think about a time when you had to overcome an obstacle. What—or who—helped you see the light?

7. The book is written from multiple points of view. How do these alternating voices drive the narrative? And how do each of the voices reflect the narrator's personality?

8. Up until the very end of the story, Max refuses to believe that Harper really is inhabiting Linnea's body. What do you think ultimately changes her mind?

9. Throughout her life, Linnea has had to struggle to survive, and baking has become not only a means of creative expression, but also a therapeutic outlet. How does the symbolic significance of the culinary arts manifest itself throughout the novel?

10. By the novel's end, Max and Linnea have become close friends. Beyond what happened at the campground, what do you think brought these two girls together? What has kept them close?

ALSO BY ELEPHANT ROCK BOOKS

The Art of Holding on and Letting Go
by **Kristin Bartley Lenz**

"Eloquent debut."
 –Booklist;
  Junior Library Guild Selection

The Carnival at Bray
by **Jessie Ann Foley**

"Powerfully Evocative!"
 –Kirkus Reviews, Starred Review;
  Printz Honor Book & Morris Finalist

The Biology of Luck
by **Jacob M. Appel**

"Clever, vigorously written, intently observed,
 and richly emotional."
 –Booklist

*Briefly Knocked Unconscious by a Low-Flying Duck:
Stories from 2nd Story*

"This collection will demand, and receive, return
 trips from its readers."
 –Publishers Weekly, Starred Review